PRAISE FOR
BAD MOON RISING

"As unique a place in the mystery universe as you will ever find, and in the eloquent prose of John Galligan it comes alive in a ride that is smooth, unexpected, and memorable. This book is a diamond in the rough."

—Michael Connelly, #1 *New York Times* bestselling author of *The Law of Innocence*

"Fascinating characters, a thoroughly original voice, and a riveting sense of place and atmosphere . . . Unputdownable."

—Ausma Zehanat Khan, author of *A Deadly Divide*

"Gritty and propulsive . . . Intriguing characters take a wild ride through backwoods Wisconsin in this irresistible mystery."

—*Kirkus Reviews* (starred review)

"Suspenseful . . . Readers will root for Kick as the action builds to a satisfyingly hard-edged denouement. Fans of gritty rural crime, such as Ace Atkins's Quinn Colson series, will be enthralled."

—*Publishers Weekly*

"Fast-paced and well written, *Bad Moon Rising* leaves Galligan's fans anxiously awaiting the next volume in his Bad Axe County series."

—*Mystery and Suspense* magazine

BAD MOON RISING

A BAD AXE COUNTY NOVEL

John Galligan

ATRIA PAPERBACK

NEW YORK   LONDON   TORONTO   SYDNEY   NEW DELHI

ATRIA
PAPERBACK

An Imprint of Simon & Schuster, Inc.
1230 Avenue of the Americas
New York, NY 10020

First Atria Paperback edition June 2021

ATRIA PAPERBACK and colophon are trademarks of Simon & Schuster, Inc.

For information about special discounts for bulk purchases, please contact Simon & Schuster Special Sales at 1-866-506-1949 or business@simonandschuster.com.

The Simon & Schuster Speakers Bureau can bring authors to your live event. For more information or to book an event, contact the Simon & Schuster Speakers Bureau at 1-866-248-3049 or visit our website at www.simonspeakers.com.

Interior design by Erika R. Genova

Manufactured in the United States of America

1 3 5 7 9 10 8 6 4 2

Library of Congress Cataloging-in-Publication Data has been applied for.

ISBN 978-1-9821-6653-3
ISBN 978-1-9821-6655-7 (ebook)

BAD MOON RISING

Tues, Aug 6, 12:08 PM
To: Dairy Queen (dqhkick@gmail.com)
From: Oppo (oppo@blackbox.com)
Subject: You need opposition research.

Do you want it?

I can get it.

An account has been created for you in blackbox.com.

Your username is dairyqueen.
Your password is 8&4lLMnou3_592%4$1.

PROLOGUE

Jump.
Chickenshit.
Jump off now.

He obeys. When the freight slows just enough, he cinches his backpack tight and, from the deck of the intermodal car—knowing himself as Sammy Squirrel since he hopped out at a rail yard in Portland with a backpack of essentials—launches into the scorch of high noon and lands badly, pitching onto his palms and knees and skidding down the railway berm with the slung weight of the pack driving his face into sharp rocks.

He crawls into weeds, tasting grit and blood. He shucks the

pack, topples over, closes his eyes, and grins up. The train hammers east and disappears. Sun flares scrawl Cassie's name inside his lids.

That's right. Cassie. Do it for her.

He rises and barefoots away into the heavy Midwest heat, crossing sinkholes, fallen fences, blown trash, guided toward a distant intersection, Texaco, Flying J, Arby's, Black Jack's Casino, Adult Video Warehouse, China Buffet. ALL YOU CAN EAT CRAB LEGS. In the Willamette Valley, a herd of sheep pushed down a fence and killed themselves on green alfalfa. They ate until they exploded.

This is how people are.

The human race.

Cassie wants you to stop them.

The intersection growls and gusts. Sammy Squirrel crosses unaware against the DON'T WALK sign, grubby as a bugbear from the roads and rails. Drivers brake and stare. His fresh abrasions gleam, his curly blond hair explodes in crusts and tangles, his dirty T-shirt and cargo shorts hang like shedding skin. When the honking and the glassed-in obscenities begin, the voice commands, *Stop them. Use the rock.* He flinches and walks faster. He flicks up two pairs of two fingers, peace signs, then forms two hands in the shape of a heart. The grin is fixed. It never leaves his sooty, sunburned face.

He tours Arby's looking for a plug-in, finally spies one beneath a table where a wiry man in western wear works ketchup-dipped fries past sleek blond muttonchops. His hat reads EAT THE WHALES. His shirt reads BUILD THE WALL. Under the table, this man's tooled boots are shiny.

Stop him. Use the spike.

"The hell you want?"

Peace, Sammy Squirrel's fingers promise.

Love, his hands frame.

"You come one step closer, Helter Skelter, I'll snap your filthy neck."

|||||||||||

When the shiny boots have gone, he sloughs his backpack with a puff of railroad smut, crawls beneath the table, and plugs in his phone charger. As his battery gathers from zero, he watches large people angrily overeat piles of meat. When he learned about the exploding sheep he was watching news on the recreation ward TV. *This is how people are*, the voice told him that night. *This is why Cassie died. Get a knife. Get a gun. Get a bomb and stop them.*

He broke his window. *Chickenshit.* He jumped and hurt himself landing. He ran and hid. He slept in doorways in Portland for a week, lost his shoes to a drunken man with a knife, ate from the Voodoo Doughnut's dumpster, got the name Sammy Squirrel for climbing through trees along the Springwater, began to start and tremble when the voice caught up—*That man! With the suit and briefcase! Stop him! Push him into traffic!*—then met a homeless dude who showed him how to jump a freight and found himself huddled on steel mesh, his fingers locked through it, escaping, he hoped, on a car racketing high across the chalk-blue churn of the Columbia River.

The voice had followed him.

If you're going to be such a chickenshit, just jump.

|||||||||||

He waits and waits for the battery. At six percent, he gets on the Arby's Wi-Fi and text messages his mother.

Hope all is good

Seven percent becomes eight percent on the cracked and dusty Samsung.

Cuz I'm doing good too

Becomes nine percent. His empty stomach snarls.

Don't worry

A droopy girl about his age in an Arby's uniform comes out to watch him peel a french fry off the floor. He shows her *peace* fingers, *love* hands. While she blushes, he fits the french fry through his rigid grin and chews it.

Becomes eleven percent.

Love to everyone

Drains back to eight percent.

He is staring across the intersection toward Black Jack's Casino when the Arby's girl comes back. This time she wears latex gloves and holds a spray bottle.

"Sir, I'm sorry, but you have to leave."

The phone pings: *Where are you?*

The Arby's girl goes away, looking over her shoulder. He taps fast on his phone surface.

Don't worry I'm good

"Him."

A security guard with a black beard lumbers ahead of the girl with the spray bottle.

"Him, right there."

"Hey." The guard's approaching steps rip the sticky floor. "Hey, you. You were told to leave."

His hands jump. *Peace! Love!*

"Out."

Ping: *You are not safe*

Ping: *You need your medications*

Ping: *Please tell us where you are*

He sees his own grin in the cracked phone. Five percent. He has no idea where he is. Over him the security guy snatches the girl's spray bottle and seethes. "Leave now." Then the bottle is cut loose, chemical blasts against the side of his face, down his chest, over his hands protecting his phone. When the spray stops, his face burns, his fingers drip.

"Don't pretend you don't hear me, asshole."

It's not that. He doesn't speak anymore. Back when, as it started, he had been feeling unlike himself already, angry and exhausted, nothing to say. But then came the October dawn when he had awakened to pounding and screaming on his mom's back door. He had opened it to see his neighbor and his almost-girlfriend Cassie with her black bubbled skin and behind her the hillside on fire and the entire sky full of smoke. Her horses! Her horses! He hadn't known how to help her—called 911 and stood there shaking while she screamed. After Cassie's funeral, he had begun stealing things and failing school. He had obeyed a nagging voice and let a different neighbor's horses go. He had walked through Best Buy unplugging everything. He had climbed the water tower with spray paint and written DON'T LOOK UP HERE THE PROBLEM IS IN YOUR HEAD. Next, he had lit his mom's garage on fire, destroyed her car and her boyfriend's motorcycle. *They call it back-burn*, the voice had whispered to him, over and over. *Little fires stop big ones.* He remembers woofing single words of explanation to his mom—all the family he had—while she cried and slapped his face for grinning. "I don't know you!" she had wailed, erasing his name.

Another spray in the face. "Out."

Sammy Squirrel aligns his hands so that the letters on his knuck-

les can be read clearly. Back when, one afternoon after she showed
him how to ride a horse, Cassie had inked the letters upside down,
skipping one knuckle: I AM NICE. "Cuz lately maybe sometimes you
scare people," she had said.

The guard's angry swipe rips the charger cord from the
phone. Its plug with a tail of broken cord slings across the floor
and disappears beneath a different table.

"Get out."

Peace!

"Get a job, jerkoff."

Love!

Then he is outside under the searing sun, clutching his
draining phone and ruined charger. His backpack lands
with a thump at his feet. The guard points toward the intersection.

"All the way to the end of the property. The sidewalk."

Beneath the roar of accelerating traffic his phone vibrates in
his hand.

At three percent: *We love you!*

He glances back at Arby's. The guard sustains his men-
acing glare-and-point. The girl sprays down the open door,
chasing dribbles with a cloth. Sullen diners cram trash and
waddle out.

Stop them. For Cassie. Stop them.

He zips open his backpack, reaches under his wadded bedspread, past the sharp granite chunk and the railroad spike he
has collected, under the cafeteria fork and the jagged broken
highway reflector, to reach the only weapon he believes Cassie
would want him to use.

Chickenshit.

He kneels in the path of customers on the blistering sidewalk.
He opens a plastic case the size of a book.

Loser.

Get a knife, get a gun, get a bomb.

His grin grinds. His wild blond mop falls forward. In a flurry of elbows he draws in colored chalk with all his might.

92°–101°

Thurs, Aug 8, 4:56 AM
To: Dairy Queen (dairyqueen@blackbox.com)
From: Oppo (oppo@blackbox.com)
Subject: Opposition Research

To answer your questions:

1. Someone who cannot support you publicly (per county ordinance against political activity on the job).
2. Because you need to fight back.
3. With research.
4. Blackbox is a secure encrypted email host.
5. Kim Maybee's suicide was a homicide.

So do you want my help?

CHAPTER 1

1. *Cut several fresh (bright green) dandelion leaves and put them in a clean glass or plastic container. Do not use a metal container.*

2. *Make sure that the leaves, once cut, do not come in contact with sunlight.*

3. *Urinate on the leaves until they are completely submerged.*

4. *After 10 minutes, check for red bumps on the leaves.*

They say that we hear music in the womb.

We hear voices.

We are designed this way.

The wet tympanic membranes, the yielding ossicles, the soft hard-wiring to the brain, these are created to convey to the womb the sweet vibrations of enveloping love. And so, swaddled in supportive sound, we grow.

What could go wrong?

||||||||||||

Bad Axe County Sheriff Heidi Kick rolled and gasped beneath her sticky sheets.

What could go wrong?

Seriously?

She lurched up, still three-quarters asleep. Moonlight glistened on her forehead. Night sounds grated at the screen.

It was all too obvious what could go wrong.

We could hear all the wrong things. Anger. Stupidity. The subtracting silence of despair. The pitiless gnashing of time, the thunderous indifference of nature. Surely, along with Mozart and Mommy, we also hear the insanity of the whip-poor-will, the ghoulish wailing of coyotes, the death scream when the owl hits the rabbit.

Or gunshots.

Yes, she had heard a gunshot. Because now she heard another.

From where? Inside herself? Outside?

Two hard cracks echoed across the landscape mapped inside her sheriff's brain, four hundred square miles of farm and forest, ridge and coulee.

Somewhere. Anywhere.

She fell back upon the bed. As her dream resumed, the gunshots echoed. Womb became dirt became a tomb. The Bad Axe soil she had tried to cultivate—her de-thistled pasture, her expanding vegetable and flower gardens, her new acres of alfalfa—poured over her like rain.

Hot. Dry. Black. Rain.

Heavy.

Sheriff Kick groaned and lurched up again, desperate to fully awaken. She wrested over her head and flung away her sweaty T-shirt: BARN HAIR, DON'T CARE. Red-blond strands stuck across her mouth as she pitched onto her side and groped emptily for Harley. *Help me!* But her husband the baseball hero was a hundred miles away representing the Bad Axe Rattlers at a Midwest League all-star event. He had won the home-run derby last night. Today was the game. *Opie, help me!* But her oldest child, the family's wise one, was away at summer camp.

Ten-double-zero! Ten-double-zero! Officer down! All units respond!

The sheriff could not wake up.

Shovel by shovel, the dirt massed upon her. She arched under the weight. She clenched her sheets, drove her hip bones up. Her mouth gaped.

"Unngh!"

She contracted every muscle, exploded upward. Contracted and exploded, sucked air, spit dirt, kicked, clawed.

At last she breached.

Gasped for air.

Cried in jerks and gulps like a baby.

Caught her breath.

Turned on the little rawhide lamp beside her bed.

There it was. Before sleep, she had found her diary from high school, the summer she had turned sixteen, and she had found the page where she had written down the recipe.

Cut several fresh (bright green) dandelion leaves and put them in a clean glass or plastic container . . .

"No," she whispered, touching the clasp on the diary. "I can't be. I'm careful. And we hardly ever even . . ."

But she was seventeen days late.

The recipe for lassies, her Grandma Heinz had advised her, *who don't dare go to the drugstore or the doctor.*

|||||||||||

At dawn she endured a stinging bladder as she searched the pantry for an empty Mason jar. When she found one, a pint that once contained strawberry-rhubarb jam, she dropped her cell phone into her robe pocket and hurried outside.

As she started barefoot across the dew-drenched yard, the nightmare clung to her. She tasted dirt. Her body felt sore all over. Her gut retained a sickish tickle of dread. And the dream's special effects seemed to have warped her waking world. The normally clean breath of dawn smelled like kerosene and fish. Birdsong jangled and the sunrise hissed, dissolving shadows with a crackle. She recalled how seven years ago when she carried her twin boys, vanilla ice cream had tasted like socks.

I can't be. Please just let me be sick.

Overnight, two familiar signs—KICK HER OUT and BARRY HER—had appeared on her yard. The election was still three months away, but Barry Rickreiner had been trolling her and spreading rumors since around the Fourth of July. She wondered now, who was Oppo? What did Oppo mean: *Kim Maybee's suicide was a homicide?* Should she fight back with counter-rumors? Maybe. But as much as she loathed Rickreiner, this didn't feel right. Her strategy had been to start campaigning on the first of September, at which time she meant to take the high road. Meanwhile, the heat wave had claimed all her attention.

Hurry, Heidi, before you piss down your leg.

She hastened around the corner of the old farmhouse. So as not to cast a shadow, she sneaked beneath the curtained window of the guest room, where the kids' Grammy Belle Kick slept whenever Harley was gone overnight. Belle had seemed hostile lately, suspicious, as if believing some new gossip.

The sheriff ducked under her clothesline, gave wide berth to the soggy septic drain field, and arrived upon the shady ground beneath the honeysuckle thicket.

Cut several fresh dandelion leaves . . .

Several meant how many? She preferred exact numbers.

She packed nine bright-green leaves, serrated, oozing latex, into the jar. She was ready to cut her bladder loose when she felt the buzz of her phone.

"Sorry, Denise," she blurted into it. "Family stuff. I gotta call you right back."

Her dispatcher and friend Denise Halverson said, "I think we need you now, Heidi."

"I can't—"

She couldn't even finish the sentence. She dropped to a squat, tossed her phone upon the wet lawn, reached beneath her robe, and aimed the jar against herself. Wow. Better.

"OK, go ahead."

Denise spoke distantly from the grass.

"Do you remember that priest from La Crosse who told us homeless men are being picked off the street and never coming back? He was calling the counties a few weeks ago to put us on alert?"

She remembered appreciating the passionate good intentions of the call, but it had left her with questions. The priest had said that five men had disappeared—under suspicious circumstances, he was certain—from the streets of the nearest "big" city. But wasn't the simplest explanation that transients tended to be transient? And why was he so convinced that there was foul play involved?

"Yes, I remember. He thinks someone's offering them farm work. Denise, what happened?"

"A milk truck driver scared some turkey vultures off a body in the ditch on Liberty Hill Road. Deputy Luck just got there. It looks like a homicide. It looks like the victim might have been homeless."

The jar grew warm and heavy in her hand. She heard the gunshot echoes from her dream.

"Sheriff? Are you there?"

"Let me guess," she said. "Shot twice with a small-bore rifle, probably a .22."

The phone went silent for moment.

"And the body's caked in dirt."

"What's going on, Heidi?"

"Am I right?"

"Heidi, what the hell is going on?"

She pulled the jar away and finished into the grass. She raised her face toward the house and saw Grammy Belle staring back at her. The guest room curtain fell closed. She dumped the jar.

"I'm on my way," she said.

CHAPTER 2

Leroy Fanta, having heard the call on his bedside scanner and beaten the sheriff to the scene, was lighting his first smoke of the day when he saw Heidi Kick's brown-on-tan Charger crest into the already brutal morning sun on Liberty Hill Road.

At the sight of his favorite sheriff, Fanta felt pride—and then, beneath his ribs, a hot gob of loss.

Come November, it looked as if Heidi Kick would be gone.

He could visualize the headline he would write:

Challenger's Attacks Take Down
First Female Sheriff

Except the *Bad Axe Broadcaster* did not print news anymore. It no longer needed headlines, nor an editor to write them.

After a century in service, the *Broadcaster* was no longer even a newspaper. It had become the *Happy Valley Shopper* after Babette Rickreiner had sucked it into her empire, and as of last week, after forty-three years as editor-in-chief, Fanta had become unemployed.

He should turn his scanner off, maybe. But here he was. Sheriff Kick's new rookie, Deputy Lyndsey Luck, had blocked the road with three orange cones. Fanta hustled in his old-man shamble to move them. His favorite sheriff steered past with a nod and parked behind the milk truck. Then she stayed inside the Charger, talking on her cell phone.

Now fully into his first sweat of another tropical day in the Bad Axe, Fanta energized himself with a pull on his Winston and limped toward Deputy Luck and the milk truck driver where they stood on the bridge over Hink's Creek. His joints hurt, every goddamn one of them. His fingertips prickled. His pig valve felt sticky as it flapped. His hip locked, and he had to tack left to go straight. He hadn't seen a dead body in a while, he told himself, other than his own in the mirror. What Babette Rickreiner had done to the *Broadcaster* had crushed him. He felt like a ghost as he joined the deputy and her witness.

"Where?"

Deputy Luck aimed a stolid nod at the bend in the road across from the milk truck, where the ditch bristled with wild parsnip.

"He? Or she?"

"The deceased is an adult male," reported the deputy in her just-out-of-school manner. "Caucasian, between twenty and forty years of age."

"I just seen a glimpse," the driver jumped in to explain. Fanta looked at an eager kid with a peach-fuzz beard and thirty pounds of extra fat. "I was keeping my eye out for some lost beer. I just picked up milk at Lars Hansen's, and he told me his wife drove back from town on this road yesterday with the tailgate open. A twelve-pack of Busch Light got slung out the back, and they couldn't ever find it."

Light beer, Fanta mused. Though presumed locally to be harmless, light beer figured in an absurdly high percentage of Bad Axe calamities, one way or another. Nothing light about a dozen Miller Lites in the bloodstream, and he knew the sheriff would agree. He looked to see if she was done inside her Charger. Not yet.

"I thought that twelver might have slung out on the corner, and I just barely seen something, so I backed up to look."

Deputy Luck, brown-eyed and apple-cheeked, stocky and earnest, a Green Bay girl whose go-to expression seemed to be, *Oh, cheese*, had been toiling with a short pen over a small notebook. "And your zip code?" she asked, continuing her interview of the driver.

He gave her the digits. The rookie wrote them down carefully and then double-checked. Fanta experienced another pang for Sheriff Kick. His zip code? *Oh, cheese*. A month ago, Lyndsey Luck had been the sheriff's fifth choice to replace David Morales. The Police and Fire Commission had felt jilted when first Olaf Yttri and then Morales—both outstanding chief deputies—had left the Bad Axe for greener pastures. After Morales departed in late June for a police job in Santa Fe, the commission's solution had been to overrule the sheriff during the hiring process and prioritize inexperience, because the important thing was that the new hire have nowhere better to go. The PFC had then tried to make it up to Heidi Kick by selecting a woman. Hence twenty-two-year-old Lyndsey Luck, still just a girl, honestly, whom Fanta had once seen, in the midst of an arrest, ask a very drunk and potentially violent man to spell "Bob."

She asked the driver, "How often do you drive this road?"

"Back and forth every day, seven days a week."

"So, would you say fourteen times per week?"

"Uh . . . yeah. Yeah! Good call."

With the young people getting on nicely, Fanta drew on his cigarette and, without moving, drifted away. In his head, apropos the fall election, he composed a fantasy endorsement that boasted of Heidi Kick's success. In fact, the sheriff had been too busy succeeding at the job to campaign for it, so, as an antidote to Barry Rickreiner's rude campaign signs and social media jackassery, Fanta's argument would state facts and reference cases solved, and it would "kick-start" the sheriff's reluctant defense.

He would remind readers of the runaway girl from Iowa who had been raped and murdered, and disposed of in a freezer. He would reiterate that, thanks to Sheriff Kick, four local men were doing five-to-ten for the rape, and a fifth was doing life for the murder. In the process, a hidden history of sex crimes had been brought to light—and who knew how many future victims had been spared?

The sheriff remained on the phone inside her Charger. As Fanta wondered whether the call was about one of her twin little boys acting out again, he continued dreaming up his case of support. Last spring, amid a local infection of hate, there had been the executions of a beloved retired teacher (Augustus Pfaff: shot, mutilated, burned) and the sheriff's own brother-in-law (Kenny Kick: shot) at the hands of a local white-power gang leader (Rolf Stang Jr.). Stang Jr. had in turn been fatally half beheaded (competition throwing ax) by Terry James Lord, a racist troll from Oklahoma who had flung acid in the sheriff's face. Lord had been sentenced to two life terms in federal prison. In Fanta's fantasy endorsement, he would remind Bad Axers that through all this mayhem, Heidi Kick had never flinched. Rapists and traffickers, kidnappers and racists and killers, all accounted for by a brave and hardworking sheriff, who despite her workload had never missed a high school sporting event, a Red Cross blood drive, a ribbon cutting or festival opening, or even a Lady Lions Club luncheon. These facts would glow convincingly from page seven, as Fanta's lead editorial:

Bad Axe Safe and Sound Under Steady Leadership of Sheriff Kick

Finally she stepped from her Charger, a striking almost-redhead in her mid-thirties, compact and smart in her uniform and cap, almost always bouncy and smiling but this morning wearing a frown and rigid in her body language. The weeks of record temperatures had taken their toll. Crimes of all kinds were up. And despite emergency welfare visits that had kept the sheriff and her deputies running day and night, the lives of three elderly Bad Axers had been lost to heatstroke. Her opponent had marked each death with an RIP tweet and #kickherout.

While Fanta was lost in his thoughts, Deputy Luck had left the bridge to join her boss in appraising the body. Uncomfortable with silence, the giddy milk truck driver tried to make chitchat.

"How's it going, man?"

"On the bubble," Fanta told him.

The kid scratched himself.

"Between Anger and Despair," Fanta clarified.

"Oh. Yeah. Sure."

"With daily visits from Denial and Bargaining. Babette
thinks she let me go, but I sued for age discrimination. Also, I'm
a disabled veteran, so there are ADA and VEVRAA issues. She's
filed for a restraining order, so there are injunctions flying every
which way right now."

"Oh. Right. You're the newspaper guy."

"Was."

"Oh. Right."

"I was killed in Vietnam," Fanta elaborated. "I just haven't
died yet."

"Oh. Sure."

A few seconds later, the kid tried bravely to reboot. "Well, I
guess all the news these days is online anyway. Did you see the
one about the dog that ate a golf ball?"

Rather than chew off an innocent head, Fanta schlepped over
the bridge and into Sheriff Kick's line of sight, where he hovered
suggestively. Her nod meant that he could keep coming and have
a look.

Faceup in the wild parsnip sprawled a young white man,
thirtyish but heading into premature middle age, balding with
a fringe of stiff black hair, robustly built yet wizened to hardly
more than pale skin and knobby bones, wearing nothing besides
saggy vintage underwear and one shin-high rubber boot, dry
and cracked.

Lyndsey Luck cataloged facts into her notebook. "Black boot
on his left foot. Ranger brand. That underwear looks too big.
Tattoos on shoulders, forearms, hands, and neck. I count one,
two gunshot wounds to the chest."

Sheriff Kick corrected her rookie. "That's his other left foot.
And those are exit wounds."

"Right foot, sorry. And exit wounds."

"Perfect."

Fanta studied the two small eruptions of gore: both ragged and mud-crusted, one through the lower right rib cage, the other through the opposite armpit. The rest of the dead man was flaked and clumped with dried dirt and pinkly stippled with what looked like a rash. Fanta noted a decidedly elsewhere look about the scene, as if this trauma had occurred in some faraway place and the victim had been dumped here among alien weeds. Sheriff Kick turned. The editor's weak heart sped, his pig valve flapping.

"Grape, any idea who this is?"

He kept looking just in case: busted nose, self-inflicted tattoos, his one bare foot with toenails so long that they curled. But Fanta only recognized the boot. Ranger was a brand favored by the local Amish.

"I'm sorry, Sheriff. I've never seen him before."

"Deputy, who is the truck driver?"

"Cody Jacob Wilkinson, age twenty-two, commercial license valid, driving record clean, residence on Ten Hollows Road in Town of Hefty."

"Did he see anyone else on the road this morning?"

"Negative. But he said a Linda Larsen drove through here last evening and lost a twelve-pack of Busch Light off an open tailgate and couldn't locate it. Mr. Wilkinson was on the lookout."

Sheriff Kick found a stick. She squatted on the slope of the ditch and pushed a toxic parsnip stem aside so she could see the body more clearly. As Fanta watched, she seemed to become stuck there, as if too deeply in lost thought or too affected by the death to move.

Meanwhile, Deputy Luck had stewed her way to a conclusion. "It's possible that someone else located that beer."

Fanta gravely told her, "Beer vultures." Then he winked.

"Oh, cheese," she whispered to herself and looked away.

At last the sheriff stood with a scowl, pushed TALK on her radio handset, and began telling Denise Halverson what she needed to happen. She needed any relevant missing person reports analyzed. She needed a team of deputies to search a mile of Liberty Hill Road in both directions. If there was a shell casing, a scrap of clothing, a left boot, a beer can, anything, she wanted it mapped and taken into evidence. She wanted Vernon County's K-9 team here on mutual-aid loan ASAP to see if the man had died at the end of any kind of trail.

"I'll do chain-of-custody with the body to the morgue. Dr. Kleekamp can give us a picture with his face cleaned up. We'll send it around, maybe somebody will recognize him. Meanwhile, we'll run his fingerprints through CrimeNet. One way or another, maybe we can get a name and talk to his . . . his next of kin."

As the sheriff said *next of kin*, Fanta heard a slight waver in her voice. He could guess why. The dead man had a mother. Motherhood was hard enough without your boy turning up dead in a ditch.

"Be nice to print his picture in a newspaper," she growled at Fanta as she passed him, as if to cover up the emotion he had seen.

He picked up the stick she had dropped and went painfully to one knee, feeling his swollen organs squish around, scooting as close to the body as he could without tumbling down the ditch on top of it.

He pushed the parsnip stem aside. On the dead man's shoulder was a crude tattoo, a faded red heart around one word: MOM.

||||||||||

When Leroy "Grape" Fanta arrived at the two-story brick building, circa 1908, that had been his daily wheelhouse for forty-
three years—204 Second Street, Farmstead, Wisconsin—he
could hear his desk phone ringing through the old glass door.
But his key wouldn't work in the lock.

He pulled the key out and studied it.

The phone stopped ringing, then immediately started
again.

His key looked fine. But maybe he had bent it somehow.
Or maybe there was something in the lock—though not that
he could see. The phone stopped and started again. Whoever
was calling didn't want to use the message machine, meaning
that he or she represented exactly the kind of old-school Bad
Axer who wanted a human being on the other end, who felt
cut off by the loss of the weekly *Broadcaster*, to whom saying,
All the news is online anyway, amounted to saying, *You don't
count anymore.*

Fanta grumbled around the block toward the alley where
the back door was. Lord love a duck, it was hot. Seven A.M.
in Wisconsin, and it felt like high noon on Hill 937 in South
Vietnam. He rounded the corner, saw that the bank sign read
ninety-five degrees, and he snorted. That was only weather. As
he had been pointing out in the *Broadcaster* just two weeks ago,
climate was another story: this had become the hottest summer
ever, breaking last summer's record, which had broken the record
from the summer before. Cumulatively, the relentless thermal
load had settled into the bricks and the concrete and the asphalt,
had sunk into the fields and the forests and the spring creeks,
and either Fanta was mistaken, or he was seeing rapid changes.

Lately, different birds hunted different insects in the Bad Axe, different parasitic vines twined the tree trunks, a bigger and bolder mustelid hunted a more prolific mouse population in his woodpile. Unless Fanta was mistaken, and he was not, he had seen a nutria—sleek Gulf Coast rodent, big as a beaver— ransacking the bank of the Bad Axe River. And the gypsy moths, their incessantly chewing caterpillars the vanguard of an invading horde, shrouding trees everywhere with their sticky gray tents, ominous and funereal . . . and, goddamn it, Fanta's key didn't work in the back door either.

He noticed that the knob and lock were shiny. They were different. They were new.

He labored back to the front door.

Same.

Babette Rickreiner had changed the locks on him, still with his personals inside, his whiskey and cigarettes, music cassette tapes, pictures of his late wife, a hundred years of Bad Axe history in his filing cabinets.

And the phone kept ringing.

Streaming sweat and cursing everything Rickreiner—"*Happy Valley Shopper*, my flat ass"—"*Barry Rickreiner for Sheriff* over my road-killed body"—Fanta jaywalked across Main Street to Farmstead Home and Agricultural Supply, where he shoved himself through the door. His weary pig-valve heart felt strange, unusually thumpy. Was it the heat, or the dead body, or the wounded look on the face of his favorite sheriff? Was it his Agent Orange exposure, or the carditis inflicted by the Lyme spirochetes upon his heart muscle? It was hard to say exactly which specific pains afflicted Fanta as he wallowed up to the agricultural desk. Perhaps all of them. His vision tunneled. His veins throbbed. His joints bucked and squealed like train couplings.

"What can I do you for, Grape?"

His short-term memory had been dissolving under stress. He had to think for a moment.

"One crowbar, please," he wheezed eventually at his old pal Ron Bellweather.

"The biggest, nastiest crowbar you can sell me."

CHAPTER 3

A blue body bag lay zipped on the examining table. The latest Bad Axe County coroner, the multitalented Dr. Blaine Kleekamp, both the sheriff's family medicine doc and a wildlife veterinarian, shut off the water and turned from the sink, snapping on rubber gloves.

"How's your little boy?"

Her stomach seemed to flop—which one?—and she glanced away.

School had been out for exactly 64 days—yes, she was counting—and Opie had been gone at Rainbow Kids Camp for the last 23 of those days—and the precise divisor for either of those numerators was the number of times, either 17 or 12, that Taylor had been in a time-out since. In any case, the outcome of the calculation equaled parental worry. Or could it be possible, she thought just now, that the correct numerator was the 117 days since Barry Rickreiner had filed the paperwork to run for Bad Axe County Sheriff, when the first KICK HER OUT and BARRY HER signs had appeared? Was that when Taylor's troubles had begun?

From the basement window of Strangspleen Funeral Home, the county's make-do morgue, she watched the tires of the ambulance retreat, leaving her a view of the backside of Farmers' Direct-Buy, the original of Babette Rickreiner's franchise properties, inherited from her late husband. In the Rickreiner tradition of predatory enterprise, Farmers' Direct-Buy dangled a lose-lose deal by which sinking farmers could acquire suicidal levels of debt while spending borrowed money elsewhere and defunding the local economy. The sight of BARRY HER's cash source made the sheriff remember that Dr. Kleekamp had declared himself a Heidi Kick supporter. Since Oppo claimed to work for the county, Oppo could be Kleekamp, she thought. She might trust him if he was.

Watching her through safety goggles and over a germ mask, the doctor asked, "Is his wound healing up OK?"

So he meant Dylan. One week ago, Taylor, for reasons unknown, had chopped Dylan on the arm with a hoe to the tune of eighteen stitches.

"Oh." She sighed with relief. "The little goofball is looking forward to a nice big scar. He thinks it's going to look awesome."

Dr. Kleekamp said, "Hmmm." He stripped the yellow custody tape and began to unzip the body bag. "I referred you folks to our in-system child psychologist. Any progress there?"

Now he meant Taylor, Dylan's assailant.

"Well, no, not yet, because my husband . . ."

Kleekamp stopped the zipper on its first curve and waited for what she had to say about her husband. She and Harley agreed that compared to Taylor, Dylan was somehow developing more quickly, was bigger and stronger, was reading and writing at a higher level. The other threat to Taylor's psyche, they agreed, was that meanwhile, Ophelia, Opie, Taylor's natal big sister, was at a summer camp for gender-nonconforming kids, possibly becoming an even bigger and smarter brother than the one Taylor already failed to keep up with.

The sheriff caught herself touching her stomach and visualizing her uterus beneath her duty belt, scanning it. Three days to zygote . . . Eight days to embryo . . .

But Harley resisted seeing a child psychologist. By end of summer, he had been arguing, maybe Taylor has a growth spurt, maybe Opie becomes a sister again, maybe Barry Rickreiner gets exposed, quits the race, stops picking on the Kick family. All this crazy weather and stress would break eventually, her husband believed, and they would coast into a cooler, calmer fall.

She told Dr. Kleekamp, "It's just that Harley knows all about small-town stigma and he's protective of Taylor."

"Ah, yes. Well."

"I am too," she said.

Kleekamp resumed unzipping. "We're all protective of Taylor," he reminded her, working around the victim's booted right foot. "It's just a question of the best way to take care of him. Your whole family needs to get together on this. No mixed signals."

And *now* he meant Belle Kick, Grammy Belle, who believed that all Taylor needed was a mommy who paid attention to him and showed how much she loved him by whupping him good whenever he acted out.

"Right." The sheriff gritted her teeth. What was Belle's problem lately? "Same page. Yes, I know."

Now the corpse was fully exposed. Kleekamp leaned in.

He was new at this. He mostly looked at living people. As for violent death, she knew that lately he had been collecting road-killed deer, conducting autopsies and finding evidence of some new disease—not the well-documented prion infection, chronic wasting disease, but something bacterial and gnat-borne that made the deer stagger onto the roads and get killed in collisions. On the table was Dr. Kleekamp's first murder victim, and Sheriff Kick felt his apprehension.

"Well, shot twice in the back," he said, beginning with the obvious. "Dirty exit wounds. Looks like mud and blood mixed."

He peered more closely at a pattern of small red welts across the dead man's chest, neck, and cheek.

"What's this rash, I wonder?"

"We found him in wild parsnip."

"Ah. No clothes on?"

"We found him just like that."

Kleekamp began to circle the table, prodding the victim's torso, lifting his limbs, looking beneath his filthy underpants.

"He's about thirty. Uncut hair and nails, bad teeth, needle tracks, emaciated and malnourished, scabies all over his groin . . . I'm going to guess that he was homeless."

The sheriff nodded grimly. She thought so too. She remembered the priest: *Five homeless men missing, picked off the streets of La Crosse . . .*

"Urban homeless, I mean," Kleekamp continued, "not from around here, probably."

She knew what he meant. Poverty existed in the Bad Axe—deep, and plenty of it—but no one panhandled or pushed a shopping cart or slept on the sidewalk. Her phone buzzed beneath her badge. "Excuse me," she told Kleekamp. "This is Dispatch." She answered with a finger tap. "Go ahead."

"You're in town, right?" Denise began. "Because everybody else is out on Liberty Hill Road or busy on a welfare visit."

"I'm with the medical examiner. Go ahead."

"ADT alarm is calling in an incident at the newspaper office. There's been a break-in. Can you get there?"

"I can leave right now."

"Ron Bellweather says he just sold Leroy Fanta a crowbar."

"Got it."

"Maybe you can beat Empress Rickreiner to the scene?"

"I will."

"And Heidi?"

"Go ahead."

"That priest from La Crosse is on my other line. His scanner is programmable by zip code. He heard our call and wants to talk to you. I said, 'She's kinda busy, Father.' I took his number."

"Thanks, Denise."

She slipped her phone back behind her badge. Kleekamp had turned the body over. Powder burns around the entry wounds meant the two gunshots had been at point-blank range.

"I need a headshot and fingerprints," she told him. "How soon until we have a cause of death?"

Kleekamp pushed the victim's matted hair aside and used a penlight to look inside his ear. "Hmmm." He shone the light up both nostrils. "Hmmm," he said again. He straightened up and blinked through his goggles. His mask puffed out.

"A fair while, I think. From what I'm seeing here, I'm pretty sure I'm going to have get the saw and the scissors out—"

He swallowed hard. This was no dead deer.

"—and open up his lungs."

| | | | | | | | | | |

"We meet again," Grape Fanta managed to tell her over loud orchestral rock music, something she vaguely recognized. He had limped coughing to the glass front door of the newspaper office—it had been repainted: HAPPY VALLEY SHOPPER—and let the sheriff in. She saw that he had gathered his thin silver pony-tail and zipped his cargo shorts since she had seen him an hour ago. The music fizzed from a dusty silver boom box that would have looked retro even when she was in grade school.

"We got an alarm call. Was there a break-in?"

"Sure was. Back door. I shut off the noise."

"Anything missing?"

He collapsed into his antique wooden desk chair, coughed some more, and spat into a tissue. He turned his music down.

"One laptop computer. Some fool's personal effects."

She unflapped her breast pocket, took out her notebook, clicked her pen, and began to look around.

"I see they left a crowbar behind."

One leaned against Fanta's desk. Beside it sat a battered cardboard box jammed with framed photos, coffee mugs, award plaques, pens and pencils, inhalers, and a cone-shaped lump of foam.

"It looks brand-new," she observed of the crowbar. "This could be easy. It's still got a bright new FARMSTEAD HOME AND AG sticker, so it came from across the street. Whoever broke in might be close by."

The ruined editor cleared his throat. His spotted hands shook. He had barked several knuckles. "Bastards," he rumbled.

"Any idea which bastards? Or should I ask at Home and Ag?"

"Hey, you wanna hear something?"

"Babette and Barry are on their way, I'm sure, to supervise my work. It's only about twenty minutes from Blooming Hill."

"Screw 'em. You gotta hear this."

She realized he had been listening to a message. He reached across his desk and restarted his answering machine. An angry old man's voice continued.

"'. . . turning and turning in the widening gyre, the falcon cannot hear the falconer; things fall apart; the centre cannot hold; mere anarchy is loosed upon the world, the blood-dimmed tide is loosed, and everywhere the ceremony of innocence is drowned.'"

Fanta raised his shrubby eyebrows at her. The voice went on, tremulous with seeming rage.

"'The best lack all conviction, while the worst are full of passionate intensity.' Meanwhile, the complete assholes print ads for gas-guzzling Ford trucks and thirty-six-packs of Coca-Cola—"

Fanta paused the rant.

"Who is that?" she asked.

He creaked back in his wooden chair, knit his bent hands behind his ponytail, showing her his wet armpits. He hadn't bothered to brush away the wood splinters that clung to his shirt.

"William Butler Yeats," he said. "The great Irish poet, 1865 to 1939."

He hesitated and she said, "Oh."

"Except for that last part about assholes."

"Oh," she said again.

"My mother was a Donovan, Irish all the way. Same as your father, yes? Rest his soul. And your mother's."

He seemed a little drunk. Maybe the dead body had knocked him off balance too.

"I meant the caller."

"Ah, him." Fanta shot his answering machine a wave of acknowledgment. "I think he's this crank who used to write me letters to the editor—which, as you know, the *Happy Valley Shopper* won't print anymore. That guy quoted Yeats too. T. S. Eliot as well. Sometimes Jimmy Buffet and KC and the Sunshine Band."

She tried again to inject urgency. "All those ADT alarms ring at the Rickreiner houses too. You can be sure they're on the way. They might conclude that you're involved."

He ignored the problem. "You find out anything?"

"The medical examiner has the body. We'll get fingerprints and send around a photo. I've got deputies searching the area. The Vernon County K-9 team is there too. But it's hot already, and any minute now I'll have to back my deputies off and start them on welfare visits."

Fanta slumped. He pulled both ends of his tobacco-stained mustache. "I heard we lost Joe Himmelsbach."

She nodded. Yesterday afternoon, Interim Chief Deputy Dick Bender had found the poor old man fighting for breath on the floor in front of his TV. It had been a hundred and ten degrees inside his house. If they had checked on him earlier, he might have made it.

"Shit on rye," Fanta said, his eyes red-rimmed. "And Bender's gotta feel like the Grim Reaper by now. That's three, right? He's got the touch. Maybe that means he should retire and give you another chance to hire somebody new."

She declined to comment. Her Police and Fire Commission had grown increasingly antagonistic since she had busted a whole convoy of them for drunk-driving ORVs, off-road vehicles, on

Memorial Day. When Chief Deputy David Morales had left, they had appointed Bender, a hostile party, as her interim chief deputy. The PFC was using Bender to harass her—and to stall, she felt, until Barry Rickreiner got himself elected in November.

She swallowed her frustration and took a few steps to see better behind Fanta's desk. One drawer was open exactly as far as the neck of a tall whiskey bottle. Against that drawer leaned a battered briefcase. Inside she could see a silver laptop, no doubt the "missing" one.

"So is this caller threatening you?"

Fanta shrugged. "He's got a right to be upset."

"Does he have a name?"

"If it's the fella I think it is, he always signed his letters *'FROM HELL HOLLOW.'*"

She searched her mental map and frowned.

"I can't think of any place around here called Hell Hollow."

Fanta coughed for a few moments. Then he leaned forward and said stickily, "Given his interest in poetry, I gather he's making a metaphor."

He restarted the message.

". . . big sale on strawberries, fresh off their three-thousand-mile jet trip from Argentina, cheap ground beef at only eighteen hundred gallons of water per pound, vanilla ice cream with listeria. We sleep beneath a prion moon, Fanta, a billion misfit molecules hunting each and every one of us. Awake, we can't see even the biggest broken things. Meanwhile, noon is our new midnight. But hear me . . ."

The voice choked and seemed about to fail.

". . . those who face the darkness are meant to shine the light. You will be saved by fire."

With a hard click the message ended. Sheriff Kick felt chilled and jittery.

"Do you have his letters?"

"If he's 'FROM HELL HOLLOW,' yes, I do, on file. You know"—the editor sighed, going limp with weariness and frustration—"prehistoric records, cave paintings and such."

He raised a weak wave to indicate the cavernous room behind him, where in the shadows the sheriff could see several filing cabinets, and behind them big machines and trays of cast-metal type.

Fanta sighed again. "'Noon is our new midnight,'" he quoted. "That's not bad. The thing about poets . . ."

She stepped around his desk and past the cabinets and trays of type to inspect the back door. "I'm listening." The jamb had been pried out and shredded on the lock side, the way a clumsy person in a fury might break-and-enter if he had no background in the craft.

"Poets don't just change the channel," Fanta told her with his voice raised. "They put a foot through the TV. Poets drive on the wrong side of the road. That's their job."

She returned. If the Rickreiners had left Town of Blooming Hill at the alarm, they were now about five minutes away. She took a latex glove from her hip pocket and put it on—just for show, she decided. She picked up the crowbar and faced Fanta, who fumbled with a pack of Winstons.

"Let me guess," she said. "They changed the locks on you?"

"Yes."

"Right now, are you trespassing?"

"Possibly."

"You've been let go?"

He got his smoke lit, blew a gust toward the old building's pressed-tin ceiling.

"Babette thinks so. But I've filed a few lawsuits, so at least my right to be here is legally contested."

She sighed and put her notebook away. Her phone buzzed for attention again. She had to get back to Liberty Hill Road.

"OK," she said. "Your right to be here is tied up in the courts. I can go with that."

She raised the crowbar.

"I'm gonna file this bad boy in my trunk and give it to my husband."

She kept her gaze on Fanta as he pulled on his Winston.

"I'm going to move your car around the block, Grape, so the Rickreiners won't know you're here, and so I won't have to bust you for driving under the influence. Then I'm going to call ATD and tell them it was a false alarm. Stay out of sight while I deal with Babette and Barry. As soon as they're gone, you're going to call someone to fix that back door. Then you're going to collect your stuff and leave, and you're not going to do this again. Do we have a deal?"

|||||||||||

She waited outside her Charger on Second Street for the Rick-reiners, mother and son, manager and candidate, feeling the approach of another scalding day delaminate her into layers of time. Three weeks exactly since she and Harley had made love. Seventeen days since she should have had started her period. Seven days since Taylor had stuck the hoe in Dylan's arm. Only eighty-seven days until the election. One-eighth of a day—three busy hours—since Grammy Belle had caught her peeing in a jar, around the same time that she got the email from Oppo popping the question: *So do you want my help?*

Before the sheriff could come further unglued, Babette Rick-reiner's custom-gold Silverado cornered at dangerous speed off Main Street onto Second Street and jerked to an angular stop ahead of the Charger. Something new: the big truck's tailgate

displayed a life-sized 3-D decal that made it look as if Babette
had Kenny Rogers bound and gagged in her truck box. Good
God, this woman. The horny widow. Candidate Barry followed
his mommy in a vehicle perfectly unbecoming of a sheriff, or of
any adult for that matter, a vintage El Camino, red, accessorized
with a hot-green Yamaha dirt bike tethered upright in the box.
Her opponent roared up to bookend the sheriff, who cringed
and waited.

First, pint-sized Babette tumbled out, birdy-legged and
bazooka-chested, balancing on six-inch-tall wedged sandals.
The woman was seventy, dressed twenty-four, and talked like a
trucker. This early in the morning, her look wasn't quite together:
her unadorned earlobes sagged weirdly, and she had nicked her
teeth with lipstick while driving.

"So you're just standing out here sunning your tits," she
began.

Sheriff Kick waited for meaning.

"Because you didn't catch the cocksuckers."

Ah. And ick. "None to catch," she answered, not untruth-
fully. "The building is secure. You haven't been robbed. I called
the service provider. They should have called you."

Babette rumbled her loose throat and spat a nighttime
specimen. She might have rolled her eyes behind the rhinestone
sunglasses before she said, "We came all this way . . ." She opened
her complex dental work in a yawn. "Like we got nothing else to
do but chase false alarms."

*Your choice to chase, lady. Why not trust the sheriff's department
to handle alarm calls, like a normal business owner?*

But the sheriff held her tongue. Since her first day as a
rookie—1,574 days and counting—every call at any Rickreiner
property had worked its way through some variation of these two

showing up to interfere. It seemed as if the Rickreiners always expected more than just a break-in, were always girding for bigger and more complicated trouble. The sheriff wondered if what Oppo wrote was true: *Kim Maybee's suicide was homicide.* Barry was a lowlife, but was he capable of murder? The young woman had been a girlfriend of Barry Rickreiner's in his days as a boozer and a user, and his casting-off of the wrong friends anchored his redemption story.

Now the candidate exited his ride, hauling out a Big Gulp cup to spit into before saying something unfriendly into his phone. He had his mother's exquisite body type—petite yet unbalanced—and lately, as if to get the Bad Axe ready for the sight of him in a sheriff's uniform, he had begun dressing like a cable TV cowboy—but the runty one, she would like to tell him, trying to catch up on the short-legged horse.

"... enough of your bullshit, *Sharice in Atlanta.* Get your shit together or lose our business."

The sheriff stared, always appalled. It was not among her official responsibilities to police fashion, but she could write some heavy tickets right now. Pigeon-toed men weighing under a buck-fifty should not wear flashy western boots. Chinless men should not decorate the problem with string ties. *And flaunt your open-carry permit,* she thought, *go ahead, fine, but the black Gore-Tex thigh holster is bunching up your cowboy trousers and confusing the look.* And real men did not cuss out the security system's customer-service reps into their sparkly new iPhones.

"Hey, Ma, the idiots just called. False alarm."

"What's-her-face just told me."

Barry drilled Skoal juice into his Big Gulp. Loyal Denise had attempted to demystify this pissant's run for office with jokes withdrawn from her vast mental savings account.

How does a man decide when it's appropriate to challenge a woman in power?

He looks in his pants. If he sees a penis, it's time.

But in truth BARRY HER's run for sheriff had been a while in the works: substance-abuse rehab (year one), tech-college law-enforcement training (years two and three), stints as a volunteer EMT and a part-time township police officer (years three and four). Somewhere during year three, he had ticked the family-man box by marrying a divorcée, Becky Rilke, with three prefab little ones.

"Are we gonna check the building, though?" he wondered, almost looking at Sheriff Kick on his way to read the mood of his mother.

Babette's heavily made-up nose had popped out with fat jewels of perspiration. She needed air-conditioning, fast. "I think she can handle it from here. She's at her best when nothing happened."

All three stood there baking in the enmity and the sun. Then BARRY HER seized the day. "So, hell, Ma, I guess we oughta hit the Ease Inn and get a bloody, then go put some signs around. We just got the new one: WHY ARE YOU KICKING YOURSELF? I mean, instead of just standing here getting swamp crotch."

Again he nearly looked at the sheriff. His mother one-upped his crudity.

"Might as well," Babette agreed, "since we hauled our stinking cornholes all this way."

The sheriff stared at the sides of their averted heads.

"Don't drive drunk on my roads," she said.

She felt a drip of sweat roll straight down her spine.

"And while you're out, come take the signs off my property. Try that stunt again and your stinking cornholes are going to catch a trespassing charge."

| | | | | | | | | | |

On her way out of town, she passed Farmers' Buy-Direct and then played eye-tag with the other Rickreiner properties, gaudy and grasping, disruptive trash in the still-quaint Bad Axe: Cash America . . . Supercuts . . . Dollar Heaven . . . Liquor City . . .

CHAPTER 4

The K-9 on loan from the Vernon County Sheriff's Department, a female German shepherd named Duffy, had found the missing twelve-pack of beer. Or at least half of it.

That summarized the news.

The sheriff's own deputies had found nothing of note along the roadside. Denise had repurposed one to a domestic disturbance call and sent the other three back on welfare checks. But the dog had found six Busch Lights.

"One empty at a time," explained the dog's handler, Vernon County Deputy K. Christiansen. She seemed to be a Lyndsey Luck type, a new hire, trying hard.

The sheriff felt the heat pulse against her. Both the dog and her handler were flocked with burrs and looked about to collapse. As Duffy panted, her gray-spotted pink tongue hung egregiously out the side of her mouth. Her ribs heaved unnaturally, and she stared fixedly at her cage inside the Vernon County SUV cruiser.

"Somebody got a pretty good load on," Deputy Christiansen surmised. She panted too, pointing with a fistful of wire flags across a meadow toward Liberty Hill, several hundred yards in the distance.

"Blue-and-silver cans. Like connect-the-dots. Going that way."

The sheriff looked "that way" and tried to see any kind of trail. But the meadow was wall-to-wall with head-high late summer weeds. Cicadas droned across the distance. Turkey vultures floated over it.

"I flagged the beer cans," Deputy Christiansen said. "Duffy picked up a clear trail between them. But funny thing, she couldn't find the victim's scent, as far as I could tell. She went straight from beer can to beer can, but she wasn't happy, like she thought she was doing it wrong."

Changing her voice, she spoke to the dog.

"You just couldn't smell him anywhere, could you? But you were such a good girl! You tried so hard! Such a good hot girl!"

She pointed once more toward Liberty Hill.

"We went all the way to the top. I would guess the cans kept going over the other side. But it wasn't your guy drinking 'em and tossing 'em. No scent of him, according to Duffy."

Deputy Christiansen opened the rear of her vehicle. Duffy trembled at the sight of the cage inside, eager to escape her disappointing performance.

"We came back and did a full three-sixty around this spot, but we got nothing and she's just too hot, Sheriff. The heat index was over 140 degrees before we even started. She went whining around every which way for a while and then she just sat down."

The dog looked ashamed as her handler pulled a ramp down and positioned it.

"OK, girl."

K-9 Duffy slunk up into her cage.

|||||||||||

A minute later, Sheriff Kick stood alone in the brutal swelter, squinting into the sea of vegetation.

Kids. Who else would find hot beer and bash straight off into thick weeds to drink it?

Kids on foot.

She tried to think of kids in the area, but she hardly knew this far-northeastern corner of the Bad Axe, and she hadn't seen a residence of any kind since turning off the county highway three miles back. The terrain was thickly forested bluffs flanking rocky, flood-scoured coulees, with swampy lowlands in between. As her gaze followed Liberty Hill Road to the east, she realized that Elmo Quarry Pond was nearby. Two days from now, on their way with their 4-H Club to help out at the annual Bad Axe County Farm Breakfast, the twins were scheduled to make a ritual sunrise stop at Elmo Pond to feed shelled corn to the giant goldfish, supposedly carnival-game escapees, that survived there. Opie claimed to have seen one as big as a suckling pig. This would be the boys' first brush with the myth. They were excited. Dylan had wanted to set his alarm clock five days ahead of time. Taylor had insisted he would need snacks, water, and extra clothing in his backpack.

Kids.

Right?

It had to be kids who found the beer. The body had appeared and the beer had disappeared in the same vicinity within the same time frame. Somewhere, she thought, there must be at least one kid who knew something.

Either that or the sun had boiled her brain.

She retrieved an evidence bag from the Charger's trunk. The

sea of weeds closed behind her as she used a stick to slash her way from marker flag to marker flag, collecting blue-and-silver Busch Light cans.

One . . .

Two . . .

Then a third can, drained empty within just a hundred yards.

Kids, for sure. She could imagine herself and friends finding beer at about thirteen years old. The idea would be to drink as much as possible, as fast as possible, before their incredible luck ran out. Never mind if hot light beer tasted sour as horse piss. There was alcohol in it.

Twenty scorching minutes later, rashy, sweat-soaked, gasping for breath, now with five cans in her evidence bag and verging on heatstroke, Sheriff Kick reached the base of Liberty Hill. She felt dizzy, temples pounding, and the Charger seemed miles away. But from here on she would be in the shade of the hillside forest. After a short rest, she pushed on to the top.

She had never been on Liberty Hill. A toppled fieldstone cairn reminded her of the reason for the name. Larger and more populated Vernon County began just over two miles north, and with campaigning on her mind she recalled Grape Fanta's story in the *Broadcaster* about Grover Cleveland. Barnstorming for president in the 1890s, Cleveland had passed through Vernon County giving speeches from the porch of his train car. Some proud Bad Axer had raised a large U.S. flag right here, and the candidate, gazing south across the ridgetops, had spied Old Glory and famously called this "Liberty Hill."

When she gazed south, she could see the vast tract of weeds between herself and her Charger at the roadside, and from there the vista skipped across ridgetops all the way to Farmstead. A mile or more to the east she could see a corner of Elmo Quarry—a sheer cliff of dynamite-fractured limestone—but not the deep emerald pond that filled the abandoned gravel pit. Out to the west rolled sister hills of Liberty Hill that had no roads or names. And finally from this height, looking north over rugged ground, she saw a farm.

She moved herself to see it better. She could make out, half-hidden in the isolated coulee directly below, what looked like an Amish farm fallen on hard times: collapsing outbuildings, a primitive sawmill and piles of gray slab wood, a scythe-cut hayfield, laundry on a bowed line. No power poles or wires. No tractors or trucks. She saw specks, brown and white, in motion.

Chickens?

Nothing else moved. It looked like desolation, like despair. Or was that a faulty judgment by her frazzled modern mind? What was wrong with a slower pace and a simpler life? Wasn't living off the land and depending on no one a cornerstone of American identity? Her thoughts had drifted back a hundred-plus years—subsistence farming, rustic isolation, Grover Cleveland for president—when her phone stirred beneath her badge.

"It's Dr. Kleekamp, Sheriff." The medical examiner sounded rattled. "I've got some results. Bear with me here."

"OK. Go ahead."

Kleekamp exhaled with a whoosh of relief, in exactly the manner of a rookie coroner who had just sawed through his first human sternum.

"First, I'm gonna agree with myself that he was homeless. Indications of liver disease, gum disease, lung infection, frostbite, brain contusions, basically the works. He was in real bad shape for at least several years."

She waited, thinking of the priest from La Crosse and his concern about the vanishing homeless. But she knew Kleekamp hadn't called just to reinforce his own guesswork.

"And?"

"Well," he said, whooshing again, "I disagree with another thing I thought at first. I do not think someone brought him in and dumped him off dead in that ditch. I think he was alive in the Bad Axe, alive when he landed there. And I think you should have found his other boot somewhere nearby."

"Why?"

"He walked around that terrain for a while. *After* he was shot."

"Because?"

"I'll stand to be corrected by a forensic botanist," Kleekamp said, "but he's got trefoil burrs in his underpants, and he's got wild parsnip seeds all the way down in the toe of that boot. He'd been walking for a while."

She glanced at her uniform: burrs everywhere. Her pant cuffs were full of seeds and other shreds of desiccated matter, and something prickled inside her socks.

Kleekamp said, "He was on the move, Sheriff. He had covered some ground. But with *both* boots on, because his left foot, the one without the boot, is in exactly the same condition as the right. From that, I conclude the other boot came off close to where he died in the ditch."

"OK. That makes enough sense."

"And then I'm gonna guess that your searchers found some disturbed ground close by. Maybe a large, shallow hole?"

Her breath caught. A grave? Touching her stomach, she stared down at the worn-out farm.

"Am I right?" Kleekamp persisted.

"No. No, actually not. The dog got no scent of him in the area, and we found pretty much nothing. Some empty beer cans. Did you find any alcohol in his system?"

"None. He had a meal in his stomach. All vegetable. No alcohol. You didn't find a hole in the ground within a couple hundred yards away? He couldn't have gone very far in his condition."

"Which was what?"

"These two gunshots were from close range, but neither one hit anything immediately fatal. Still, with internal bleeding, he couldn't have lasted more than thirty minutes to an hour, at the very best. Even if he hadn't also been . . ."

Kleekamp's voice faded. "Hang on!" At a distance, she heard him throwing up.

"OK," he restarted, sounding embarrassed. "I just cut open his lungs, and I'm looking inside them one more time, and unless I don't know what I'm looking at . . ."

He paused to swallow, and just then the sheriff caught a flicker of something blue-and-silver far down the steep slope toward the farm. She wasn't really listening as her medical examiner explained about aspirated dirt . . . that he had only one way to explain how a man could have this much dirt in his lungs—

She didn't need to hear it. She had been there.

"He was buried alive," she interrupted.

She had surprised Kleekamp into silence.

"He was shot twice and buried alive," she said, beginning to move. "He escaped his grave somehow, traveled on foot, then not on foot, and landed in that ditch."

She wasn't sure how the phone call ended. All she paid attention to now, descending toward the isolated farm, was the glint ahead of a blue-and-silver beer can.

CHAPTER 5

"Liar," began the same caller's voice the moment Grape Fanta picked up the phone.

"Corporate tool," the caller added, a fiery lash to an old lefty such as Fanta.

Fanta said, "Well, now it sounds personal. You probably don't realize that you and I are on the same side—"

The man talked over him.

"It always said on your masthead 'We the People.' I sent you a letter. You didn't print it. I sent you another letter. I didn't see that either. All I see is what's for lunch at the nursing home. Beer and trucks for sale. Who hit a deer, and how much property damage, that's the important thing. The deer are sick by the millions, Fanta, but you're keeping your little scorecard on collisions with automobiles. Insurance. New bumpers. How much smaller can you think? Changes in latitude require changes in attitude, Fanta. That's what my letters were about. Noon is our new midnight. We'll be sub-equatorial before we wake up. You used to print the people's letters. But profits over people, that's your game now. Well, I'm the game changer."

As the caller broke into a wheezy cough, Fanta used the opening to talk back.

"Listen, friend, I've gladly printed your letters. I agree with a lot of what you have to say. But what's happened here at the newspaper is that it's not even a newspaper anymore. You apparently haven't heard that—"

The voice came back, nearly shouting over Fanta as if the man were deaf.

"The G8 summit is in two weeks, Fanta! You know what they'll be talking about? How to drive down oil prices—"

"Actually it's the G7 now," Fanta put in. "Russia's out."

"Oil prices! Not the climate refugees, Fanta, not the billions of displaced people soon to be on the move. When I think of this—"

"Those are issues that I've always—"

"'—a vast image out of *Spiritus Mundi* troubles my sight: somewhere in sands of the desert, a shape with lion body and the head of man—'"

"I've read Yeats too, my friend."

"'—while all about it reel shadows of the indignant desert birds.' How about the shadows of the gypsy moths, Fanta? Shrouds in the trees. They'll strip us bare. But it won't matter. We've already sold our soul. Feedlots on the ridges, *E. coli* in the aquifers, spongiform in the brain. And now the goddamn ticks are going to kill us with a new spirochete." The caller's labored in-breath whistled. "But . . . oh, well, at least lawn mowers are on sale and there's another pancake breakfast. At least we're racing tractors on the fairgrounds. At least—"

A grinding patch of static cut off the speaker. Unsure what

had happened, Fanta used the opportunity to say, "Well, now, I've been infected by Lyme disease myself, so—"

"—instead of the truth. You're a corporate tool now. You work for the forces of destruction—"

"The hell I do. I—"

"You work for Koyaanisqatsi, Incorporated."

"The goddamn hell I do. You have no idea—"

"—afraid to print my letters. The People's letters. We the People, Fanta. If things go according to your plan, the People die, and only the rich will make it through the night. Well, let me say this: They had better goddamn hope so. The sun is upon us. Noon is our new midnight. Like the great martyr Thich Quang Duc, I will bring the light."

Another static hiss and some fumbling.

"Can I talk now?" Fanta asked.

A solid click.

"Hello?" Thich Quang Duc rang a bell. Vietnam in the sixties. The self-immolating monk. "Listen, how about you tell me who you are? You're the fella that signs off '*FROM HELL HOLLOW.*' Am I right?"

The second click was the hang-up, he understood, because next came the dial tone.

Fanta stared at his antiquated answering machine. *Aha*, he realized. *I've been talking back to a recording.* A recording playing to a recording. One cassette tape to another.

The guy had recorded himself reading a letter and played it over the phone into the machine.

Fanta sat back in the old desk chair that after decades had become an extension of his aching, creaking body. He lit a smoke and sucked on his Walker bottle. He put his feet up, his journalist's brain coming alive.

FROM HELL HOLLOW.

What was the story here?

God, how he loved to ask that question.

Whose story was it?

The lovely subject-object dance. Viewpoint. Where did the storyteller stand? How did the story and its teller connect?

Vietnam? He considered the intriguing eligibility of his own narrative as a parallel: A Bad Axe farm boy, 1969, proud to be drafted, returns home damaged by a futile and fraudulent war, having slaughtered fellow humans, inhaled Agent Orange, lost a kidney and a bone-hunk from his right leg, transforming into the kind of young man that no one around the Bad Axe ever expected to see, a longhair with DOW SHALT NOT KILL on his Volkswagen bumper, an angry voice in the taverns saying un-American things. And from there forward, in exchange for one of the smallest salaries in the history of journalism, the former farm boy spends the next forty-plus years breathing fire from the rooftops . . .

Ugh.

This was pain talking, the over-exercised rhetoric of loss and grief.

Local Man Wallows in Self-Pity

Fanta watched his headline drift away. *Tell the truth, asshole.* He was only ever of average ability, average disability, and average courage. He had ended up as an average alcoholic widower, staggering around at the end of his rope, unable to let go. From here he tried again.

He was the common man.

An honest pilgrim.

He the people.

Ugh.

Ugh, ugh, ugh.

Martyr-to-Be Self-Eulogizes

He swallowed a mouthful of Walker, shot smoke from his nostrils, and chuckled darkly at a favorite memory.

Back when his beloved wife, Maryanne, was alive, whenever he had become overwrought at his typewriter and was being a jerk, mixing a metaphor, dangling a modifier, confusing *its* and *it's*—this was the eighties, Maryanne typesetting on the clumsy Compugraphic machine on the balcony over his desk—whenever he botched the angle on a story, waxed too poetic, wrote a steaming dump of a headline, his dearly departed would reach into her bra, extract her foam-rubber left boob—now in his box of recovered personal effects–and chuck it down upon his head.

He chuckled again darkly.

Something had just hit him on the head.

The story was not just *FROM HELL HOLLOW*.

The story was himself, the veteran-veteran Grape Fanta, finding *FROM HELL HOLLOW*, meeting the man, engaging him, their encounter, their dialectic, their reconciliation, that was the story.

Could he find the man?

Of course he could.

If he looked, there would be clues in the letters. To the extent that he had ever given any thought to the matter, he had always guessed that his screed-writer was a homesteader, a reclusive subsistence farmer, educated, radical, pacifist, contrarian, perhaps Amish-like in his willful disconnectedness, howling from the wilds of the Bad Axe.

These guesses still seemed right. As the Vietnam War had shredded the nation, as students rioted and cops fired tear gas, there had been a back-to-the-land movement, and after Fanta had returned home and kicked around in despair for a time, the idea of checking out and homesteading, becoming a society unto himself, had beckoned. He had pursued meaning through journalism instead. Maybe *FROM HELL HOLLOW* had done the same through nature. And look at both of them now.

Fanta's cigarette ash reached his fingers and he jolted. He tilted up out of his chair and stared dizzily toward his bank of filing cabinets.

A man goes back to the land, the land infects him with spirochetes and prions.

A man seeks sanctuary, sanctuary attacks him.

A man seeks truth, finds pain, and madness.

A man like that, Fanta thought, *he and I could talk.*

CHAPTER 6

The sixth Busch Light can from Lars Hansen's lost twelve-pack had been drained and jettisoned on the way down Liberty Hill to the distressed property in the hollow below.

When Sheriff Kick arrived in the farmyard, she found the torn beer box and the other six empties strewn in heavy grass around a body sprawled facedown, unmoving in direct sun.

Sweat in her eyes caused the sheriff to wince and blink for a clean look. It was a young female in plain Amish dress. The girl's eyes were shut. Her cheek rested in dried vomit. But her nose whistled as she breathed slowly in and out.

The sheriff blinked again. The girl's face and hands, her bare feet and ankles, were covered with bites and rashes. Her long-sleeved gray dress and black bonnet were stuck all over with the same burrs that were attached to the sheriff's uniform. A blurt of oxidized fluid had dried across the dull-blue dress, which was freshly wet in back where she had peed herself not long ago.

Her dirty feet looked a hundred years old. She had a mustache and a few long black chin whiskers. But her shallow bust and lithe body made the sheriff guess she wasn't much more than sixteen.

"Hello? This is Sheriff Kick. Are you all right?"

Getting no reply, she looked around. The farm was a dilapidated mess but it still seemed to be a working operation. A swaybacked horse had been tethered near a stand of tall cottonwoods, but the shade had shrunk and left the creature to suffer. From that same brutal glare, a handful of shabby chickens hid beneath an iron-wheeled wagon. A cow bawled somewhere. Both men's and women's clothes hung from the drying line, and the sheriff stared at this an extra moment. The Glicks, her Amish neighbors on Pederson Road, never hung men's and women's clothing on the same line, as the local bishop had decreed this to be indecent. Several strips of rags, long and narrow, hung with the clothes.

Her gaze drifted away. The outhouse path, heading into the shade of a huge old honeysuckle, appeared trodden. People lived here, she suspected, at least one male and one female.

She dropped her bag of beer cans, knelt and touched the girl to reassure herself. Yes, she was breathing.

"Hello? This is Sheriff Kick. Can you wake up? Hello?"

She got her arms beneath the girl and hauled her limply upright, surprised by her weight, worried by her gurgling stomach, then lugged her in a fireman's carry to the porch of the house, which offered shade but little space amid dense clutter. She pushed aside old boots and harness tack, crates of wilting cabbages, a basket of wilted greens, and laid the girl down. Sweat stung her eyes. She paused to mop a sleeve across her face and gather in a few deep, scorching breaths. She felt a little dizzy as she knocked on the door.

"This is Sheriff Kick. Hello? Hallo? Goedemorgen?"

She reached to turn the doorknob—had nearly touched it when an electrical shock jumped to her sweaty fingers and snapped her hand. Inside the house an alarm bell rang. Her breath stuck as she saw the red stripe across her inner fingers. The drunken girl moaned and shifted on the porch floor.

What had just happened?

Keep breathing, Heidi.

As her lungs hauled at the heavy air, she unsnapped her holster.

"Hallo! This is the Bad Axe County sheriff."

Was the doorknob booby-trapped? Why? How? The Amish didn't use electricity—except when they did. Like the Amish couldn't own a telephone or a car, but they could use your telephone and ride in your car. Their clothing could not have buttons, but safety pins were OK. She had lived around the Amish all her life without ever understanding the nuances of their Ordnung.

"Hallo? Goedemorgen? Ist hier jemand?"

She had no probable cause to enter the house. She walked out into the farmyard. The sawmill had not been used in years. All the wood, both sawed and unsawed, had weathered to gray. The sawdust piles had rotted.

She turned toward the barn. The structure was in the Amish style, plain architecture, unpainted and weathered, just an ordinary barn, yet the silence from the open door made her feel that something was wrong. She used a sleeve to mop her face again. Her lungs labored, her heart sped. Silent barns spooked her, odd for a farm girl, for an ex–Dairy Queen, maybe, except that when she was seventeen her mom and dad had been found shot dead inside their own.

Never mind, Heidi. Turn that off.

As she approached the door, the contrasting brightness was too strong for her to see inside.

"Is anybody in here? This is the Bad Axe County sheriff."

She took a last breath of sunbaked air and stepped in. Now the air was cooler, but it hardly smelled like a barn. In her mind she should be inhaling the scents of manure and cow piss, hay and grain and milk. But these were only traces beneath the dull artificial smells of metals and plastics. As her eyes adjusted, she saw a cord hanging from an overhead light fixture . . . as if daring her to tug it.

"I'm here to help. Is anybody back there?"

She hesitated to touch the cord. Then she pulled it. The bulb winked on and a grinding sound began. She found its source: a sawed-off pump-action shotgun fixed to some kind of geared armature, mechanically coming level with her right hip and racking itself to shoot. An instant before the weapon exploded, she dived back through the doorway, hearing shot strafe the barn wall.

She lay still for a few moments. The blast echoed in her ear membranes. A red-tailed hawk screamed in the sky. What was wrong here? She rose unsteadily, her feet feeling a long way down. Her eyes found the electrical source. There on posts in the high grass behind the sawmill was a solar collector, homemade-looking, silently gathering power from the sky. The sawmill roof sheltered what had to be the inverter, faintly snapping as it fed a rack of heavy gray batteries.

The hawk screamed again as the sheriff stepped back out beneath the ruthless engine of the sun. Through weeds beyond the sawmill she saw a square-bladed shovel stuck up in freshly dug earth and first thought, *Shallow grave, his lungs filled with dirt.* But the fresh earth was only fill dirt above a narrow trench, leading away through pastureland thick with bull thistle to a wellhead. OK, the trench was bringing power to a pump. Running water? Once more she felt confused about the Ordnung. Were they truly Amish, whoever lived here?

Now, light-headed and panting as she rounded the barn, she could see the outhouse deep in honeysuckle shade. Through its moon-sliver window, she saw light. Closer, she saw a glowing bulb. She drew her service pistol and stepped into the shade, feeling a shiver as she stopped ten feet from the outhouse.

"Hallo?"

Her dizziness, the starkly contracting light and shade— maybe she was seeing things. She stared at the moon-shaped cutout in the door. Yes, there was a light bulb burning inside.

"This is the Bad Axe County sheriff. Open the door and let me see your hands."

No movement. Silence except for buzzing flies. She closed the distance with unsteady steps and opened the door herself.

The sight stopped her breath. On the toilet hole slumped a man in Amish dress, his trousers past his knees and folded over the tops of his rubber boots, his gray beard so long that it feathered and re-joined blood-stuck around the forged steel shaft of the gimlet jammed into the center of his chest.

She looked back toward the house. The girl lay unmoving amid the clutter on the porch.

No one else had appeared.

The man's eyes were shut. His lips were mashed together. He breathed faintly through his nose.

She touched the radio handset on her shoulder and heard the hiss that told her no contact.

Could she do first aid? She wasn't sure what. Maybe unfold him? His bare haunches had sunk through the toilet hole toward the stinking pit. The outhouse was a two-seater and his head had lolled right, dumping off his wide-brimmed straw hat to catch in the second toilet hole beside him. Flies swarmed in and out around the hat. They jumped from his face to his blood-gobbed beard and back. Had this happened overnight? Predawn? It seemed he had been reading. His Bible lay upon the outhouse floor, blood-soaked and swollen, double-thick inside its frail leather cover.

"Sir . . . ? Can you hear me?"

She backed away, touching her radio again. No. She retrieved her phone, held it toward the sky. Not that either. She stepped in something and looked down. From the dried orange crust in the grass, she gathered that the girl had begun vomiting here. After seeing this? After doing this?

"I'm getting help, sir. Hilfe bekommen. Hang on."

First she untied the swaybacked horse, which rolled its bloodshot eyes and tried to bite her before she pushed its head away and slapped it toward shade. Then she broke into a jog along the farm's narrow dirt inroad, heading steeply uphill through dense hardwood forest.

As she ran, her body felt both weightless and twice its normal weight, and every intake of air became a deeper communion with the inferno in her chest and the questions inflaming her mind. What the hell had happened? Had the girl gotten drunk and stabbed her father?

The driveway summited at a swing-arm pole gate. As she pushed through, the frame dragged a broken chain. When she let go, the gate coasted squeakily, weighted by fieldstones, and banged shut behind her.

She ran on in frustration. She hadn't even known that these people existed. They didn't call 911 with their problems . . .

After a short downhill curve, the driveway leveled. In another two hundred yards she crossed a wood-plank bridge and stopped at the forest's edge. As she begged for breath, she realized she had returned to Liberty Hill Road. Three hundred yards to her left, east, she could see her Charger.

An Amish buggy traveled slowly past it, away from her.

"Hey!"

The buggy jolted and sped away, wobbling severely. She goaded herself back to a trot.

"Hey! Stop! Halt! I need to talk to you!"

By the time she reached the Charger, the buggy was a quarter mile gone.

But here she had radio reception. As she raced the Charger to close the gap behind the buggy, she told Denise what she needed—backup deputies, two ambulances, and, since the old man seemed close to death, probably Dr. Kleekamp again.

"Ten-four," Denise said, hesitation in her voice. "But, wait— an Amish, a buggy, is fleeing you?"

"I don't know. I think so."

"Well, don't spook the horse."

"Right." She lightened up on the gas. "Stay on with me, Denise, please."

Sweat burned her eyes. She took turns smashing one shut and keeping the other open. The Charger's wheel felt slick in her hands as she followed the road along a meandering creek. At last she eased up behind the buggy, twenty yards back, hoping to come alongside.

"I'm on his bumper," she told Denise. "But this is a first."

Normally an Amish driver would slow and move his outside wheels onto the shoulder, but this one accelerated and stayed centered on the narrow road, not letting her around.

"He won't pull over. What now? I can't do siren and lights."

"Loudspeaker?" Denise suggested.

"That might freak out the horse," she worried. "And these ditches are steep. I'm going to wait. Maybe he just doesn't realize I'm here."

But she didn't believe this. The driver knew. Then she finally held both eyes open long enough to notice that a shattered spoke caused the left rear wheel to spin in figure eights. This was what wobbled the buggy, and she could see its canopy shredded along the left side. Weeds and brush dragged from the undercarriage, shreds flying loose as the horse began to gallop.

She told Denise, "He knows I'm here."

She switched on her speaker. Her voice blurted harshly out.

"This is the Bad Axe County Sheriff's Department. Stop your vehicle."

Whether that spooked the horse or whether the driver whipped it to go faster, the creature surged into another gear. The buggy followed erratically, skimming and jumping among the ruts in the road, with a corner ahead. The sheriff glanced at her speed: almost thirty.

"Denise, that backfired. Now he's fleeing for sure. I'll just fall back and follow wherever he's going. That poor horse can't run much longer. We'll talk when he stops."

But the horse didn't slow down. The buggy skidded into the corner, then tilted onto its outer two wheels, showing its underside stuck with wild foliage ripped from the earth. In the depth of the corner, with the buggy twisting hard, the horse threw a wild-eyed look over its shoulder. Seeing the Charger, it gathered at the haunches and lunged for even greater speed. The buggy tipped all the way over, slid on its side, and went airborne over the deep ditch, taking the bellowing horse with it.

Sheriff Kick stopped the Charger.

She whispered, "Fuck."

"Heidi, what happened?"

She touched her wet forehead to the backs of her wet fists around the wheel.

"Heidi? What happened? What do you need?"

She racked her radio handset angrily. She used her phone instead to call back Denise.

"I still need all that stuff I asked for a minute ago. Plus a large animal vet with a euthanasia kit."

She climbed from the Charger. The horse had torn loose. As the sheriff slid down the ditch, the animal struggled up and limped away on three legs, lathered and wheezing and rolling its eyes at her. His front left leg was broken under the knee.

"I'm sorry, boy. I'm so sorry."

The buggy had landed upside down, one wheel still spinning.

She found no one inside it.

The frightened horse must have been pulling it empty, ghosting about this deserted region of the Bad Axe at least since dawn, because caught beneath the brake bar, where a driver would sit, was a boot.

A rubber boot—a Ranger—the left boot, cracked and split by age. The seat was smeared with what looked like dried blood. Her victim had been driving this buggy before he ended up in the ditch.

But that was all she had. She collapsed into the weeds. Her face had gone numb. Her heart fluttered and she shivered. Her thoughts became mired and sluggish. She heard a vehicle slow on the road above, but she could not convince herself to stand. Whoever it was would stop and help. She couldn't stand and wave. She couldn't move.

Yet the vehicle didn't stop—and this rallied her. A sheriff's cruiser, an upside-down Amish buggy in the ditch, a limping horse in the meadow . . . what kind of person doesn't stop to offer help?

She crawled up the ditch bank. But her vision had blurred. The vehicle was too far gone. An old white truck, maybe?

She slid back down, collapsed beside the overturned buggy, and looked about helplessly. With the sun directly overhead, she had not one centimeter of shade to crawl under.

As she faded into shuddering blindness, a phrase from Fanta's caller, *FROM HELL HOLLOW*, came back to her.

Noon is our new midnight . . .

101°–106°

Thurs, Aug 8, 12:39 PM
To: Dairy Queen (dairyqueen@blackbox.com)
From: Oppo (oppo@blackbox.com)
Subject: *Why Would You Not Accept (Free) Opposition Research?*

Objective: Neutralize (minimum) or Destroy (optimal) opposition candidate

Theme: Kim Maybee (1989–2015), her alleged "suicide," and her intimate relationship with Barry Rickreiner

Background (per *Broadcaster,* coroner's report): Morning of April 3, 2015, Kimberly Karen Maybee, 26, found comatose in her rented home, Town of Leaning Rock. Transported by Farmstead EMS to La Crosse, poisoning suspected, extracorporeal hemodialysis and resin hemoperfusion performed unsuccessfully. Died of massive organ failure at 11:47 AM.

Investigation (BASD files): Remains of buttermilk in a glass found inside home of KM contained pesticide 2,4-D (brand name Killex). Investigators also found opiates and opiate-delivery devices and diary with writings expressing thoughts of self-harm. From interviews, investigators determined KM was in suicidal frame of mind. No indications of foul play recorded.

Autopsy (coroner): Signs of alcohol/drug use. Massive organ failure. Deep bruises on chest, back, and legs. Oh, and by the way: *she was four months pregnant*.

Cause of Death (coroner): Suicide by Acute Self-Intoxication.

Want more?

Say YES, and stand by for **Problems with This Story**.

CHAPTER 7

The railroad cop who catches Sammy Squirrel trying to hop out from the Burlington Northern yard in La Crosse is an ornery man in a rumpled gray jumpsuit, with a heavy black pistol on his hip, a rifle in the window behind him, and an artificial right arm.

"Get in."

He drives slowly around in his heavy Ram utility truck, making threats.

"You wanna know what I could do to you?"

His ID badge reads *Railroad Special Agent Ruben Cobb*. He seems sixtyish, a small man but tightly bloated, with fresh shaving cuts and a gooey crumb of sandwich stuck in the corner of his mouth. Half a Cousins sub broils between his dash and windshield.

"You ain't gonna talk? Well, then, I'll talk, and I'll tell you what. If we have to stop a train to remove one of you dirty bastards, federal law allows us to bill you for the costs."

Sammy Squirrel looks past the sandwich out the window. It's so hot that the tree leaves are limp. At least they're green, though. They won't burn. It's so hot that the truck tires rip the asphalt.

"You know how much it costs for a loser like you to stop a whole damn freight train and throw the schedule off?"

By now he knows that in the presence of someone like Ruben Cobb, the voice puts up its feet and takes a break. The backpack rides on the truck floor between his scabby knees: his tattered bedspread, his dead phone, his rock, his railroad spike, his fork and shattered reflector, his case of colored chalk. He sits still and grins.

"It costs a million bucks an hour. You think that's funny? You got a million bucks? You even got a million brain cells? A cockroach has a million brain cells. You're wacko, huh? You're some kind of loon?"

Special Agent Cobb pilots his truck down a private road between the tracks and a mighty river, brown and flowing invisibly. His rubber hand, stiff and gray, detaches from the steering wheel and lands on the seat between them. It's so hot that the weeds have fallen over in the ditch, so hot that blue-green scum bubbles atop the backwaters of the river. The sandwich on the dash gives off a smell that Sammy Squirrel can chew.

"What did you do, kill somebody?"

He shakes his head no.

"Ha. Sure. Then where you headed?"

His hands reply. *Peace. Love.*

"Oh, Lordy." Special Agent Cobb laughs high and squealy. "Son, you were trying to hop a train to Duluth. That where they're hiding all the peace and the love these days, Duluth?"

As they drive on, the rubber hand inches closer. They cross the tracks into a small old city where every other building is either boarded up or a tavern. Soon the city trails away and Special Agent Cobb accelerates from stoplight to stoplight through a depressed industrial zone, rusty warehouses and tilting fences pinched against the tracks by rocky bluffs.

"You hear about the train that went through a forest fire in Idaho, and when it got to the next yard they found three of you assholes in a hopper car, barbecued to death?"

Sammy Squirrel aims his locked grin off his right shoulder toward the river. He doesn't feel much anymore except sudden stirrings of deeply buried sadness and rage, and these moments belong to the voice. Now expecting it, he keeps his gaze cast far away and spies amid the shoreline scramble of trees an approaching mass of blue poly tarps, sheets of black plastic, tents of many colors, a homeless camp. His eyes stay on the camp as the truck passes.

Red light. The truck stops. That rubber hand bumps him on his bare thigh.

"Burnt bums. Ha! Guess what. Smelled just like chicken."

Green light. Another leg bump. Off they go. Sammy Squirrel twists to watch the homeless camp until he loses it in the dense riverbank forest. The truck speeds up.

Stop this tool. Stop him.

"You heard about Hobo Heaven? In Washington State? It's a tunnel in the mountains, eight miles of smoke and fumes. When the train comes out the other side, all you scumbags are dead as smoked fish, every time, gone to meet your maker. Hobo Heaven."

Are you chickenshit? Take his gun and stop him.

Already the homeless camp has faded a quarter mile back. Ahead hangs one last stoplight. Then the road becomes a two-lane highway, heading steeply up away from the river.

Use your bare hands.

Loser.

At the last red light, Agent Cobb prods again with the rubber hand and makes a nervous wheezy giggle. "I'll bet you'd like a little cash. Huh? Bus money? So you can go find your peace and love?"

This last stoplight turns green. Agent Cobb isn't looking at the light, so the truck doesn't move yet.

"I'll bet you'll take thirty bucks for the bus to Duluth, am I right?"

Break his neck. Cassie wants you to.

As the truck begins to roll, Sammy Squirrel jerks his leg away. He lunges across the seat with his hands like claws. He snatches the sandwich, shoulders open the heavy truck door, dives out after his pack. He pops up on the gravel shoulder and runs.

CHAPTER 8

Deputy Lyndsey Luck, the first to arrive at the chaotic scene on Liberty Hill Road, knew the difference between heatstroke and heat exhaustion, a distinction the rookie clarified at great length while Sheriff Kick shivered and panted in a swirl of abstract vocabulary, not listening.

"Bottom line," her deputy concluded breathlessly, "we either need a third ambulance because you're heatstroked, or you're going to be OK in ten minutes. So, may I?"

When the sheriff nodded permission, the deputy touched her skin, took her pulse, looked in her pupils, asked the sheriff where she was in time and space. *Midnight in hell*, she wanted to say, but she got the answers right. Yes, she felt cold. No, she did not have a headache.

"Good news. You've got heat exhaustion. That's the easy one."

The deputy led her boss across the road into the ankle-deep

creek and sat her down in a reef of lush green watercress. Deputy Luck stripped off her own tight uniform shirt, then her vest, then peeled off her undershirt. She soaked the undershirt in the creek and draped it over the sheriff's head. As the shirt came down inside out, the wet fabric glowed bright as a movie screen. The sheriff could read its silhouetted lettering.

DEATH

ROE

SURVIVOR

She flinched and felt her shivers spike. Deputy Luck put her vest and shirt back on. A minute later the deputy returned from her cruiser with the bottle of electrolyte water that she carried everywhere. Slowly, the shivers settled and Sheriff Kick began to feel coherent again.

The second deputy to arrive, twelve-year-veteran Rob Schwem, drew his cruiser close by along the shoulder above the creek. Over his idling engine he hollered down, "If it's that un-marked driveway a half mile back, I went in there a few years ago checking up after a flood. That's the Goodgolly family. Gabriel Goodgolly and his daughter, Patience."

Deputy Luck conveyed the sheriff's mumbled response up to Schwem.

"That does not sound Amish."

"I hear they converted to Amish. Or they tried to. Where does she want me?"

Schwem's cruiser roared away to meet the two ambulances heading for the Goodgolly farm. A minute later, Interim Chief Deputy Dick Bender parked across the road. Bender drove the department's oldest vehicle, an '05 Avenger that somehow looked dog-eared. Without discussion, he drew his service weapon and walked out from the overturned buggy into the high weeds of the meadow.

They heard the horse snort, then a gunshot.

When he arrived above the creek, Bender said in a raw voice, "Dr. Geyer's on vacation." The sheriff waited. Bender always dropped another shoe. Benderisms, she and Denise called his hostile little habit. "I'da thought," he said eventually, "that the person in charge would have known a basic fact like that."

Sheriff Kick peeled Deputy Luck's undershirt off her head. She went to hands and knees in the watercress, stayed there enduring a weird cramp between her hips, then stood unsteadily inside her wet pants. She waited out a wave of dizziness, then looked up to the road. Bender appeared grim, his narrow shoulders deflated.

"Thank you for taking care of the horse, Dick. Can you tell whose buggy that is?"

"It says GOODGOLLY under the dash rail." Count three. "All you had to do was look."

The frightened animal probably tried to go home. It would have found the gate shut.

"OK," she told Bender. "Let's get Roads out here with a front-end loader to pick up the horse. Then diagram the accident and take the buggy into evidence. There's a rubber boot in there. Make sure that gets bagged."

Bender stared through his smudgy glasses, running fingers through his thin hair. She sometimes felt like he was sizing her up for a lampshade.

"Pick up the horse and do what?"

"Take it in on Goodgolly's land and bury it."

"Wouldn't have hurt you to say so in the first place."

"Right as always, Dick."

The sheriff tested her balance, then bear-crawled up the creek bank onto sizzling gravel. Bender pulled away. A pair of vultures coasted high above the horse. Sirens twined nearby, closing on the Goodgolly farm.

"Meet you there," she told Lyndsey Luck.

She rushed to put on dry pants and chugged a warm Powerade from her trunk. As she got behind the wheel, her full faculties were coming back. The dead man in the ditch had been on the Goodgolly farm. He might have stabbed the old man and stolen the buggy. But then who had shot him and buried him? The old man? Who did what to whom? When?

She Y-turned the Charger. From this angle she got a weak bounce from the tower in Farmstead to Schwem's phone.

"We're treating Patience Goodgolly as a person of interest in two crimes," she told him, "homicide and aggravated assault. Don't let her out of your sight."

"Well, that's the thing." Schwem's response crackled back through gaps and static. "Denise reported a stabbing victim sitting on the pot in the outhouse, did I get that right?"

"An old man, yes."

"Well, I opened the door, all I saw at first was a Bible and a hat, and a lot of blood. Then I heard something. Sheriff, now the old man is all the way down inside the toilet pit."

She surged the Charger.

"Are you sure?"

"He's down there groaning in the doo-doo. He had to be folded up and pushed hard. I can see a bunch of other stuff down there too. A shovel, a rifle, some beer cans. Maybe some clothing—"

She heard her deputy gag and spit.

"But there is no Patience Goodgolly," Schwem continued.

"She's on the porch of the house."

"Not there, Sheriff."

"Look inside the house. Don't touch the doorknob."

"Too late for that," Schwem told her with a high laugh. "But at least I got my hair permed. She isn't in the house. Or anywhere."

"She has to be."

"Sheriff, I'm telling you, if there was a girl here, she's gone."

CHAPTER 9

In the office of what had become the *Happy Valley Shopper*, Leroy Fanta lit a new Winston, leaned across his former desk to set the smoke in his former ashtray, and opened another manila file folder labeled *Letters to the Editor*, this one from 2017. He peered in, accompanied by a Procol Harum cassette hissing forth from his dusty boom box with "A Whiter Shade of Pale."

A man like FROM HELL HOLLOW, Fanta repeated to himself, *he and I could talk.*

But how to find him?

Well, was he lost?

Was he hiding?

Fanta skimmed the 2017 letters, seeing the usual. Taxes were too high. Farmers deserved more government support. People should stop eating meat. People should eat more meat. We should all support the soldiers.

FROM HELL HOLLOW could have used his real name.

Most letter-writers did. Most newspapers did not print anony-
mous submissions. But in his capacity as editor-in-chief, Fanta
had violated this norm. In his view, truth needed both light
and dark to fully flower. Whistleblowers, right? Don't we make
laws to protect them? Deep Throat took down Nixon. *FROM
HELL HOLLOW*'s screeds amounted to dropping a big, fat
dime on our lethal human weakness for business-as-usual. Let
him speak.

But was the man escaping contact, or seeking it? Was his anti-
Fanta vitriol a bluster, or a threat, or was he sending out cries for
help? Was he directing Fanta? Or misdirecting him? Or both? Or
none of the above? This would make an interesting front-page story.

Local Madman Seeks Same

By this time more than a little drunk, the ousted editor
composed this and other mock headlines as he worked his way
through 2017.

Local Dead Man Suddenly Full of Piss,
Vinegar, Johnny Walker Red

If that nasty little toad Babette Rickreiner could publish a
pretend newspaper, he could write pretend headlines. He could
rant and prance, swoon and mutter. He could fudge his promise
to the sheriff and defiantly haunt the front window when the
candidate's cover-story family, Becky Rilke-Rickreiner and her
marshmallow brood, schlepped past en route to the public pool.

Bad Axe Voters Seek Whiter Shade of Pale

He could loom and fog the glass like a bogle.

| | | | | | | | | | | |

In a little less than two hours, while handyman Jim Steffke fixed the back door, Fanta had culled *FROM HELL HOLLOW*'s letters to the editor, photocopied them, replaced the originals, then annotated each copy and placed it in a folder, gradually constructing a mental matrix to guide his journalistic manhunt.

At noon-thirty, he took a lunch break: a chocolate bar, more whiskey, a smoke, and a self-scathing mock headline.

Longtime Vegetarian Counts Tobacco
as a Vegetable

Pre-Vietnam, all the meat he could eat.

Post-Vietnam, never another bite.

Go figure.

Should he find it odd, he wondered, how *FROM HELL HOLLOW* raged at him, of all people, Grape Fanta, champion of the loser, truther to the tool, hugger of the tree, hunter of the Tofurky, outcast in the land of his birth for all deviancies above-listed, and more?

No. It wasn't odd, he decided.

It was perfect.

His correspondent was a wounded man, jilted by his dreams, howling into a mirror.

Fundamentally, Fanta thought, in seeking his ranting letter-writer he was seeking himself—if, forty years ago, instead of choosing to seek salvation in newspaper truth-telling, he had sought salvation by embracing the land—if, instead of *Happy Valley Shopper* firing him and changing the locks, his dream-bending demise had turned out to be tainted wells, infected meat, and bug bites.

Fanta did a little more research: farmers' market registrations, permits for small-time agro such as beekeeping, membership rosters of the local Lyme disease support group and the local anti-vaxxers group, phone calls to a select list of bartenders, a survey of public records for arrests on anything drug- or alcohol-related.

By early afternoon, with his file folder of *FROM HELL HOLLOW* letters in hand and a particularly stirring 2019 specimen on top, he was locked and loaded.

Seen out the office window, the display in front of Farmers Bank said 1:27 P.M. and 102 degrees.

Ha. Weather. Don't give me weather. Give me climate. Don't give me your little tiny time. Give me now.

He took a final few nips of Walker, then experienced a nostalgic crying fit while using his cozy old toilet for the final time.

At last, he set sail into the dangerous outside air.

Several Local Back-to-Landers Short-Listed for Melancholic Delirium

| | | | | | | | | | |

There was no breeze, not even a whiff on the ridges. The Brobdingnagian windmills along Jegers Road were stuck in the sky. In farmers' yards, the SUPPORT OUR TROOPS flags hung as limply in Fanta's view as the facts and the reasonings behind them. Cattle stood in trout streams or shoved for real estate on tiny islands of tree shade under gypsy moth *shrouds*. Good word by *FROM HELL HOLLOW*, he mused, to describe the gray clots of fibrous webbing suddenly everywhere in the Bad Axe, inside of which the moth larvae stripped leaves from the doomed trees. *Shrouds*.

He drove slowly through his changing world. The rusty green Tercel's AC roared, its trail of drips mingling with transmission fluid, engine oil, and whatever else the ancient car leaked lately.

Fanta's first choice was Darvin Montag, who had scored highest in his *FROM HELL HOLLOW* matrix. But he knew he had figured wrong the moment he saw that Montag's mailbox had been lovingly crafted to look like a miniature Norwegian storehouse, fondly called a stabbur.

He paused the Tercel to knock back a bit of extra Walker from the bottle in his glove box and have a look. A man could only support one true hobby, he theorized. Especially a madman. Wisconsin's own Ed Gein, for example, did not both construct lampshades from human skin *and* craft quaint nostalgic mailboxes.

But since he had come this distance, he drove down Montag's driveway anyhow, meeting several large dogs keen to shuck him from the Tercel and rip his bowels out. A whistle slowed them, and out of copious yard junk appeared big old Darvin dressed in bathing trunks and a tie-dyed undershirt and sloppily brandishing an assault rifle.

Fanta called out over the dogs, "Hey, Darv. Hot enough for ya?"

"Shush up, knuckleheads. 'Lo, there, Grape. Yeah, sure enough, if she gets any hotter, I'm gonna have to take some stuff off that I'd better oughta leave on."

Fanta said, "Well, lemme get off your property before that happens."

He turned the Tercel around with both old men grinning.

||||||||||

Strike two became Kent Sutherland with his fresh DUI conviction and his brace of unvaccinated, homeschooled children. No one was at home at the end of a long dirt driveway in Town of Daisy. But Sutherland's affairs looked generally tidy and spoke of adaptation, especially the robust-looking alpaca herd blinking from a shady hillside. When Wisconsin became Central America, Sutherland would be ready. Adding to this, the potted flowers and whimsical doodads meant, *Here lives a happy woman*. If a man's woman was happy, to Fanta's way of thinking as he popped his Walker, the apocalypse was not nigh.

As he drove on, Moody Blues in his cassette deck, "Story in Your Eyes" whirling from his old speakers, he asked himself: *Why do people rant?*

He had tossed himself a setup question, a softball. A ranter himself, he knew why. Costumed in righteous outrage, a rant expressed pain and fear, isolation with these feelings, cries for help. When a man ranted, he asked you to rant with him. When a man ranted, he showed you a wound. He wanted the salve of sympathy, the first aid of agreement.

These were decent turns of phrase, Fanta thought. A man who sent a ranting letter to the editor was looking for a hug. He craved the embrace of, *That is so true*. Every week, the newspaper came out, the whole community widened its arms to listen, and the man *felt better*. Nothing changed, of course. But he could keep ranting, writing, sending, imagining, and feeling better— until the newspaper disappeared.

So that explained the rage and blame well enough. But Fanta had a strong hunch that *FROM HELL HOLLOW* would be a more complex sort of cat. The letter he had selected for special focus—crimped half-open atop the file folder on the Tercel's passenger seat—could have been dictated by John Milton to his obedient daughter, the great blind poet raving and hacking through thickets of metaphor to find his visionary *Paradise Lost*. Some men groomed their madness, Fanta decided. Definitely not Darvin Montag or Kent Sutherland. But some men built an altar to their big idea and sacrificed themselves.

He aimed a squinting glance at *FROM HELL HOLLOW*'s letter, its penmanship so large and childishly precise that he could review bits of the screed as he steered his wonky old Tercel. The letter had been sent four months ago, just after Babette Rickreiner had bought the *Broadcaster* and banned opinions. Hence Fanta had just opened it today. In his poetic style, *FROM HELL HOLLOW* voiced remarkable claims.

> *I am afflicted with the plagues of our Mother. In putrefaction's fever I see the path and the purpose of my full decay. My flaming out will light the world. Allegory? Watch me.*

These were not the words of some unread, light beer–swilling soybean farmer. He should discount Wally Rumpf right now, Fanta advised himself while turning onto Rumpf Hollow Road. But his journalist's habit was to work the process. Experience had taught him that he never knew until he knew.

He spied Wally Rumpf. Way out across his field the man balanced eight feet off the ground atop the back wheel of his spray tractor, taking a piss into pesticide-saturated soybeans. Drifting over the field with the sour scent of dimethoate, lethal to bees, came country music, our great collective head-in-the-sand. So now Fanta knew: *FROM HELL HOLLOW* was not Wally Rumpf. He turned his key and headed back for the high ground of the highway.

He had progressed this far when the Farmstead Volunteer Fire Department's Pumper #2 screamed past the other way. Helpless before his instincts, the old newspaperman turned around and chased the fire truck.

|||||||||||

Minutes later, Fanta had composed another mock headline.

Meat Beats Heat

A cattle truck full of steers had broken down on the side of the highway. The poor doomed steaks-to-be had been roasting to death, prematurely, until the VFD had arrived to strafe the perforated trailer with Pumper 2's full power, wetting the steers as they stamped and bellowed and for their inscrutable reasons started mounting one another. As Fanta rolled down his window he amended his headline.

Meat Beats Heat, Meat

Over the dozen onlookers settled a torrid mist of atomized manure. While Fanta held his breath and watched, an old white pickup, northbound, slowed as if to rubberneck. He was admiring the truck, an International Harvester, sixties vintage—a version of the last truck he ever drove, traded it for a VW after coming home, always wanted another—when the heavy vehicle jerked to a squeaky stop right beside him and he understood that the driver meant not to look at the wet steers but apparently to glower purposefully at him, the editor.

This kind of thing happened. "Disgruntled Reader Shoots Messenger." Was she vaguely familiar? Through her open window she fixed him with an especially bitter glare: knit brow, fevered cheeks, damp forehead, wild blond-gray hair twisted in a braid down her back, a faint twitch of calculation in her aqua eyes, a wrinkle in her chapped lips. Braless cleavage descended through the stretched neck of a soiled men's undershirt. Her hands were work-gnarled, her forearms scratched and veined.

Fanta was about to say hello when from beyond came a harsh

splat. The fire hose had turned on again. The steers bellowed and assaulted one another. Manure mist descended. Did she give him a nod? *A heifer clambers up*, he recited, feeling her baleful inspection. *Nighthawk goes out, horses trail back to the barn.* Good words by Gary Snyder. *Spider gleams in his new web.* He had renewed his intent to greet her when the woman hit the gas and the white truck rumbled away, showing him a license plate too muddy to read and a rusty oil drum wobbling in the bed.

Well?

Ruined Scribbler Follows Hunch

Fanta U-turned on the highway, bumped over the pumper truck's thick hose, and floored the Tercel up to its full-out putter, racing to catch up.

CHAPTER 10

The ambulance bearing Gabriel Goodgolly took the rough driveway slowly. The EMTs had left the gimlet right where it had been inserted, its corkscrew shaft jammed into uncertain tissues of the old man's chest.

Sheriff Kick, two deputies, and three EMTs had carefully tilted the outhouse sideways off its base. In the grass beside it lay the items recovered from the pit: a .22 rifle, the six Busch Light cans and their torn carton that had been in the yard, and a square-bladed trenching shovel, the one she had seen standing up in fresh dirt behind the barn. Someone had rearranged the scene.

"Photograph it all. Then rinse it off as best you can and take it into evidence."

Deputy Luck, pale and gulping breaths behind her germ mask, answered, "Yes, ma'am."

"Not 'ma'am,' please. Call me 'sheriff.' There's a water pump. Maybe you can find a hose."

"Yes, ma'am."

The sheriff gazed across the scorched farmyard. Patched trousers, gray undershirts, heavy dresses, shapeless bloomers, and narrow strips of soiled fabric hung limply from the clothesline. An open stretch of cord showed where something had been removed. A clean dress, probably. Patience Goodgolly had vanished.

"Schwem, go with Roads and help Bender recover the buggy."

"I'm on it."

She called him back.

"Did you see anybody on Liberty Hill after I sent you this way?"

"Negative."

"An old white truck?"

"Negative."

She stripped her gloves and mask and dropped them into the pit. The re-staging of the crime scene had happened quickly, between the time she had run to call for help and when Schwem had arrived. How much time had passed? Twenty or thirty minutes? Had Patience Goodgolly fooled her by playing possum? Where had she gone? And how had she gone there?

The sheriff had no way to judge the normalcy of what she saw inside the house, the startling severity of the kitchen and the sitting room, shabbiness and tidiness bluntly intertwined. She had known Amish all her life but never been invited inside a home. What had Schwem said about this family? *They converted to Amish. Or tried to.* She gave herself a tour. In a bedroom she found two single beds with bedding, each with a wooden chair at the foot, each with an electric lamp on a wooden nightstand at the head, and a rag rug along the plank floor between.

Electricity. That wasn't Amish. Or was electricity OK if it came from solar? Down in Crawford County where she grew up, the bishop had been famously strict—and infamously known to bend his own strictures to make himself comfortable. The juicy hint of hypocrisy among the English back then had been the rumor that Bishop Hershberger entertained Amish maidens in his backyard Jacuzzi.

But if she hoped to uncover scandalous secrets inside the Goodgolly home, her inspection disappointed. She cataloged exactly three minor oddities: a half-knit garment for a baby, a 1992 Florida license plate hung on a nail, and a full Mason jar of buttermilk in an icebox.

None of these pointed to anything. She saw no other evidence of a baby. The girl had not walked barefoot to Florida in the last thirty minutes. Buttermilk was out of fashion but still commonplace on farms. Sheriff Kick photographed the license plate—turquoise-and-red, OHGEOMYI, Palm Beach County, hung next to a crucifix—and moved her search to the barn.

What to make of the animatronic shotgun? Security? Guarding something? For sure it was not the weapon that had put two clean .22 holes in the man found in the ditch. Deciding to leave it for now, she moved around the apparatus into the workshop behind. The gimlet came from here. Several similar hung with other traditional hand tools on the barn wall above a workbench. Arrayed on the bench were the partly assembled bare bones of a solar panel. The barn floor was dirt. One of three livestock stalls contained a semi-fresh horse turd and dark smears on the door and sidewalls that could have been dried blood. But as a former farm girl, she knew there could be many explanations for blood in a barn. Outside, the entire south-facing roof flashed with homemade collection panels.

When she cornered behind the barn, a bony Holstein lumbered toward her from behind barbed wire, the cow's swollen udder showing that she needed to be milked. Beyond the animal, a disused tractor road trailed away into tall late summer weeds. A few hundred yards off, the meander of box elders meant a creek flowed there. A steep bluff towered beyond. Nothing else to see.

The sheriff climbed between loose strands of barbed wire and let the desperate cow butt her ungently in the chest. It was a hard thing, the way life just went on indifferently in the aftermath of horrible crimes. She knelt and milked the cow onto the sun-scalded clover beneath her udder. As happened lately at odd moments, Taylor came to mind—her troubled little boy, what he needed she just couldn't figure out. Around a month ago he had begun dressing differently, compulsively overdressing for a little boy, if she had to put a negative label on it. He would no longer expose his bare legs in a pair of shorts. He always wore his brown hat with *Cabela's* in gold script. He kept on his little Levi's jean jacket in the heat, and his little work boots, and he coasted about silently, enigmatically, wincing at the world like some mini-desperado.

Squeezing teats by old muscle memory, she asked herself again when this all had begun. And why? She and Harley had mostly found it cute until one July morning Amos Glick had picked up Taylor hitchhiking for real out on Pederson Road. "I was pretending," he had claimed.

She sighed and gave the cow her done-slap. Life went on.
And on.

She did not need more of it.

She bumped her Charger back out Goodgolly's driveway.
When she reached Liberty Hill Road, she called Denise.

"Be on the lookout for an older model white pickup."

"Is that all we have on it?"

"I didn't see it well."

"Ten-four," Denise said. "BOLO on an old white pickup.
Meanwhile, hon, four other items for your attention."

"Is that all?"

"Well . . . for now."

"Go ahead."

"Somebody's been putting bowls of water out on Main
Street for dogs. Some lady from Madison stepped in one outside the antiques store. She turned her ankle and wants to file
charges."

"And?"

"Permission to bribe her with free tickets to Rodeo
Days?"

"Granted."

"Secondly, a complaint call about campaign activity on
county time and property. Guilty party is a Kick supporter. Just
FYI."

"Vigdis Torkelson? At the library?"

"Yup. Homemade button. *I'm With Heidi Kick-Ass.*"

"I like it. Who complained?"

"Well, how can I explain?" Denise answered. "OK, how do
you sink a submarine full of blondes?"

"Um . . . tell me."

"You knock on the submarine door."

"Oh. So you mean it was Becky Rilke-Rickreiner?"

"Bitch wasn't even in the library. She was just walking past with her kids on the way to the pool. She had to make a special trip inside to read the button."

The sheriff sighed. "Are any of these items important?"

"Numbers three and four are keepers," Denise said. "Three, Dr. Kleekamp submitted fingerprints, and CrimeNet sent back four machine-matches needing human review, which could take a couple of days."

"Are there mug shots?"

"Yes. And our guy looks like he— Hang on," Denise interrupted herself. "Just sec."

She disappeared for the time it took the sheriff to drive alongside and then over Spring Coulee Creek. She normally saw fishermen but not lately. She had heard that for the first time in her life the water had become too warm for trout. So did they die? Or where did they go? Denise came back.

"Our victim looks like he could be one of them. You'll see from the mug shots when you get here."

Sheriff Kick hesitated. Another mile south, she would turn off the highway to go home. She could see the intersection through thermic waves wriggling up from the asphalt. She glanced at the Charger's clock: already after four P.M.

"Denise, I need to stop by home. Harley's out of town, his mom is helping out, and I need to check on the kids."

"You can do that here," Denise said.

"What?"

"Item number four is your ma-in-law just showed up here looking for you. The kids are in the van. I guess they're waiting for you."

Her heart sank. Lately, the moment anything went wrong

on Belle's watch, the erratic old woman loaded them up and brought them to their mom the sheriff as if to say: *Here, look at what you've done.*

Denise said, "I guess there was some trouble with Taylor at the pool."

CHAPTER 11

For several miles, with "Gypsy" by the Moody Blues haunting the air from the Tercel's dashboard cassette player, Fanta followed the white pickup at a ticklish distance, heading north toward Farmstead. He stipulated aloud over a chugging chord bridge that he was probably chasing a farm wife on a run to Piggly Wiggly. Oh, well. He was "retired."

But just outside the town limits, the woman hit her brakes and cranked the heavy truck due east onto a private right-of-way with signs that read: POWER CORRIDOR—AUTHORIZED VEHICLES ONLY.

Fanta followed onto narrow gravel, casting the Tercel's shadow ahead. As the truck hammered beneath high-voltage wires and their towering supports, the leveling rays of early evening shone hard upon its dusty rear window and the corroded oil drum in its box. Its side mirrors glinted. But he was staying well enough back, Fanta hoped. He took his time, losing her in a thick deciduous blur, following her dust cloud more than her truck itself. He stole glances at the letter.

> *It's the deer prions. The bacillus knocked the door down for the Chronic Wasters to go horizontal. Not much time left for me.*

Trailing the white truck through the hot, buzzing forest, thick with mosquitoes and ticks, hung with mummy shrouds of the moth worm, Fanta realized that *FROM HELL HOLLOW* was referring to "horizontal transfer." He was talking about animal infections going sideways, infecting humans. A vet gets kennel cough. An equestrian gets equine encephalitis. That kind of thing. Exceedingly rare and fundamentally terrifying. Not rats carrying a human disease. Not at all. Humans getting a rat disease, the body undefended.

He shuddered. Lyme disease and a pig valve were all the horizontal action he could handle.

He had to watch the "road" through the power corridor. Primitive at best, it made for rough going, sharply up and down over washboards and deep ruts, around fallen trees and rocks, but somehow the rusty-jointed old Tercel successfully crossed three coulees in the transcendent style of the heavy wires overhead and emerged backlit, dusty-windowed, and leaking strains of symphonic rock onto a county road and then into the bygone hamlet of Mastodon.

Burn slowly the candle of life . . .

So went the lyric now, the next track.

> *My flaming out will light the world . . .*

This was what *FROM HELL HOLLOW* had promised.

The white truck coasted into the lot of Mastodon's ancient American Legion post and stopped.

Fanta, having nervous fun now, ducked the Tercel into the driveway of one of Mastodon's three remaining houses, a dumpy little prefab with its curtains shut. He snugged up beside a long-haul rig parked on the yard along with epic quantities of dog shit and one of Rickreiner's BARRY HER signs, plus two new ones: FREE FRANK and VICTIM'S MATTER. Good God. These referred to county board member Frank Truss, Town of Sumac, a bona fide wife-beater who deserved his night in jail and much more—and of course there should be no apostrophe on the wholly illegitimate word *victim*.

Fanta unbuckled his seat belt with a sigh and slung out into the ass-scorching air. He shambled several steps and peered around the end of the semitrailer to find that the woman had also left her vehicle . . . and stood behind it, between the truck and the low brick American Legion building. Up to what?

Fanta checked the picture window of the prefab for curtain movement, for hellhounds, then set sail across the trucker's yard for a better angle. He wallowed up behind an LP gas tank racked crookedly on cinder blocks. From here he could see her. And she was . . .

Hallelujah!

Making Calls of Duty

This had been his real headline a few years ago when he had done a story about the Mastodon American Legion Post, where there was still a working pay phone, one of the last of its kind anywhere.

The woman stepped close to the phone, the helmet-shaped, faded blue fiberglass pod fastened to the bricks, with its coin slot, its graffiti-altered dialing and payment instructions, and its hard-plastic receiver on an armored cord.

Gene Oostertag had since passed away, but at the time of the story, this phone was used by the region's last surviving World War II vet to call his sixty-five-year-old grandson to pick him up after his Friday-night old-fashioned at the bar.

The woman was making a call. Or at least the receiver was off the hook and in her hand. It took Fanta a few moments to understand what she balanced on her other hand, black and rectangular, the size of a large book, held level beneath the receiver.

Then he got it.

Of course. What else could it be?

He celebrated his discovery by not stepping in dog shit as he hustled back to the Tercel.

She had been holding the phone receiver over a portable cassette tape recorder.

Liar! I sent you a letter. You didn't print it.

FROM HELL HOLLOW at this moment ranted in recorded form at someone, somewhere—possibly another media outlet, or possibly Fanta again.

Over the next hour, while Fanta sweated inside the Tercel, eyeing the prefab window, eager to go, she made several more calls, answering his question. *FROM HELL HOLLOW* spread his rants around.

At last the woman finished. She drove out the other end of Mastodon and he gave her a long lead. Then he followed the white truck away.

CHAPTER 12

"What happened at the pool, Mom?"

Belle Kick unplugged a Marlboro Gold and gushed accusing smoke.

"Your little boy pushed a lady in."

"Which little boy?"

"Which little boy do you think?"

The sheriff's pulse rose beneath her sticky skin. The van's AC roared and dripped beneath the hood. The heat had peaked at a brutal 106 degrees. The temperature had since dropped a bit as the sun lowered, but the humidity had risen a dozen percent, and from now through dawn were the hours when the elderly had breathing problems. She looked at Belle, seventy-four years old. The heat wave had forced her into loose cutoff jeans shorts and a baggy white bikini top, both from a time when apparently she had the goods to fill them. She had tied up her long gray hair into an angry-looking knot. Her fringed leather cigarette purse hung like shredded meat about her hollow waist. A pair of old blue flip-flops exposed her hammertoes. Her red face gleamed with sweat.

"Mom—"

"First of all, he would not change into his swimsuit. Then this kid started talking to him and he pushed the kid into the water. I said, 'Taylor, no pushing.' He took a lap around the pool and did it again. Then the kid's mom called him a blankety-blank-blank little monster."

"What kid's mom?"

While Belle rolled her eyes, the sheriff felt the blankety-blanks like gunshots, her anger rising. What kind of mother calls someone else's kid names?

"Which mom?"

"Oh, just take a guess," Taylor's grandmother said. "Becky Rilke-Rickreiner, that's who. Big as a house. Sitting on the edge dangling her fat feet in the water. She screeches bloody murder at your son, and I'm thinking, good, now the bitch feels better, your son learned his lesson, and it's over."

"Mom—"

"But, no," Belle rasped. Sweat dripped off her nose. She almost had to bite the weighty air to get enough inside her lungs. "Your son waits awhile. He bides his time. Pulls his hat down. And keeps walking circles around the pool in his little cowboy jacket."

The sheriff glanced at her watch and felt her stomach twist. She was needed as a mother now. But nearly the whole day had slid by and she had so much left to do. A dead man's name to be discovered, his family to be notified. Another man in critical care who needed questioning. A suspect at large, Patience Goodgolly, who needed to be found. On top of this, she needed to get together with Denise and Rhino on a better strategy for deploying deputies to visit the vulnerable, many of whom didn't know to ask for help. And she still hadn't made her daily visit to the high school gym, open as a public cooling center, to thank the on-site volunteers and the drivers who brought people in. She still hadn't managed to get herself a pregnancy test. And Harley's all-star game hadn't ended yet. A hundred miles away, he would be home by nine at the earliest.

"Around and around the pool your son goes," Belle continued, "walking faster and faster."

She sucked a hot-on-hot breath through her cigarette.

"Then he runs up behind Becky Rilke-Rickreiner and, boom, he shoves her into the water. Two hundred pounds easy, grease and all, freaking tidal wave. It's only three feet deep, but she thrashes around screaming like either she's going to melt or she's going to drown. She gets out, and guess what? She calls 911."

Sheriff Kick glanced toward the building. Poor Denise, she thought, taking that call. BARRY HER's bride had a five-hundred-dollar fine coming, at least by law. You don't call 911 just because you got wet—unless your husband is running for sheriff and you want to start something. The sheriff hoped Denise had let it slide. She made a mental note to Oppo: *YES*. She would reply right away. *YES, I WANT YOUR HELP.*

She looked back at Belle.

"And?"

"And nothing. We came here to turn ourselves in."

Harley's mom said this bitterly. Her bikini top tied in the middle, and she lifted a string from it, bent her neck, and mopped above her eyebrows.

"Mom, what's wrong?"

"Now we're going home to run through the sprinkler."

"Good idea. But is something else wrong? Are you mad at me for something?"

"Assuming you even have a sprinkler," Belle accused.

"We do have a sprinkler. It's hanging on the wall with the tools in the barn. Mom—"

"If he was one of mine, I'da whupped him good right there."

"Thanks for the advice."

"Folks talk."

"I know."

"You couldn't have written a better campaign ad for Prick-reiner. And you don't even have your own ads. Seems you won't do a damn thing to save yourself."

"I'm busy, Mom, actually doing the job. I didn't plan to campaign until September. But I know. I see what's happening. I know I need to do something."

She turned away from Belle and rolled open the van's sliding door, getting a double good deal: her beloved boys, and a blast of cool air. Taylor glowered over a Sprite can, half-crushed while he still drank from it. Dylan, his twin, observed cautiously.

"Hi, guys."

She kissed Taylor on the forehead. She kissed Dylan, then she kissed Taylor once more. His temper was one thing, his struggle with impulse control. That seemed normal enough for his age. It was his premeditation that troubled her and Harley. Last Saturday, to "accidentally" injure his brother, he had chosen the weed hoe, the one with the sharp triangular point. Dylan must have said something, she and Harley agreed. But neither boy had wanted to explain.

"We love you," she whispered into Taylor's small ear.

He twisted his head away.

"When you go home," she whispered, "you need to go upstairs to your room and close the door and not come out until you write a note that says you're sorry to the boy and his mom. You can ask Grammy Belle or Dylan to help you with the spelling."

She paused, feeling clueless. How could you have "identical" twins, yet one could spell perfectly, and the other wasn't even close? And yet Taylor, in all kinds of intangible ways, seemed to be the more perceptive one, more aware of hard truths. How did this happen? She felt panicky, without knowing precisely why. She needed Harley, his ability to calm his excitable mom, his steady and good-humored hand with the boys, his strong arms around her—she needed him now.

"And then," she continued into her little boy's ear, "you need to write a note to Dylan and your grandmother that says you're sorry that they had to leave the pool before they wanted to leave the pool. You may not come out of your room to run in the sprinkler until you've finished this. Two notes that say, *I'm sorry.* Do you understand?"

Taylor crinkled his Sprite can and took a sip, scowling hard.

"Do you? Say, *I understand.*"

"I understand."

Her heart hurt. This didn't feel right.

"We all love you," she said out loud and heard Belle snort. "Even when we don't like something that you do, we all always love you, Taylor. *Always.* No matter what."

Her eyes stung as she rolled the van door shut.

She turned to face Belle.

"What is it?" she demanded. "What are you not telling me?"

"Kumbaya and all," the boys' grandmother answered testily, stepping on her cigarette. "But none of this nonsense is what I really came to say to you."

The sheriff tensed. It seemed a week ago that Belle had seen her peeing on the dandelion leaves, then tossing out the jar's contents and rushing to put on her uniform to go investigate some other mother's dead child in a ditch.

"OK, Mom. I'm listening."

"I gotta tell you, mother-to-mother," Belle rasped, "that I always felt two kids was more than plenty. Let alone three already."

Belle fixed her with a challenging glare.

"But four kids? Or five?"

"Mom, I'm not sure I'm actually—"

She felt her insides twist harder. She couldn't even say the word. She couldn't be. She had no room for another. The family had no room. The world had no room.

"Well, you shouldn't be unsure at all, should you?"

"What does that mean? I shouldn't be unsure?"

"You shouldn't even be wondering if you're knocked up, should you?" Belle challenged her.

"What are you talking about? How is this even your business?"

Belle held her glare. "Should you?" she challenged. "Should you even be wondering if you're knocked up or not? After your husband had his tubes snipped?"

The sheriff's mouth fell open. She commanded herself to pause, to breathe, to evaluate—but instead she blurted, "What the hell! Mom! Harley hasn't had a vasectomy!"

Belle huffed and stared toward the highway. She did that thing with her bikini string again.

"Not one that you know about."

"What? *What?*"

"Don't play dumb."

"Mom!"

"Don't 'Mom' me. Your husband is *my* child. *My* little boy. And I heard from a good source about your fun and games with that Spanish deputy, that Speedy Morales fella. That's why he left. That's what I heard."

The sheriff turned a hissing circle, actually stamping her feet.

Morales left because they had an affair? That's what people were saying? Supposedly Harley was snipped—some barfly's bullshit fantasy. The boys watched with stricken faces.

"Who is your 'good source'? One of your alcoholic friends? And you believed it? Who?" Her temples pounded. In a matter of seconds, her entire uniform, cuffs to collar, had become sweat-pasted to her skin. "Tell me who!" The boys stared from the van, Taylor in a deep scowl. "Who would start that? Why?"

"Call me old-fashioned," Belle answered her grimly, "but I also always felt that one man was enough."

"Mom, no!"

Belle put her wrinkled hand up in a stop sign, something she must have seen on TV.

"I can't imagine where you even find the time."

"Mom!"

"We all love our boys."

Harley's mother started toward the van, working the keys from the pocket of her cutoffs. She looked back.

"We all love our boys," she rasped again, "so trust me on this, Miss Piss-in-a-Jar. I've got only one left. You hurt my last boy with your tramping around, then I guarantee that around here 'Ex-Sheriff' is the nicest name anyone will ever call you."

106° – 95°

Thurs, Aug 8, 5:33 PM
To: Dairy Queen (dairyqueen@blackbox.com)
From: Oppo (oppo@blackbox.com)
Subject: *Suicide vs. Pesticide*

Problems with the Story:

1) *Politics*. At the time of Kim Maybee's "suicide" our elected coroner was a pharmacist, McKee; following year, McKee lost his license for over-prescribing opiates;

2) *Investigators*. Generous term for Sheriff Gibbs and Chief Deputy Elvin Lund, aka "two monkeys f^cking a football";

3) *Irregularity*. EMS response was compromised when an EMT trainee showed up and talked his way into riding transport with KM, his "old friend." This EMT was your opposition, Barry Rickreiner, just re-married and in the final semester of his Criminal Justice degree;

4) *Prickreiner*. Nothing "old friend" about KM and BR. KM was f^cking BR in exchange for oxy (see 1 above, McKee) during BR's engagement, after his marriage, and up until KM died. Repeat: *KM was pregnant at time of death*.

But Ask Yourself: With oxy in plentiful supply, and more firearms than people in the Bad Axe, would you drink Killex?

Stand by for the fairy tale.

CHAPTER 13

It felt as if Harley's mother had kicked her in the heart, the guts, and the womb, all at once, and she couldn't breathe.

"I'm OK," she lied to Denise.

The cold indoor air had given her goose bumps. Across her desk, Denise showed her the mug shot of a twenty-seven-year-old man named Daniel Allen Greevey, one of the CrimeNet preliminary fingerprint matches, who closely resembled the dead man they had found in the ditch.

"Yes, that looks like him," she agreed. "Go ahead. I'm fine."

Denise wasn't buying her lie, but she continued reading the profile she had put together.

"U.S. Navy veteran, last known address two years ago in Lowell, Massachusetts, where he did six months for assaulting a woman on a sidewalk. Since then—"

The sheriff forced a shaky exhale and Denise stopped.

"Heidi, how do you know when a woman is having a bad day?"

"I'm overheated. I'm fine."

"She has a tampon behind her ear, and she can't find her cigarette."

"Thanks, Denise. I just need to cool off."

To avoid her dispatcher's disbelieving eyes, the sheriff stared out the window—*seventeen days overdue*—and saw that since this morning two signs had appeared in the soybean field: BARRY HER and the new one: WHY ARE YOU KICKING YOURSELF?

No, she agreed with Oppo, *drinking Killex is the last way I would choose to end my life.*

She glanced at Blackbox on her phone to see if Oppo had replied. Yes. She was eager to read the message, but turned her phone face down on the desk.

"OK, I'm with you," she told her dispatcher. "Daniel Greevey. Assaulted a woman in Massachusetts. Since then?"

"Since then, he's shown up on charge sheets all over the country: vagrancy, panhandling, public intoxication, public urination . . ."

For sure homeless, as she and Dr. Kleekamp had thought. She tried to focus on Greevey's mug shot. He appeared both ancient and young, tough and vulnerable. His nose had just been broken, perhaps in the arrest. His eyes burned with intense and angry bewilderment. What on earth was he doing in the Bad Axe, falling out of Gabriel Goodgolly's buggy?

"In March of this year," Denise resumed from her notes, "Daniel Greevey underwent a psychological assessment at a VA hospital in Fresno, California, results inconclusive. As of this June, he was cited for trespassing in St. Paul, Minnesota. After that, he turned up at Our Lady of the River, a Catholic mission in La Crosse."

Her dispatcher raised her eyes to the sheriff's.

"So. Yeah. An hour ago, Heidi, we got another call from Paul McCartney."

The name made her think Denise was setting up another joke. *What did the other Beatles say when John got married again? Oh no!*

"I'm not kidding," Denise clarified. "The priest from La Crosse, his name is Father Paul McCartney. He wanted information about our homicide that I wouldn't release without your OK first. He got salty with me. Our Lady of the River is a homeless shelter. He runs it."

"What does he want?"

"He thinks he can ID the body."

"Send him Dr. Kleekamp's photograph. Let's start there."

"I knew you'd say that. So I offered. But he insisted on seeing you in person."

Denise made the sign of the cross.

"He's here, Sheriff. When he called, he was already on his way. Father Paul McCartney is out there with his hair on fire."

CHAPTER 14

After delivering her recorded message from the pay phone in Mastodon, the woman navigated her old white pickup widely around the municipality of Farmstead and into the northeastern corner of the Bad Axe, turning eventually onto Liberty Hill Road and passing the ditch where hours ago at dawn Fanta had observed the dead man.

Nipping his Walker steadily, with Blind Faith taking over as his melancholy soundtrack, Fanta followed her through fading light along Liberty Hill Road to Skull Rock Road to Leavings Road to Muchlander Road, circumscribing a wide half circle around Liberty Hill itself and entering what to Fanta's way of thinking represented the *beyond-here-be-dragons* wilderness of the Bad Axe. With no traffic anywhere, he had been stealing glances at *FROM HELL HOLLOW*'s letter.

To survive to my end, I have undertaken a profoundly

spiritual therapy, a sharing of souls, from many,
One. Today, I partake of the Body of Chris . . .

Fanta reached across and nudged the bent page, still getting
its breath outside the envelope. So interesting how the *t* in *Christ*
was missing, and then it showed up below the fold as the cruci-
fixiate extra *t* in the continuing phrase: *. . . so that I may sustain*
my appointment with marttyrdom.

Or was that a fanciful reading?

Fanta stayed on the tail of the truck. Few ever came this
way, he guessed, mostly hunters intending to trespass. The land
had always been private, the roads always ill-used, and the few
misguided attempts at farming had long been abandoned. Elmo
Quarry Pond, a mile or two away, was the only destination Fanta
knew of. He had skinny-dipped there in high school. Local leg-
end told of ten-pound ex-carnival goldfish lurking in the pond's
turquoise depths.

To the bittersweet wail of Stevie Winwood, Fanta trailed
through the rugged landscape.

Well, I'm near the end, and I just ain't got the time . . .

He put his windows down, sensing slightly cooler air. Natural
karst geology had sequestered this whole region in steep and tangled forests, flood-scoured coulees, obscure caves, and churlish
swamps.

. . . I'm wasted, and I can't find my way back home . . .

Indeed, he was thinking. But the white truck had slowed, and
now it stopped. Reacting late, Fanta had perhaps drifted too close.
He stuffed his brake and skidded on the gravel. The two vehicles
idled a few hundred yards apart, Matchbox toys to one another,
but Fanta felt enormous and foolish. He should have driven past
raising a perfunctory wave. He had given himself away.

Abruptly as he thought so, the white truck jolted forward,

cranked right, and blasted through a shallow roadside creek, bucking and spraying, then plunged into weeds so tall that Fanta could only see the top of the cab as the vehicle progressed.

Well.

Had he spooked her?

In another hundred yards, she drove the truck into hardwood forest and disappeared.

Puzzled, Fanta eased forward to see. She had turned onto an old logging road, maybe, a faint suggestion only. But he saw neither a bridge nor a ford across the creek, nor evidence that such an accommodation had ever existed.

As for the land, no ownership was indicated, no posting, no rural address marker. No way did anybody live here. The truck had just blasted off through swells of goldenrod and wild parsnip, leaving only mashed-down parallel tracks that pitched over peak and trough before shanking into the forest.

Fanta sat a while, hearing "Sea of Joy." Wasn't it true? Joy was always keen to drown you, mid-rapture?

But, OK. He stopped the cassette. Where was this, exactly?

His joints ached as he reached to sort the heavy book of plat maps from the mess on his backseat. With the tome upon his lap, he flipped pages. This was Town of Leavings. He had stopped in Section 15, facing east. The road she had taken, if it was a road, did not exist on the map. In any case, she had headed north toward Sections 10, 9, and 8, a large property that the plat map identified as owned by Golly Bros.

The name—Golly—snagged in Fanta's mind.

Then he remembered. The Golly brothers? The twins?

He lit a smoke to think back. His book of maps was old. That had to be the problem. Jim and Jon Golly were long gone, as far as he knew, otherwise that pair would have scored high in his investigative matrix—the dominant twin, Jim, especially.

Fanta's phone showed a weak 3G signal. He aimed a swollen finger at his saved number for the Bad Axe County Library. He rummaged through his memory while the phone searched. The Golly brothers had looked alike but behaved differently. Jim was the brash and charming know-it-all, while Jon was the taciturn and seemingly pious go-along who kept his brother in the vicinity of reality.

"Library!"

Vigdis Torkelson's startling bark sounded in his ear over keys clicking lickety-split.

"Good evening, Mrs. T," Fanta began, addressing the eighty-something woman who had taught him English lit in high school. "This is your former star pupil and former editor of the former *Bad Axe Broadcaster*."

"Devoured by Babette's Feast," she growled. "And hideous, just hideous, that her little honyaker would try to take our sheriff's job."

"Honyaker?"

"Something that we used to call what is now, I believe, called a jerkoff, or possibly a fuckhead," said the fearless Mrs. T. "Though I suspect that he is actually much worse. He was my pupil too, you know, three decades after you."

"Not to be a tattletale," Fanta played along, "but the candidate's newest sign says VICTIM'S MATTER. With an apostrophe."

"Perfect."

"But hey, Mrs. T, it's too late to call the county clerk, so I wondered if you could access current land deeds . . ."

He gave her the parcel numbers and waited.

Ah, yes, the Golly story. Or the *almost*-story. The gregarious brother, Jim, had been irate when Fanta had deep-sixed the profile piece he had been working on. When was this, 1994? They were homesteaders, new to the Bad Axe, and Jim had wanted the attention. Never one to turn down a people piece, Fanta had interviewed the brothers about their saga, which—Jim doing the telling—was that their car dealership in Jupiter, Florida, had been destroyed in Hurricane Andrew, and thus as early climate refugees they had used their insurance settlement to buy land as far away from hurricanes as they could find it. They planned to homestead in the heartland.

It had begun with all the ingredients of a good feature. The gist of Fanta's early drafts, pre-fact-checking, was a mildly skeptical introduction to two eccentric bachelor brothers, businessmen from latitude 26.9, who approached "living off the land" as if that were something they hadn't mastered yet only because they had been too busy selling cars. Fanta intended to imply, gently yet with certainty, that the land would have its say, but that no matter what difficulties the Gollys faced, Bad Axers, a welcoming people, would stand by to support. Warm. Cute. Hopeful. Wish the brothers well.

But their "facts" had not checked out. Simply put, Jim Golly was a liar. The "car dealership" had in fact been a nightclub that ran strip shows. "Destroyed" checked out, but Hurricane Andrew might have had the help of a professional arsonist, and "insurance settlement," Fanta had come to suspect, probably amounted to lipstick on insurance fraud. Plus Jim Golly had five DUIs, two assaults, and a drug conviction.

Fanta had simply scotched the story. Not his business otherwise. Jim Golly had bitched and cajoled until he had seemed to comprehend that Fanta had his facts straight and was doing him a favor. The talkative Golly's PR campaign had ceased. Jim's twin, Jon, had seemed relieved.

Fanta blew smoke toward the creek, wondering if the Tercel could ford it without busting an axle.

As expected, the land had kicked the Golly brothers' asses. He couldn't remember exactly when they had given up, sold out, and left the Bad Axe. Not until after Ronald Rickreiner got his throat slit, for sure, because Sheriff Gibbs had included the Gollys on a list of suspects who were debtors to Babette's husband and Barry's—

"That property is owned by James and Jonathan Golly," interrupted Ms. Torkelson.

"I'm sorry?"

"They hold the deed on that land."

"But they're long gone," Fanta informed her. "Back to Florida, I think. A decade in the Bad Axe, they decided hurricanes weren't so bad after all. I recall an Amish family taking over their old homestead."

He twisted on his car seat.

"But that's around the other side of Liberty Hill. Anyway, that can't be right."

The other end of the call went quiet, even the keyboard. He had just accused Vigdis Torkelson of speaking in error.

"I'm sorry, Mrs. T," he corrected himself. "Really? This land is still owned by the Golly brothers?"

|||||||||||

After the call, Fanta sat through another cigarette, watching the sky singe red and remembering FROM HELL HOLLOW's recorded voice.

Could he be looking for Jim Golly? He felt his favorite thrill, his writer's hunger for a complex character. He had never liked Jim Golly—who could?—but the man's fabricating mind had fascinated Fanta. Yes, Jim Golly had gabbled poetry and song lyrics. Yes, he had been strident, ahead of his time, about melting polar ice caps fomenting stronger hurricanes and destroying coastal livelihoods. Jim Golly had impressed him as one of those larger-than-life characters with no niche in polite society—Paul Bunyan with his blue ox, plowing out riverbeds and eating flapjacks the size of football fields—a well-read braggart whose modest twin, Jon, seemed to be less a separate person than he seemed to be Jim's doppelgänger, Jim's representative in the small and mundane world where the rest of us lived.

Now the voice from the telephone message came back to Fanta.

Noon is our new midnight.

If *FROM HELL HOLLOW* was Jim Golly, Fanta mused, then with that one phrase Jim Golly had shucked the known universe inside out like an old paper sack. Day devolves into night, night into day.

That's what poets did. Yeats. Milton. Lorde. Oliver. Mrs. T had taught him that. Poets knocked you down. Poets lunged into the road, made you hit them with your car, made you stop and back up to see what you hit.

Prions. Spirochetes. Ehrlichiosis.

Poets infected you, triggered fever dreams that showed you the truth. Poets crawled under your skin and made you tear yourself open to bleed them back out. Poets were often massive assholes too.

You work for Koyaanisqatsi, Incorporated.

Fanta grinned and said aloud, "The hell I do. But nice try."

He swished back a hefty shot of Walker and stared through the tall weeds into the moth-shrouded forest. Then he shrugged.

Big deal. So I bust an axle?

CHAPTER 15

"When, Sheriff?"

The man's voice rose angrily.

"When?"

With the description *hair on fire*, Denise had perfectly captured runty, rusty-haired, overboiling Father Paul McCartney, hardly thirty years old, director of Our Lady of the River Catholic Mission.

"When-when-*when* does somebody step up and do something?"

She felt tired, anxious about Taylor, desperate for Harley to get home, worried what Belle might say to him about her fabricated affair with David Morales and her potentially real pregnancy. Was Taylor hearing the Morales rumor? Did that explain his trouble?

She stared at Father McCartney in his Roman collar, cargo shorts, striped tube socks, and Teva sandals. She appreciated his concern for the homeless, but she didn't have the energy for his histrionic language. *Who*, specifically, did the reverend father want to do *what*?

"Father," she said, just managing to stay patient, "we found a dead man this morning. What *we* are doing, the Bad Axe County Sheriff's Department, is we are *investigating a homicide*."

"Investigating," he repeated sourly.

"That's correct."

He had already implied a difficult history with the cops in La Crosse, who didn't take his concerns seriously. He had already made it clear that before her desk stood a warrior, prepared to fight all comers. Good for him. She felt this sincerely. But she was not his bone to chew.

"We are investigating *one* homicide, in *our jurisdiction*."

"Five men!" he exploded. "Five of God's children since last summer, disappeared into thin air! When do we stop *investigating* and do something?"

So he proposed that she should *stop* investigating? And do what? What kind of *something*?

She held her tongue. Denise, sensing her need, had brought her an ice-cold Mountain Dew as she ushered in the priest. Sheriff Kick sipped from the bottle and looked away. Denise was heading off-duty now. Beyond the sheriff's office window, etched against the vehement red surrender of the day, her lovely friend trundled out into the soybeans, uprooted the BARRY HER and WHY ARE YOU KICKING YOURSELF? signs and delivered them to the dumpster.

Feeling renewed by this, the sheriff asked Father McCartney, "What makes you so sure that those five men didn't just move on? They're homeless, transients. Isn't that what they do?"

Her question tormented the young priest, the paucity of her understanding apparently beyond reply. He paced back and forth in front of her desk, muttering and fulminating. Bless his heart. She meant that. He cared. More people needed to care.

"What makes you think there might be crimes involved?"

He drew a long and weary breath. "Sheriff, I have been serving the homeless community since Jesus was a boy."

Less than ten years, she guessed, given his age. "Thank you for your service."

"I recognize when a man has turned the corner in his spirit and begun to change. These five men had stopped moving on. They had stopped running from the Lord. They were sober. They were working and saving money. That they would disappear under those conditions is suspicious, is it not?"

She didn't feel sure but declined to debate. She pushed Dr. Kleekamp's photo of the dead man's face across her desk.

"Is this someone you recognize?"

The priest's eyes closed. His lips moved silently for several moments. When he opened his eyes again, they were blurred with tears.

"Of course. That's Daniel Greevey. Danny."

"When did you last see Danny?"

"July the twenty-sixth, five-thirty in the morning, drinking coffee as he walked out the mission door into the sunrise."

His precision seemed defiant, as if challenging her to question the symbology of his last Daniel Greevey sighting. The priest gripped his hands together and awaited her response.

"Where was he going?"

"To the job line."

"The job line?"

"Corner of Industrial and Third, about a mile from the mission." He touched Greevey's paper face. "Men who want work line up there on the curb five days a week. People who need help, contractors, homeowners, landscaping crews, drive up, make an offer, off they go. Danny . . ."

Outside, Denise's truck door slammed. Off she went. Down

the hall, Rinehart Rog, Rhino, settling in for the night shift, had turned on his radio to a Milwaukee Brewers game.

"Danny was working," said Father McCartney. "He was going out every day. He was putting money in the bank. He was clean and he was getting good with the Lord. He walked out the door on the morning of July twenty-sixth, and he never came back."

"Did you—"

"Yes, of course."

She sipped Dew.

"Just like I notified the police when the other four men disappeared under the same exact circumstances. The cops don't give a damn. A homeless man goes missing, nobody cares. Easy targets."

This she believed: easy targets.

"So what do you think happened to Danny?"

"I have no idea. Except he got picked up in the job line."

"Tell me more about the job line."

She heard Velcro. Up from a cargo pocket came his cell phone.

"I'll show you."

He squared the phone on her desk.

"I've been to that curb, taking pictures, asking questions, every day since Danny disappeared. If the police won't solve this, I will."

He began to flip through photographs so fast she couldn't follow. Down the hallway, a thin voice on the radio described Ryan Braun hitting a long fly ball . . . going, going . . . caught. *Please hurry home*, she silently begged Harley.

"According to what I hear," said Father McCartney, "and what the La Crosse cops refuse to hear, is that at one point or another, every one of the men I've lost got into . . . into this . . ."

The priest stopped his spin of images.

"This vehicle."

He swiped back to a long shot of an old white pickup.

"Excuse me, Sheriff."

Rhino's massive frame filled her doorway.

"I'm sorry to interrupt. We just got a call from the *Tri-County Press*, the newspaper down in Cuba City."

She frowned. Cuba City was sixty-some miles southeast of Farmstead, across major highways, across the wide Wisconsin River. Cuba City was another world.

"Can I call them back?"

Rhino frowned and fiddled with his thick bison beard. "Um, I think you'd better take it."

Father McCartney rolled his eyes with dramatic effect as if to say, *Brushed off again*.

Rhino watched this and applied his placid gaze an extra instant to let the father know he might be out of line, making faces at the boss. Then her dispatcher's explanation rumbled out.

"From the description, Sheriff, it sounds like one of their reporters was up here doing a story and just stumbled onto that Goodgolly girl we're looking for."

CHAPTER 16

Fanta double-hit his Walker for courage, then backed up his Tercel and took a run at the shallow creek. A crashing splash, some crunching and grinding, some weird slippage that felt like his own body coming unglued—and then he had made it across, with both axles intact and no worse damage than a galloping pulse and a funny wobble in his pig valve.

Once a fresh smoke burned, he aligned his tires with the truck's path through goldenrod and eased it into gusts of pollen and swirls of insects.

He felt unusually alive as leaves scratched and squealed along the car's flanks and bees thumped the windows. The flagrant sky slipped overhead, dry things snapped beneath the tires, and the contours of the rocky earth gently pitched the creeping Tercel this way and that. It was his habit and perhaps his obligation to miss Maryanne, his beautiful and feisty late wife, anytime he felt himself approaching a "sea of joy." But, presently immersed, he asked himself a jaunty question: Did he miss Maryanne right now?

Strangely, and without precedent, no.

And he knew why too: because he felt his most private and most sacred ecstasy—experienced just once before—flooding back into his soul. He had never told Maryanne how the most authentic moment in his life—perhaps the only pure moment in his life—had been rising from the boiling mud of a rice paddy into a hail of Vietcong bullets, rising up and fighting back without regard for rules, safety, survival, hot to wreak death upon others and with exquisite indifference to his own.

He had never shared this bizarre and shameful experience with anyone. How could he? He had killed other human beings while in a state of ecstasy. Then, after no more than sixty seconds of nirvana and a half dozen Vietcong cut down, he had been hit, a leg bone shattered, and the feeling was gone. He had lain in abject terror for hours under U.S. Army C-123s raining defoliant. Before he knew it, he was back in the Bad Axe, back in the slow and secretly dull grind of living, with his new bride Maryanne to remind him not to piss and moan, to stop yearning constantly for more.

So, no, he did not miss his beloved at this moment, as his car bumped in beneath a primeval umbrage of maple, birch, and hickory, as his rusty bumper pried through tangled buckthorn and blackcaps, as a profusion of KEEP OUT and NO TRESPASSING signs exploded in his peripheral, because this was a moment truly beyond Maryanne, the plunging again of his exhausted soul into that terrible, secret sea of death-indifferent joy. He shouldn't be here. So what?

He leaned toward his window to drink it in. The feverish shade screamed with insects. From above, sunset torched the treetop shrouds.

Noon is our new midnight . . .
Wow. Once more he tickled open the letter for a peek.

Changes in latitude, changes in attitude.

Jimmy Buffett, of course. But in the letter's context, the line read as a prediction of mass movement by climate refugees, a vision of the clashing of displaced peoples with invaded peoples, of global conflagration.

He flipped the letter over. In his bizarre postscript, *FROM HELL HOLLOW* had written: *Please forward to General Secretary, Group of Eight, Hotel du Palais, Avenue de L'Imperatrice, Biarritz, France. To be opened at noon, August 26, 2019. Dear Mr. Secretary: Look out the window.*

Fanta stomped his brake. A sick whitetail buck staggered toward the Tercel. The creature's ribs and hip bones showed through a ratty coat hung with odd polyps, warty and black, wobbling as the animal lurched toward collision. The buck's head lolled. His jaw dripped. Fanta softly tapped the Tercel's horn, but the deer blundered on until his splintered antlers struck the Tercel and he jumped back in blind fright.

Fanta gaped in sorrow at the ravages of chronic wasting disease. The buck's brain, gone spongiform, performed little better than a sopping loaf of bread. The infected prions massing in the tissues of his eyes brought a closing darkness, while fibroid demons tried to escape through his skin. Weakly feisty, the poor creature blustered forward and once more challenged the Tercel's grille, jousted with his ruined antlers, then careened away into the underbrush.

Fanta continued, but his sea of joy had begun pitching and plunging steeply.

We sleep beneath a prion moon, Fanta, a billion misfit molecules hunting each and every one of us. Awake, we can't see even the biggest broken things.

He pressed on.

Like the great martyr Thich Quang Duc, I will bring the light.

Indeed, that had the ring of something Jim Golly might say. One thing from Fanta's background research *had* checked out: Both brothers had been drafted. Jim had fought in Vietnam, been wounded, and been discharged on a psychiatric waiver. Jon had safely pushed paper in Guam.

Just where the road degraded into rubble and began to rise steeply, Fanta had to stop the Tercel again.

The white truck blocked his path.

Abruptly breathing loud and fast, he found himself outside the Tercel, gripping its doorframe.

"Hello?"

A barred owl answered close by. *Who cooks for you? Who cooks for you all?*

"Hello-hello?"

He heard the big bird's wing beats.

"I'm just trying to say hello!"

He crept forward and looked into the truck cab, seeing the portable cassette recorder on the seat and a bale of recycled newspapers on the floor. In the rear box beside the rusty oil drum he saw a coiled strip of cloth. He picked it up, let it dangle and uncoil, long and narrow and spotted with rusty stains that might have been blood, or maybe just rust—

His inspection stopped with a sharp metallic double-crunch, same as the cocking of a firearm from a hidden place in the jungle.

Fanta retreated to his car and sat behind the wheel, twisting his head every which way, seeing no one yet, seeing no way to turn around. He waited, waited. He was terrible at backing up his car even under ideal conditions. But if no one appeared, he would have to try. He twisted again. On the backseat he saw his reporter's notebook. OK, then. At least he would not have come all this way for nothing.

A minute later, he left a torn-out page of the notebook beneath the truck's ragged wiper.

It seems you want to talk to me. So let's talk. I'll be back here tomorrow, at "new midnight" sharp. Leroy Fanta.

He was turning his suddenly exhausted body when in a raw blur—red hands, silver braid flying—the woman lunged and cracked his head with a rifle stock, then stood over him hissing, the barrel jammed deep into his soft gut. She tossed her head back, aimed her face at the fire-tipped treetops.

"Papa!" she shrieked. "Papa!"

Fanta drifted in semiconsciousness, staring up a filthy knee-length dress at her thick and hairy legs. To spare both of them, he closed his eyes. His head was cracked, he could feel it. His brain bled. This was it. He couldn't rise.

"Good day," a man's straining voice broadcast from somewhere. "Good day to you, sir."

The woman stepped off Fanta. He let light back into his eyes and saw a nude and bloated old man limp around the pickup wearing only orange water shoes, feeling his way as if mostly blind. A massive black dog stayed close, the handle on its leather harness just in touch with the man's wriggling fingers.

"I was cooling off in the creek," the man announced, each word a throttled puff through ragged lungs.

Fanta managed to half sit. The woman kicked him down.

"Be nice, Faithy."

Fanta gaped in revulsion. The man was hairless, spotted all over like an old banana. A great red goiter hung below his ear. Like the whitetail buck, his torso was shagged with sacs of empty gray skin, mosquitoes riding him by the dozens. He released the sidewall of the pickup and thrust an eczematous hand into empty space above Fanta. He was offering to shake.

"Golly," he said. "Some might call me the bad Golly. But you can just call me Jim. Or, as Faithy does, you can call me Papa."

CHAPTER 17

In her Bad Axe Hospital ER room, Patience Goodgolly lay dully angry-eyed and pale, hooked to monitors and IV fluids.

"She's stable. She'll be just fine. Dr. Patel has more information, and she'll be with you in just a few minutes."

Sheriff Kick accepted a plastic bag that weighed hardly anything. She told the nurse, "Thank you." Her hands trembled as she looked in the bag: the girl's dress and bonnet, nothing else.

She felt spooked. Thanks to the *Tri-County Press* reporter from Cuba City who had traveled all the way to a residence in the Bad Axe for a story only to stumble upon Patience Goodgolly, the sheriff's case had just shanked inward on itself. Apparently disconnected elements—Patience, a white truck, an unreported missing man—had overlapped in ways she could not yet understand.

Waiting for the doctor, she tried Leroy Fanta's cell for a third time, but Fanta wasn't answering. That worried her. A newsman always took calls from the sheriff, even a retired newsman. She left a message.

"Grape, I need to talk to you right away about this man ranting at you on the telephone. It seems he was ranting to other news outlets too. I think we need to find this guy."

Based on a tip from the *Tri-County* reporter, there was a chance that they were looking for a Town of Zion resident named Larry Hubbard, who drove an old white pickup. She had deputies searching for him, visiting taverns and fishing piers along the Mississippi. Several of the deputies knew "Derp" Hubbard already from various incidents, but their information was a poor match for the profile of Fanta's raving caller. So far, Hubbard was a roofer, sometimes, and a milker, sometimes, but more consistently a poacher and notorious drunk. He was a high school dropout and a violent fan of the Green Bay Packers. The first bartender contacted had not laid eyes on him in a month.

Meanwhile, Patience Goodgolly—found by the *Tri-County Press* reporter inside Hubbard's cabin—continued to glare emptily at the sheriff. She did not speak English. Or she would not speak English. This still wasn't clear.

Beyond the girl's window, Sheriff Kick watched the Cuba City reporter heading across the hospital parking lot toward her car. Her newspaper had been getting these crazy calls, Maggie Smithback had explained. Except they weren't *that* crazy, she said—in case anybody wanted the opinion of a former farm wife, happily divorced and finally doing her dream job. Down around Cuba City lately, she had told the sheriff, hundreds of wells were testing off the charts for *E. coli*. The region had become a chronic wasting disease hot zone, and just about everybody she knew had Lyme disease. Widen the viewpoint, Maggie Smithback had continued, and half a million bird and insect species had disappeared throughout the world in the last twenty years, while Venice would be underwater in the next twenty. These were facts. So this poor man might be sick, the reporter had explained, but he had not been making stuff up. In fact, she thought he sounded like a prophet. That was why, looking for a story, Maggie Smithback had traced one of the calls to Larry "Derp" Hubbard's landline. With her editor's blessing, she had journeyed to his cabin in the Bad Axe, hoping to interview him. Hubbard wasn't home. So the reporter had snooped a bit, looking into his windows, and that's how she had discovered—

"It's nice to see you again, Sheriff."

She started at the doctor's voice behind her.

"But we never seem to meet in happy circumstances, do we?"

"No, but I'm always glad to see you're still here," she told Dr. Alka Patel, whose young family had struggled mightily to adapt to the Bad Axe.

The doctor lowered her voice.

"So . . . the patient is dehydrated and possibly malnourished. Also badly sunburned. Her blood-alcohol had to be through the roof because it's still only down to point-zero-seven. She has no recent injuries that we can tell. However, both her left arm and her left cheekbone have been broken in the past. Her wrists and forearms show clear indications that in the past she has been cutting herself, a sign of severe psychological stress. My most acute concern"—Dr. Patel glanced at the girl, who watched them with a scowl—"is that before we washed her, we found blood on her vagina and her thighs. We documented this. If it turns out to be a criminal case, let us know."

"Thank you."

"We're ready to do X-rays now, and after that, if you want to do a rape kit, we need to get working on consent right away. When that's done, we need to keep her calm and restful through the night. Do you happen to know how old she is?"

"No idea. But maybe I can find out. Can I have five minutes?"

Dr. Patel smiled wearily. "The nurse will be waiting outside the door. I'll get the SAFE kit."

Sheriff Kick smiled at Patience Goodgolly and moved slowly into the sullen atmosphere the girl projected. The *Tri-County* reporter had discovered her unconscious on the floor with her hands bound to the frame of Derp Hubbard's bed. In short order, after Maggie Smithback's 911 call, Denise had established that Hubbard drove a 1966 International Harvester deep-bed pickup, white, not unlike the picture Father McCartney had shown her, and matching the BOLO they had put out after Patience had disappeared from the Goodgolly farm.

When the sheriff's notebook and pen were ready, she called Interim Chief Deputy Bender at the Ezekiel Lapp farm and put her phone on speaker with the volume all the way up.

"Are we ready?"

"Funny question when half of us have been waiting thirty minutes."

"I'm sorry about that, Dick."

He snapped, "No images. Voice only."

"I understand. We're just on speakerphone. Hello, Mrs. Lapp, and thank you."

"I'm glad to help." The Amish schoolteacher added softly, "Wie bischt du, mein Schat?"

The sheriff kept her eyes on the girl, who clearly understood the disembodied pleasantry—*How are you, my darling?*—and still scowled.

"First some questions for you, Mrs. Lapp. Do you know the Goodgollys?"

"We know of them, yes. A father and a daughter. We see them at the market now and again."

"Are they . . . are the Goodgollys Amish?"

"No, ma'am."

"But, the lifestyle . . ."

"They are English who tried to join the Amish. But they have wrong ways. Our bishop has instructed us to shun them."

"Where did they come from?"

Mrs. Lapp remained quiet for several seconds. The phone speaker crackled faintly.

"The man has said Ohio and given an Ohio name. But this is one of their wrong ways. Our bishop has discovered from speaking with plain folk in Ohio that this is not true, and he tells us these people are the Goodgollys. He orders us to stay away from the Goodgollys because God will punish them for their sins."

Watching Patience Goodgolly's expression, the sheriff concluded she understood at least snatches of this.

"Young lady, I need to ask you some questions."

Mrs. Lapp conveyed this. The girl's reply was barely audible. "Lauter, bitte," requested Mrs. Lapp. The sheriff moved her phone closer.

The girl repeated at a slight increase in volume. Mrs. Lapp cleared her throat and began to translate uncomfortably.

"You wear pants, she said. She will not talk to you. You can talk to me, and I can talk to her, but she won't talk to you."

"Because I wear pants?"

Mrs. Lapp double-checked. "Yes."

The girl spoke again.

"And also, she says, because you carry a gun."

Mrs. Lapp listened to more.

"She also says she doesn't like you. She believes that you wear pants because you fornicate with women."

The sheriff bit her tongue. The girl now flung her sheet

toward her knees as if too hot, revealing her scarred wrists and forearms as she glowered toward the red sky at the window.

"Please ask her how old she is."

Mrs. Lapp did so.

"She doesn't know how old she is."

"What happened to her father?"

"She doesn't know."

"Who took her away and tied her up in that house?"

"She doesn't know."

"Where did she get the beer?"

"On the road."

"Why was she on the road?"

"She was walking."

"Why was she walking?"

Patience Goodgolly turned her head and glared directly at the sheriff as she spoke.

"She said . . ."

Mrs. Lapp hesitated. A nurse stepped in.

"She said that she was walking because she can't fly."

To hide her surprise, the sheriff picked up her phone and saw that a notification had appeared. Harley had come home. Thank God.

I heard what happened at the pool, he texted. *Taylor is still upstairs mad as hell. When will u b off?*

She exhaled and stepped toward the window, trying to bring her focus back. *Because she can't fly.* It wouldn't work to press the girl while she clearly felt angry and stubborn. It would be better to wait until her medical condition and age were fully known. But what next? In the parking lot beyond the window, hordes of some large insect had appeared to swarm about the newly glowing lights. The sky above looked infernal.

Off soon, she texted Harley. *Home in 30.*

"Thank you, Mrs. Lapp."

"I told her to be nice," said the Amish woman. "Sie nett. I told her you were not the kind of sheriff we always had before. I told her to always sie nett to people in the uniform."

"Thank you. OK, Deputy Bender, we're done for now."

She touched her speed dial for dispatch.

"Any luck on Larry Hubbard?" she asked Rhino.

"Even his own mother hasn't seen him since he went turkey hunting in May. But several folks believe they've seen his truck around since that far back, though they can't say for sure that Hubbard was the one driving it. One witness said they thought he had grown his hair out."

"How about our warrant to search his house?"

"We got it. I sent Schwem. Rotten food in the fridge. Nothing else so far. But Schwem's just getting started."

"OK. The news here is we're going to do X-rays and a rape kit, and then we're going to let her recuperate through the night. I want a deputy . . ."

She hesitated. With Schwem occupied by an unexpected chore, she was officially shorthanded, and another pressure-cooker night would trigger all the usual calls. But Gabriel Goodgolly lay in postsurgical care three doors down, potentially stabbed by his daughter, who at the moment had fixed the sheriff with what felt like a death stare.

"I want a deputy here, Rhino. In ER, to spend the night right outside this girl's door."

CHAPTER 18

Leroy Fanta became aware again when the massive black dog collected a mouthful of his right thigh.

"Tippy, off!"

The dog released him. His glasses were gone. The woman gripped them as she turned out his pockets, gathering up his change, his pills, his flip phone, his overstuffed wallet.

"He followed me."

Her voice was raw and toneless.

"I brought him to you."

For a moment, Fanta's watering eyes focused. In this lurid instant, *FROM HELL HOLLOW*'s screeds had coalesced, and the great poet Yeats had been answered: *What rough beast slouches towards Bethlehem to be born?*

Jim Golly.

"A thousand pardons, friend," the "bad Golly" wheezed. "Faithy, stand down. Tippy, I said off. Let the man alone."

"He left a note," she rasped.

"Well, read it to me, woman."

Fanta's tears of pain thickened, blurring and melting the Gollys and their dog. He tried to rise.

"'It seems you want to talk to me,'" she read sluggishly, stepping back over Fanta. "'So let's talk. I'll be back here tomorrow, at new midnight sharp. Leroy Fanta.'"

"Ha-ha!" Jim Golly celebrated. "Back to work on our story, yes? Tippy! Off! Faith, help him up. This is the newspaperman. Indeed, Mr. Fanta, let's get back to the story. Come, come, I've been cooling off in the creek."

"No." He coughed as he came to his knees, gripping the bumper of the white truck and tasting blood off his scalp. "No, Jim, thank you. I believe I'll head back out now. Sorry I intruded. As I said, I'll come back tomorrow."

It seemed as if Golly hadn't heard. He emitted a hiss. Tenderly the dog took Fanta's entire hand in its mouth.

"Come cool off in the creek. Faith, get wine. Tippy, bring Mr. Fanta."

|||||||||||

Under a double umbrage of dusk and shade, as caterpillars gnawed the glowing canopy, Fanta drifted in and out of awareness, blood dribbling off his scalp and spreading pinkly through his wet shirt while he sat on the creek bottom in a cold, stony riffle.

"A man goes back to the land, Mr. Fanta, and the land attacks him. Our weary Mother makes an example of the fool. Makes a prophet of him. How's that for an angle?"

Golly wallowed in a deeper pool, dammed by stacked cobble. There he soaked his gray skin flaps, his bloated hands. Splashing himself, he canted his skull to peer through the swelling murk of night.

"After twenty years of venison, my eyes are kaleidoscopes, Mr. Fanta, from the infected deer prions massed in my corneas. You, my friend, are carved into a dozen pretty pieces."

He hummed and splashed himself some more.

"But it's a gift. The gift of vision. This is how you write it up in your story, yes? *The man was given a gift. He was chosen to see.*"

"Sure. Yes."

"Mother chose me. This is why I must live at all costs."

"Yes, yes."

"I've done nothing wrong."

"Of course not."

"Nothing unjustified."

"No."

Fanta recalled Jim Golly's recorded voice. *Liar!* This is what liars did. They accused others. Jim had lied to him years ago about the brothers' background, while his quiet twin, Jon, had sat watchfully by.

"Jim . . . where is your brother?"

"Shall we stick to the story? *Jim Golly was chosen to suffer, to see the truth, and to burn brightly for the world to see.* How does that sound?"

Just then his silver-braided Faith appeared out of the dim forest understory, bearing along with her rifle and her dull frown two wooden cups and a tall green-glass bottle.

"Woman, you look hot."

Obediently she stripped and stepped naked into the creek and from Jim Golly took a cracking slap on her flank. Randomly, it seemed, Fanta realized why the old white pickup was familiar.

That was Larry "Derp" Hubbard's truck. He was sure of it. He knew Derp, a prolific trespasser and poacher, and an occasional performer over many years in the weekly sheriff's report. Maybe it wasn't much to look at, but the vintage International Harvester had great nostalgic value for him. He had made Derp an offer.

"Cheers," Golly said, raising his cup.

Fanta complied, tasting elderberry wine with a mineral edge.

"Here's to France," Golly said. "That I make it."

He meant to the Group of Seven, the G7 assembly of world leaders. Fanta remembered this from the letter he had brought along. The summit would take place in Biarritz, France, in two weeks. This nude and delusional ex-Floridian sitting in a creek in Bad Axe County believed he was going there to change the course of world history.

Dear Mr. Secretary: Look out the window.

But why was Faith Golly driving Derp Hubbard's truck? How had the Gollys acquired the man's most prized possession?

Then Golly began to rant, and Fanta could only weakly agree. Yes, the glaciers were melting, the oceans were rising, and the coral reefs were bleaching. Yes, the insects and the birds were diminishing, and the deserts were expanding. Yes, refugees were moving and borders were hardening. Yes, Venice was drowning, Lady Liberty had got her ass wet in Hurricane Sandy, and the Choctaw bayous were underwater.

"Am I wrong, Mr. Fanta?"

He was not wrong. These were all facts from Fanta's articles and columns. Yes, in twenty years Phoenix was going to be like Pakistan, Pittsburgh like Dar es Salaam. Yes, there was no more Paradise, California, and yes, in twenty years there would be no turning back.

"Faith, more wine."

Yes, in the Bad Axe the whitetail deer herd was grievously infected, and the Lyme ticks had exploded, and the bacilli had

evolved into something newer and worse. And yes, there was
E. coli in the aquifer, plus Roundup, atrazine, nitrate, and more.

"Mother wants us out, Fanta. No more shitting in the nest.
Precious little time to fix it."

The gypsy shrouds muttered above. Fanta looked up into
them and said, "Why do you have Derp Hubbard's truck?"

"Never heard of the man."

"That white truck is his."

"Faithy, he's asking for more wine."

The great dog, Tippy, rose and padded yellow-eyed along the
creek bank to stand six inches from Fanta's neck. The creek's cold
rose straight up his spine to meet the dog's hot breath. The dead
man in the ditch, he thought. That ditch wasn't far from here.

It's OK, he told himself. *You were killed in Vietnam. You just
hadn't died yet.*

CHAPTER 19

Heading back to her family, Sheriff Kick made the call she had been dreading. Inside a home in Massachusetts, the phone rang one and a half times.

"Hello?"

"Hello." She tried to keep her voice even, unemotional. "Is this Colleen Greevey?"

"It is."

"My name is Heidi Kick. I'm the sheriff of Bad Axe County, in southwestern Wisconsin."

"I see. Yes. Hello."

His mother sounded defeated. Probably she had answered this same kind of call a dozen times before.

"Are you the mother of Daniel Allen Greevey?"

"Yes, yes, that's me." She sighed heavily. "What is it?"

"Well . . . I'm afraid I have some sad news. Are you in a place where you can talk?"

Through the silence, the sheriff sped north along the highway, waiting for a cue to continue. The sunset was complete. The sky had transitioned to an exhausted black-and-blue. The roads, fields, and forests breathed back their accumulated heat, making the night air so heavy that she could feel the Charger straining against it.

"He was a good boy . . ."

Daniel Greevey's mom made it only that far before she crumpled.

"And we . . . did everything we knew . . . how to do. No matter what . . ."

The sheriff said, "I'm so sorry."

She waited with the details while the grieving mother wept.

"No matter what," Colleen Greevey managed at last, "he'll always be my little boy. He will always be my baby."

|||||||||||

At home, the sheriff's husband had pulled their plastic kiddie pool into the center of the front yard and filled it with water from the hose and what appeared to be all the block ice from the chest freezer.

She stopped at the spilling rim of the pool. Harley's dirt-stained Rattlers uniform had been shucked on the grass. He and Dylan sat in the pool dumping cups of cool water over each other.

"Mommy! Look! Me and Daddy are skinny-dipping!"

Harley had fastened a bread sack around Dylan's arm to keep his stitches dry. The brother who had chopped his arm with a hoe was nowhere to be seen, but light shone from the boys' upstairs bedroom.

"That must feel good."

"Daddy said you and him used to skinny-dip."

"Did he say that?"

"Daddy said you guys—"

But Dylan fell silent when he saw her looking up where Taylor was. Nightjars whizzed above the roof. The sky had darkened enough for a few stars to prick through. A lone coyote howled.

Harley said, "Come join us."

"I think I'll take a shower."

She went inside, wrenched off her duty boots, peeled off her uniform shirt and her vest, and climbed the stairs in her sweat-sticky sports bra.

"Mommy's home."

She tapped on the door. When she opened it, Taylor glowered up from a scene he had constructed with Legos and action figures on the bedroom floor. Her already heavy heart sank deeper. He was supposed to be composing two simple apologies. This was the consequence she had designed. But pen and paper sat untouched on his dresser. Between his widespread legs on the floor, a Lego figure stood at the side of a Lego road, a Lego truck approaching.

"Sweetie, how's it going? Did you already—"

He jumped up and bulldozed the door into her, pushed her back until the latch clicked shut.

She flashed with anger. How dare he treat her that way? Then the anger gave her guilt, and the guilt made her even sadder. How did you ever know if you were doing the right thing? You could miss or mistake something, so easily. And then it could be too late. Colleen Greevey's sobs still resonated. She had to bite her lip.

She calmed herself enough and called through the door, "Finish up so you can come out and cool off with us in the pool, OK?"

She decided not to shower just yet. Outside, she pulled a chair off the porch, unzipped her pants and rolled the cuffs up, took her bra off—this was family—and sat with her bare feet in the pool.

Harley gave her a minute. Then, underwater, he pulled her toe. "Feels good, huh?"

"Yeah. Feels good."

But it didn't. Everything felt broken. She missed Opie's old soul, whoever Opie was turning out to be. One little boy was angry, the other was worried into silence. Right now their little family felt out of balance, and as if to confuse things—

She jerked in the chair and her foot splashed. For a few busy hours she had forgotten. She touched her bare skin below the navel.

"What, hon?" Harley looked at her with concern. "Are you OK?"

"Nothing," she lied to the man who loved her, feeling another layer of guilt. But at least she could tell that Belle hadn't passed along her rumors yet. "I'm fine."

She would get up before dawn, she decided, put on civvies, and drive the family minivan to Walgreen's in La Crosse, where hopefully no one knew her. She would buy a test to confirm, then tell Harley.

More coyotes joined the lone howler. Soon they listened to a full creepy chorus. Then others rejoined from across the hollow.

"It's going to be OK!"

Dylan blurted this. She leaned and rubbed his little shoulders.

"You're right. Thank you, sweetie."

They sat awhile longer. The coyotes kept it up until Taylor startled them, bellowing out the window, "I'm not sorry! For anything! Ever!"

His voice echoed. The coyotes stopped to listen. The sheriff and her husband stared at one another through the gathering night. Taylor's twin brother poured water over his own head, again and again.

Then Dylan whispered to his mom and dad.

"You guys, come on. It's what you always say. In the morning everything is gonna be OK. Right?"

95°−103°

Fri, Aug 9, 4:33 AM
To: Dairy Queen (dairyqueen@blackbox.com)
From: Oppo (oppo@blackbox.com)
Subject: *The Rickreiner Fairy Tale*

The Fairy Tale: Opposition tells a story of suffering and redemption. Father murdered. Son loses his way. Heroin is injected. Crimes are committed. Rock bottom is achieved. Opposition breaks bad habits, leaves bad friends behind, earns degree, deserves your job.

Characters:

Ronald Rickreiner, father: farm-to-farm agricultural products salesman; throat slit, May 2003 (body in vehicle pulled from manure pond)

Barry Rickreiner, son: opposition

Babette Rickreiner, mother/widow: campaign financier and manager

Murder suspects: multiple farmers in debt to Ronald Rickreiner

Omissions:

Father's Usury: Ronald Rickreiner credited seed, pesticide, fuel, etc. to struggling farmers at interest rates up to 40% and collected on property liens for non-payment

Toxic Impact: cash netted from repossessed farms

invested in Liquor City, Supercuts, Farmers' Direct Buy, Dollar Heaven, etc.

Revenge by Pesticide: suspects passing from sudden, multisymptom illnesses include Kermit Vick (2003) and Horst Millhouser (2004); for similar symptoms, see Kim Maybee autopsy report; Ronald Rickreiner's product line included Killex

Brand-New Information: Oppo has just learned that former Rickreiner debtors and murder suspects Jim and Jon Golly (cleared by monkeys f^cking football; departed Bad Axe circa October, 2003) still own their property in Town of Leavings.

PLEASE STAND BY . . . AND DON'T DRINK THE BUTTERMILK . . .

CHAPTER 20

By morning, as incandescent dawn gilds the great brown river and bruised men shuffle out of tents to meet the day, Sammy Squirrel has a new name.

Hot Dog.

Last night someone threw him one.

Oscar Meyer all-beef.

He didn't even chew.

||||||||||

Sunk in a foamy Mississippi backwash, he soaks his mosquito bites and his train-jump scrapes and watches the lever of daylight pry up the lid of night and tip it into yesterday.

Yesterday . . .

He sieves his fingers through the murky water. Yesterday? He sifts his bare feet through the silky-warm bottom mud, feeling small sharp things buried, jerks his knees up and grips them, afraid of teeth. Unanchored, he drifts and spins—a mile of brown water, a rust-and-blue barge, a tall green bluff, a coasting pelican with its surveilling black-bead eye, the tent camp. Yesterday has fallen off the spinning earth, vaporized by the new sun.

"Come on, now, Hot Dog."

The boss of the homeless camp, Abraham, a crooked-spine black dude with a gray beard, calls down the riverbank.

"Bath time is over. Get out that dirty soup, son. Get some coffee in yuz. Then we gonna go get some jingle."

|| | | | | | | | | |

Sammy Hot Dog shoulders his backpack and follows a loose tribe of shabby men as they limp and scuff and banter along a dirt trail away from the river. They travel through sweltering shadows of bottomland forest, over glinting tracks, through cracked lots between tunnels of rusted fences, up sour-beer alleys to the designated street corner where a few men already loiter, cupping stubby smokes and jeering at the others for being lazy and late.

"This the jingle train, Hot Dog. Go on, now, line up. Your turn is gonna come."

He watches how the jingle train operates. Up pulls a work truck, a foreman looking for a roofer, a landscaper, a flagman for a paving crew. The deal takes place out the window. A door opens and a man has a job. The line moves. Or up pulls an SUV, minivan, or sedan, a homeowner needing a lawn mowed, gutters cleaned, furniture moved. The cops roll by and seem to be searching. Ninety-plus degrees and climbing fast, someone says. The cops roll by again.

"Hot Dog, how old you is?"

He lies with ten fingers twice.

Abraham cracks up.

"Oh, hell, no. I give you sixteen, best. Child, them cops

out feeding today. They catch you, they be sending you back to wherever you didn't want to be."

Somebody calls, "Hey, Abe."

Abraham looks across the street at a young man in cargo shorts and socks-and-sandals taking cell phone pictures. "That man gonna mess with you too," Abraham tells Sammy Hot Dog. "That's a good man, but his mission bigger than yours. Drift back a little. You ain't wanna get your picture taken."

Minutes later, trouble starts on the jingle train, shouting, shoving, and threatening, then two weary black men dancing in the street, shrieking and throwing fists. The cops are back like blowflies, four cars this time, lights and sirens, officers vaulting from their squads as if to stop a war. In a flash the two men are facedown on the scalding pavement, getting cuffed. The young man taking cell phone pictures confronts the cops.

"Fighting with each other is a crime? But not when they disappear? Five of these men have disappeared. I told you someone is hunting them. And you do nothing!"

Two officers attack the man, one swiping his phone to the ground, one drawing a club. "Go ahead," he defies them. He points to cars stopping, drivers with their phones out.

"Get on, now, Hot Dog," Abraham tells him in a hushed voice. "Don't run. Don't get yourself chased. But this gone bad and you better get back to the camp."

A block away, drifting numbly with no idea where the camp is, he hears the voice.

Cassie wouldn't stand for that shit.

A heavy woman in a blue smock watches the commotion through a drugstore window, her hands at work lifting boxes of vape cartridges from a box with a label he can partly read: *WARNING: According to the Surgeon General, women should not . . .* And *she* gives *him* a disgusted look through the glass.

Use the rock.
Smash it.
Use the fork.
Stop her. Kill that look.
No? Then you're the one who should have burned.

CHAPTER 21

At just after six A.M., Sheriff Kick lied to her husband. She whispered into Harley's ear, "Let's surprise the boys with milkshakes for breakfast."

"Mmmm?"

The window fan whirred loudly. Behind it the birds had just begun to sing. She would try to hold her bladder for an hour, all the way to La Crosse.

"I'm up anyway. I'm going to run to the Pronto and see if they have ice cream. If they don't, I'll find some somewhere."

"Heidi . . . what?"

"Milkshakes for breakfast."

||||||||||

She checked her Blackbox email for Oppo as the minivan rolled through ground fog on Pederson Road. Nothing new yet, probably not until she got better reception on the ridge. For now,

the suggestion that Barry Rickreiner had fed Killex to his pregnant drug buddy, to protect his new marriage and keep the shine
on his redemption story, and that he had then talked his way
onto the EMS ride to make sure Kim Maybee didn't survive—
this felt too toxic to touch. But did she believe these accusations
fell within BARRY HER's potential? Under Babette's influence? Yes,
she did. Did she find it plausible that the previous sheriff and his
chief deputy could have made such a mess of the Kim Maybee
investigation? Yes. *Like two monkeys fucking a football.* Wasn't she
obliged to pull the string that Oppo had been dangling? Election
campaign or not?

Goddamn, she had to pee.

And she needed advice.

"Call Leroy Fanta's cell," she told her phone.

But once more the call rang to his message service. Odd,
she thought again, that a die-hard newspaper guy wouldn't pick
up for the sheriff. Fanta always had, day or night. Again she
asked him to call her back, hit END, and yanked the van into
the Coon Valley Kwik Trip, where she hustled to the restroom.
She would still buy a test, but as for hormones in her urine she
had blown her morning chemistry and the results would have
to wait until tomorrow.

|||||||||||

In La Crosse, the Walgreens parking lot was nearly deserted.
Not that anyone should know her this far from the Bad Axe, but
good. She rushed in, then had to wander a bit, searching. When
at last she found the tests there were four kinds on the shelf. She
studied the box that said *99% accurate, 5 days sooner.* That was
the one.

She brought her purchase to the counter, where a broad-
beamed middle-aged woman bent over a box of vaping car-

tridges, muttering as she unpacked them and stocked them on a low shelf beneath the chewing tobacco and cigarettes.

"Hello?"

The woman rose and turned—and, after all, the Bad Axe County sheriff wasn't far enough from home. Sizing up the situation, Harley's high school prom date, Kiersten Kindergaard, eased into a little grin.

"Did you find everything you were looking for?"

"I did. Thank you."

"Do you have our Balance Rewards card?"

"No, thanks."

"For each purchase, you get points that you can redeem—"

"No, thank you."

"It's easy. You just give your phone number and then you get points—"

"I don't want a card."

"OK, no worries. That'll be fourteen dollars and eighty-seven cents. Do you need a bag?"

"Yes, please."

"Not a problem."

As she dropped the test kit into a way-too-big plastic Walgreens sack, Kiersten Kindergaard sighed and said, "Another little one. Congratulations. Some girls have all the luck."

| | | | | | | | | | |

She exited Walgreens by the main door and a scene on the sidewalk startled her. A sharp-edged heavy chunk of pink granite. A rusty railroad spike. A metal fork. A broken piece of road reflector. Nearby under a dirty blanket huddled a teenage boy, a wide-eyed and unwashed, a skinned-kneed, barefoot child, scrawling with chalk on the sidewalk.

She stopped and stared. His face seemed tear-streaked but

he grinned. He had drawn a many-colored peace sign, three feet wide. The earnestly lopsided drawing made her heart ache.

"Can I help? I'm a . . ."

What did she mean to say? She was a mother? A cop? *The cops don't give a damn. A homeless man goes missing, nobody cares.* Did she tell him that she knew of a homeless shelter run by a priest who would watch out for him?

"Do you need help? Can I take you somewhere?"

Deliberate as an ocean snail, he withdrew beneath the blanket. Then with invisible motility he moved his wrinkly shell and covered his drawing. From underneath, he hissed, "Chickenshit!"

| | | | | | | | | | |

"Call Leroy Fanta," she commanded her phone yet again just minutes later, because southbound on the highway, heading home with a heavy heart, she had just honked at the editor's old green Tercel heading the opposite direction into La Crosse. She thought Fanta looked more than usually disheveled as they whipped past each other and she caught a glimpse of his long gray hair tangling in the window breeze.

She left a new message: "Grape, is everything OK with you? That was me honking. I have some historical stuff to ask you about, so call me back."

She let a long moment pass, a long bolt of asphalt beneath her, feeling speechless but not complete.

"Grape, please, I'm worried."

She saw an email had dropped in from Oppo, sent at 4:33 A.M. Not now. Not on the highway.

She touched speed-dial 1.

"Denise, never mind, please, why I was in La Crosse, but I just ran into someone who needs Father McCartney."

CHAPTER 22

Sammy Hot Dog throws his bedspread off and fills his lungs with a gasp. The street and sidewalk are empty again. The drugstore parking lot is empty again. The woman in the smock still watches him out the window. He knees back from his drawing and stands. He has added something—actually subtracted something—that he remembers Cassie often said.

He sees his ragged image reflected, superimposed over her blue bulk behind the glass. While they stand fixed, the reflection shows a car puttering past behind him. The woman inside makes a sour face, shakes her head, and turns away.

The car softly beeps.

Chickenshit. You do nothing.

Beeps again.

He turns and squints against the hostile brilliance. A rust-riddled old green car has stopped along the opposite curb:

CAUTION: I BRAKE FOR PEACE.

The car backs up a few feet in his direction.

Stops.

Beeps once more.

He shades his eyes. A second faded sticker tilts his rigid grin:

MAKE LOVE, NOT WAR.

"Are you looking for work?"

The driver calling to him is a hippie woman with a thick gray braid. She rests her forearm in the open window and waits for him to cross the street and come abreast.

CHAPTER 23

Heading home, Sheriff Kick read Oppo's latest on the screen of her phone with the minivan rolling along Pederson Road. The dawn fog had dissolved. The eastern coulee wall cast a jagged shadow across the Glicks' potato field, the sunstruck plants wilting precisely as the shade line withdrew. The six barefoot Glick girls were out there already, bent in their curious right-angle posture, picking beetles off the leaves. Amos and Dawdy Glick and the two boys were in the apple orchard on the rise behind the house, spraying something—vinegar, probably—on the caterpillar tents that had appeared overnight. A few hundred yards on, a freshly road-killed doe lay mangled in the ditch.

Oppo's "Rickreiner Fairy Tale" told of events that occurred in the Bad Axe while she was in high school down in Crawford County. But even before BARRY HER's campaign and redemption story, she knew by osmosis that his father had been murdered, possibly by a farmer who had owed him money. She never knew that suspects had died from mysterious Kim Maybee–like symptoms.

Something orange caught her eye in the newspaper tube beneath the H+H KICK mailbox. She stopped the van and stepped out into a wall of green heat. The tube still said *Broadcaster*, though lately an unwanted *Happy Valley Shopper* had begun to appear inside it. But this wasn't Babette Rickreiner's *Shopper*. What she extracted turned out to be Harley's blaze-orange three-hole ski mask, for deer hunting in extra-cold weather. Had he dropped it on the road—in August?—and some Good Samaritan had picked it up and put it in the newspaper tube?

She climbed back aboard with the mask and started down the driveway. Was Oppo suggesting that Ronald Rickreiner's murder was still an open case? That his son and wife had taken revenge on suspects in the same way that Kim Maybee had died? Had other suspects been poisoned and lived? Was Oppo implying this by telling her that twin brothers named Golly, in debt to Ronald Rickreiner but long gone from the Bad Axe, still owned property around Liberty Hill? And the father and daughter living there now were named *Good*golly?

What the hell was that about?

"Call Leroy Fanta," she told her phone a fourth time as she parked the van in front of the house next to her brown-on-tan sheriff's Charger. No point in leaving another message. She hid the pregnancy test inside the Charger's glove box, safe there until tomorrow morning.

"Yay!" Dylan cheered as she came in through the mudroom. Noisy box fans blew air across the kitchen. "Milkshakes for breakfast!"

Shit. Instead of ice cream, she had brought back Harley's orange mask.

"Um . . . ice cream is all sold out."

"You were gone for an hour and a half," Harley observed with a head-tilt and a squint. Her van-cooled body had begun to sweat. A brand-new baseball trophy stood on the table.

"Don't tell me you were MVP."

He shrugged. "The ball keeps hitting my bat." He put his hand out for the mask. "Where'd you find that?"

"In the newspaper tube."

"What? Why?"

"You tell me. Ice cream is sold out everywhere. So instead I'll make chocolate-chip waffles."

"Yay! Yay! Chocolate-chip waffles!"

Harley said, "Hm. OK. You do that. While I feed the animals."

He stepped close and whispered under the fan noise as he kissed her on the ear, "You're acting weird, hon. I haven't seen my mask since last winter. Obviously the boys were playing. Don't forget I'm on your side. And remember we need to talk about the 4-H trip tomorrow."

When the waffles were on the table, with link sausages, butter and syrup, a pitcher of cold milk, a bowl of blueberries, and coffee for Harley and herself—everybody with their bare feet in the fan breeze under the table—she began a family discussion of Taylor's situation, starting with the fact that he had not yet composed his notes of apology for pushing Barry Rickreiner's stepson and wife into the pool yesterday.

"I understand," she said, "that some people might seem like enemies because they don't want me to be sheriff anymore."

"It might seem like they're attacking your mommy," Harley clarified. "But this is, um . . . normal. That's just how it's done. It's called politics. We're just not used to it around here."

Dylan stared wide-eyed back and forth between them. Taylor glared down at his waffle from close range.

"In politics," she expanded, "one side always tries to say why they're the best and the other side is the worst." God, that sounded stupid—yet all too true. "But in the end, we're all trying to do our best. We all want what's best for everybody." That was stupid too—and *not* true.

"But *you* don't say *he's* the worst," Taylor pointed out.

"Hon . . . is someone saying bad things about me? I mean, besides putting out those silly signs? Those are just signs."

Harley said, "Is someone saying bad things to *you*, Taylor Kick, or to you, Dylan Kick, about your mommy? That's what Mommy means."

She ground her teeth because Dylan had also looked down at his waffle and both twins had gone silent. In other words, *yes*. She could feel Harley wanting to share a look, but she kept her eyes fixed upon the boys. She had no idea exactly what they were hearing, or how they would process the kind of rumors that were out there. She needed Opie, who excelled at age-seven psychology and could reliably parse out what the twins were thinking. If the boys were getting bothered, she had to push back. She wasn't sure where Oppo was leading her, but if Rickreiner's campaign was hurting her kids, then bring it on.

"So anyway," she groped, "two wrongs don't make a right. We all know that. But for sure, it's OK to be upset when you feel hurt by someone. It's OK that Taylor got angry. It's just not OK how he showed he was angry. And now he isn't quite ready to be sorry for his actions. Am I right, Taylor?"

Her little tough guy frowned and shrugged and meticulously impaled one blueberry on each tine of his fork. It escaped no one that Dylan had done this same thing a few minutes ago.

Now Dylan tried to help his brother out. "Sometimes I'm not ready to be sorry either," he said. "Sometimes everybody's not ready to be sorry."

Taylor didn't bite. Harley said, "Trying to say how you feel can be hard. I know it is for me. I know that when boys feel bad, they sometimes try to hide it. I sure do."

At this, Taylor thrust his blueberry-tipped fork explosively toward the center of the table.

"Look!"

His brother grimaced.

His dad, hiding the same feeling, said, "Very cool."

His mommy said, "Tell you what. Tomorrow is the 4-H trip, right? You guys are going to get up super-early and go help set up the Bad Axe County Farm Breakfast at the Olsons' farm, right? I know you're excited about that. And on the way you're going to stop at Elmo Pond and feed the giant goldfish. Oh, my gosh, some people say that when they got dumped in the pond they were the size of your thumb, and they grew to ten pounds. That's exciting. Maybe you'll see one."

She paused for air. Taylor had dropped his scowl and both boys looked at her in perfect eager twinness, equal in their anticipation. She made eye contact with Harley. He read her mind and nodded.

"So it's going to be like this," she said. "That trip is a privilege, and privileges become ours when we earn them by doing what we're supposed to do. So, Taylor, if you want to go on the field trip tomorrow, you'll need to have your apologies written by then."

Another pause. Her heart thumped. Her stomach had begun to feel weird again.

"Does that sound fair to everyone?"

Dylan nodded.

Harley nodded.

"Taylor?"

"Look!" he insisted, thrusting the forked blueberries farther toward the center of the table, his face bunched and sweaty. *"Look!"*

"We see, honey." She swallowed a lump of distress. "That's awesome."

Then Taylor dropped the fork, pushed his chair back, and stomped up the creaky old stairs to the boys' bedroom. The door slammed. Harley unplugged a fan from the kitchen wall and followed him up.

As soon as he dared, Dylan said, "Good job, Mom. He's doing it."

|||||||||||

Toward the end of her journey into Farmstead, she took a call from Dr. Patel about Patience Goodgolly.

"This is Sheriff Kick. Go ahead."

"Good morning, Sheriff. First some good news, I think. She allowed us to fully examine her for injuries. We found no indications of forced intercourse. We don't believe she was raped. At least, not in the conventional sense."

The sheriff stiffened and gripped her steering wheel.

"What do you mean, not raped in the conventional sense?"

"Well, first of all," the doctor said, "the young lady is not a virgin. She has no intact hymen. And the blood on her was not from tearing it. She is either menstruating, Sheriff, or she's pregnant and she's spotting. But she wouldn't let us draw blood."

"I see."

"If we knew how old she was, and if she was a minor, there could be a statutory rape charge, yes?"

"Yes."

"So if we suspected pregnancy in a minor, maybe then we could establish yes or no with a blood test, for purposes of a criminal investigation."

She had that right. "Dr. Patel, isn't there some way you can tell me how old she is?"

"She is not a tree, Sheriff. Somewhere between fifteen and twenty. And she has not lived a normal life, so external indications may not be reliable."

Now entering Farmstead, the sheriff stared at the bank sign: 8:17 A.M. and 96 degrees. Overnight, the gypsy moth caterpillars had completely webbed the fledgling maples that the city had planted along the sidewalk in April.

Dr. Patel continued. "We found what appear to be cotton fibers inside her. This would suggest that she is, or was, menstruating and was using something nontraditional, or perhaps just non-modern, to absorb."

"Yes. Yes, I see. So that's the good news. I'm waiting for the bad news."

"I'm not sure if it's bad news, Sheriff. But we can tell you that this young woman has given birth before."

"I'm sorry, what?"

"Possibly more than once," the doctor said.

No one spoke on either side of the conversation.

"And finally, Sheriff, one of the nurses on duty this morning speaks German, and she is at this moment translating for your deputy, who I believe needs your assistance right away. Miss Goodgolly is now communicating adamantly that she is twenty-one years old, and that she wants to go home, and that seeing as she has not been charged with a crime, nobody can stop her."

Another pause.

Dr. Patel added, "Which, as I understand the law, is correct. So we're releasing her."

CHAPTER 24

In the vivid morning light, the surfaces of Hell Hollow looked a long way down. Captive but still alive, dizzily upright upon his sock feet but hobbled at the ankles like a horse, Leroy Fanta didn't dare move for fear of falling.

Through a blur both visual and cognitive, with a tremendous headache and a flinty taste in his mouth, he watched his old Tercel tremble into view among the sod structures that made up Jim Golly's hidden Middle-earth.

Faith Golly drove it. A passenger was on board. Without his missing eyeglasses, Fanta couldn't tell what flavor.

Flavor . . .

The word came from last night—*flavors*—the surreality of his meal with Golly slowly coming back to him.

Faith aimed his feeble car between the white IH pickup and a mud-spattered third vehicle, nosing it into the black throat of

Golly's sod barn. The Tercel disappeared as if swallowed by the earth.

Fanta stared helplessly into the blur. Who rode in his car with Faith?

What should he do?

How could he stop this?

He hobbled.

He fell.

|||||||||||

Last night, in "conversation" over dinner, he had learned about Jim Golly's self-prescribed prion-replacement therapy.

"I have the chronic wasting," Golly had said. "The Lyme bacilli trashed my immunity, and the infected ungulate prions invaded. I stopped eating venison several years ago, but it was too late."

He had orated around a thickened purple tongue, reminiscent of the buck that had attacked the Tercel's grille. To dress for dinner, Golly had wrapped himself in a filthy tunic that might have once been saffron, and Fanta had remembered the allusion from his recorded rant: the Buddhist martyr Thich Quang Duc, the self-immolating Vietnamese monk.

"But infected prions," Golly had declared, "can be replaced."

Of course Fanta had no appetite. He had felt concussed and sick. Unable to manage utensils, the diseased man across the table had eaten with his hands in the manner of a blind old circus bear, balling and dabbing and scooping with his jittery, tumescent fingers.

"Replaced like this," Golly had said, demonstrating, and one minute later an entire foot-long steamed zucchini had disappeared down Golly's warty throat.

"See?"

"I see."

But Fanta had not understood, not yet. He had not been able to stop the trembling caused by something, he thought, in his few sips of wine. Now and then, beneath the table, the mighty dog had licked his burning feet and gone back to sleep.

"There are alpha and beta prions," Golly had at some point asserted.

Nonsense, Fanta had said to himself.

"We humans have the alphas. The ungulates—the deer, the cattle—have the beta prions. Unless one is afflicted as I am, this is the natural hierarchy of nature. Alpha over beta, in all things epidemiological." He mashed the word but continued as if he hadn't. "This prevents horizontal transfer. Shepherds don't get blackleg. Cat ladies don't get feline distemper."

True and not true, Fanta had said to himself.

Something prevented horizontal transfer, as a rule of thumb. *Something* saved humans from goat pox, porcine brucellosis, bovine pleuropneumonia, et al. But that something was not the alpha-beta nonsense hallucinated by Golly.

"A chronic-wasting man," he had raved on, meaning himself, "can replace his bad betas by tapping fellow humans for more good alphas, which can be consumed indirectly in the zucchini, the tomato, the melon, in any vegetable or fruit that has been properly farmed."

There had been a pre-dinner tour. Golly grew the vegetables he was eating in small rectangular plots seemingly hidden in tall grass and wildflowers across the narrow coulee bottom.

"Horizontal transfer," he pronounced, "can be undone by vertical transfer, from lower human to higher human." He pawed up sweet corn, stripped by Faith from the cob. "As you see."

Fanta still had not seen.

Tapping fellow humans?

Lower humans?

He had filled his lungs and spoken.

"May I have my glasses back, Jim, please? And my car keys and wallet? You can keep the shoes."

"Faithy, the man is asking for more wine."

By then, Golly had swallowed at least a gallon. Yet he was not so much drunk and oblivious as he was effortlessly dismissive of reality. He was completely at ease with his delusions.

"It's time for me to go, Jim."

"Faithy's getting us more wine."

Fanta had looked at his plate of untouched food: the stewed tomatoes, the stripped sweet corn, the soft squashes, the oozing slices of melon. He had looked at Golly's wine-purpled tongue. He recalled a line from the letter he had brought along on his search for *FROM HELL HOLLOW*.

Today I partake of the Body of Chris . . .

Was he understanding now? Chris without the *t*? A guy off a street corner, not the symbolic Son of God?

Wanting to bolt upright, Fanta had felt stuck to his chair. He had seemed to weigh a thousand pounds. He had felt his pig valve flutter and stick. He had heard himself croak, "Tapping fellow humans? What does that mean?"

Golly raised his hairless eyebrows. "Food is medicine, yes? Read the Chinese. The fix is in the flavors. But, alas, my vegetarian therapy has been too indirect and too slow. Look at me. I won't make it the two weeks to get to France unless I accelerate my treatment. But now, Mr. Fanta, you . . ."

He canted his skull and peered across the table, seeming to study Fanta closely: *My vision is kaleidoscopic . . . you are carved into a dozen pretty pieces.* "You don't look much better than me."

"What is your treatment?" Fanta had demanded. "What's in the food?"

"Faithy, give him wine."

"Lower humans? Who are they?"

"Wine."

"No. No wine. My glasses, Golly. Give me my keys, my wallet, and my glasses. I'll follow the road back to where I left my car."

"But Tippy doesn't want you to go."

The huge dog awoke.

"I'm leaving now," Fanta had asserted, and continued in his dizzy head: *And sending my friend Sheriff Kick in to visit you.*

"But Tippy doesn't want you to leave."

He had tried once more with all his might to rise. It was more wine, the next green bottle itself in Faith's grip, that had clobbered him.

||||||||||||

He hobbled—*What flavor was arriving?*—and fell into the scalding morning sun. With his bruised brain pounding, Fanta watched through a blur as out of the sod garage emerged a dirty-shaggy-hungry kid, some mother's beautiful lost boy.

The kid grinned. He had been homeless, it appeared, hardworn by the road but still at a fresh age, a teenager. He held a tattered black backpack. The child took in Golly—the horror of the man—and he took in the half-buried sod huts amid the isolation of Hell Hollow, and still he grinned. He pushed knotted blond hair from his eyes. His bones and muscles moved. He made peace signs with his fingers. He made a plus sign. Then fixed his hands into the shape of a heart.

"Amen," intoned Jim Golly as he shambled forth in his soiled saffron robe. He spread his arms to the boy.

"Welcome, Lamb of God."

CHAPTER 25

As Sheriff Kick sped her Charger along the highway, she looked into her mirror at young Patience Goodgolly glowering in the backseat, knowing she was closer to sixteen than twenty-one, wishing she could find a way to prove, for the girl's own good, that she was a minor. *She is not a tree*, Dr. Patel had said. As soon as Denise came on duty, she had checked birth records in Bad Axe and surrounding counties. Nothing, not a surprise. So Patience Goodgolly was as old as she claimed to be, and per the district attorney, who wasn't ready to charge her with a crime, she was going home.

The anxious girl twisted on the backseat to see Deputy Luck trailing in her Tahoe. She was going home, but the sheriff didn't plan to leave her there alone.

She has given birth before . . . possibly more than once.

The sheriff opened her partition window.

"So, are you pregnant again?"

Patience Goodgolly's head whipped around so hard her bonnet strings slapped her face.

Now I know she understands me. Armed with this information, Sheriff Kick turned off the highway onto Liberty Hill Road. She slowed to twenty miles an hour to navigate the rutted gravel. Deputy Luck followed into the Charger's dust cloud. The girl clenched her jaw and stared sullenly into the mirror. The sheriff leaned, opened her glove box, removed the plastic Walgreens bag, and hung it in the window space.

"The doctor said you have been before, and you might be again. So there's something in this sack that might interest you. It's a way of telling whether you're going to have a baby or not."

She let that settle in, decelerating to roll so slowly that red-winged blackbirds on their second or third broods rose from cattails in the boggy ditch to screech and flutter at the windshield. Farther on the Charger passed a new weed that the sheriff didn't recognize, tall and fibrous, with an ugly brownish platform for a blossom, invading the asters and the joe-pye.

"It's a pregnancy test, and you could have it," she told Patience Goodgolly, "if you wanted it."

She dialed the Charger's nose into the Goodgolly driveway. They rolled under a canopy of shade until they reached the swing gate. The sheriff turned her engine off and took her keys. She lugged the heavy gate to the edge of the driveway, where it stopped against a cairn of sandstone slabs. She made eye contact with Deputy Luck: *Close it after you.* When she sat behind the wheel again and looked into her mirror, Patience Goodgolly held the test kit in her lap.

Soon the Charger came to a stop in the desolate Goodgolly farmyard. The sheriff cleared her door locks.

"Would you like me to read the instructions to you?"

With the box in her fist, Patience Goodgolly burst from the car. Lifting her dress hem, she galloped across the burnt grass and up the porch steps. She opened the door without shocking herself and slammed it behind her.

Deputy Luck approached the sheriff's window.

"Keep her here and keep her safe."

"Yes, ma'am."

"Let's work on 'Yes, Sheriff.'"

"Yes, Sheriff, sorry."

"You might want to park in the shade."

"Oh. Right."

"No radio or phone in here. If you need help, you'll have to call from the road."

|||||||||||

"Infection is our biggest worry," said the nurse hustling after Sheriff Kick down the intensive care unit hallway toward Gabriel Goodgolly's room, "but it looks like he'll recover."

"He has some things to explain."

"He's on heavy pain meds."

"I understand," the sheriff said. She stopped at his doorway, turning on the nurse. "Some private things to explain."

Inside Goodgolly's room, she carefully parsed the setup on his IV stand. None of it looked new to her. She glanced over her shoulder toward the door. Then she pinched off his painkiller drip and waited.

Within two minutes, the man's blue eyes came fearfully open. Again she glanced toward the door, then bored her eyes back into his. They flickered side to side, as if searching.

"Yeah, you," she assured him. "This is Bad Axe County Sheriff Heidi Kick, Mr. Goodgolly. Guten tag. I've been learning things about Patience."

She showed him his pinched-off drip.

"Do you feel me?"

He shut his eyes.

"You're going to answer some questions."

He turned his head. She snatched a handful of rough gray beard and turned it back.

"I've got a whole menu of criminal charges, Mr. Goodgolly. I've got murder, assault, kidnapping, incest, rape, and I haven't even turned the page yet. Let's start with who you are."

He turned his head again. She yanked it back.

"Your name."

He winced. His lips parted.

"Gabriel."

"I don't think so."

"Gabriel Goodgolly. Before the Lord."

"That's not going to do it. I know about the property deed. Are you Jim? Or Jon?"

"Please . . ."

Please? She flared hot. "Have you been raping your daughter or your niece?"

He swallowed hard and stayed silent.

"Same charge either way, so let's move on. Tell me where the babies are."

This time she let him roll his head away. She watched his tears without sympathy. His hands—swollen joints, spotted skin, fingernails like claws—clenched the sheets.

"Answer me."

He whispered something.

"Louder."

"I'm Jon. Jon Golly."

"That's a start. And what makes you the 'good' Golly, Jon?"

He winced. Beneath the sheet his back arched, then resettled.

"Jim," he said.

Her phone stirred: a text message from Deputy Luck.

"It's Jim that makes you the good Golly? Where is Jim? What has Jim done to be the bad one?"

Jon Golly shook his head and whispered. She bent over him. "What? Say that louder."

"Immunity from all prosecution."

He winced and swallowed.

"Or not one more word from me."

She stared at him, for a long moment sucked into a whirl of worry about her own twins keeping one another's secrets. She lifted her phone from behind her badge.

I think I might need help because she

Deputy Luck's text ended there. She was in trouble.

Refocused, the sheriff released her pinch on Jon Golly's drip.

"Peace be with you, Mr. Golly. While it lasts. I'm coming back."

| | | | | | | | | | |

She tore her Charger over twelve miles of melting asphalt to reach Liberty Hill Road. She nearly lost it on the first gravel corner, reined herself in over the next two miles until she cleared a rise and saw Deputy Luck's Tahoe in the ditch beyond Goodgolly's driveway. She skidded up beside. Her rookie deputy lay in the creek that ran beside the road, a brown mass amid the hard glints reflecting off the shallow current.

Her phone stirred again. The rest of Lyndsey Luck's text had just arrived.

offered me a glass of buttermilk

CHAPTER 26

"Ambulance and backup, Denise. Liberty Hill Road, same damn place as yesterday."

She jumped from the Charger before it stopped moving, reaching back for PARK.

"And get a deputy to the same farm as yesterday. It belongs to Jon Golly. Get me everything we have on him and his brother, Jim. Run both names through CrimeNet."

She plunged down the bank and crashed into the creek. Ankle-deep was plenty deep to drown in, and Lyndsey Luck lay on her face. The sheriff hauled her rookie over and dragged her by her shoulders onto cobble. For a weird instant they stared into each other eyes, as if neither believed the other existed on the same life-death plane. Then Deputy Luck convulsed and spewed a multicolored geyser that hit the sheriff's chest and face. The deputy took two retching gulps and tried to exhale. Then her eyes widened and she froze. Her heart had stopped.

The sheriff lunged, dragged her to higher ground, and fell upon her with chest compressions while her mind searched for what she knew about poisoning and came up with nothing. Between pumps she dug two fingers down Luck's airway. Something was stuck down there, too deep to reach. The sheriff tore her deputy's uniform shirt and vest off, pumped, rooted with her fingers and poked the obstruction deeper, pumped, gave up, and put her mouth over the deputy's, pinched her nose and inhaled hard, then pumped, pumped, for so long that her body and Luck's body seemed one. She had no idea how much time passed before she felt pressure, crowding, annoying interference.

An EMT shoved her aside.

"Sheriff, help is here."

She collapsed into a reef of watercress. For a while her phone had been buzzing.

She gasped, "Go ahead."

As she listened to Deputy Schwem, she closed her eyes against the relentless assault of blinding light and searing air. Via the faint signal bounce around Liberty Hill, Schwem was telling her that for the second time in two days they had lost Patience Goodgolly.

|||||||||||

The swing gate was open. The clothes were off the clothesline. On the grass in the shade of the cottonwood lay a drinking glass, empty, filmed with drying butterfat.

The ambulance still wailed in the distance as Deputy Schwem emerged from the barn.

"Solar power," he said. "I'll be darned. And there's this weird electric robot thing in there."

"Did it point a gun at you?"

"I think it tried. But it didn't have a gun."

"She has it, then. Did you find that old horse?"

"Negative."

"Then she's on it. Anything to see inside the house?"

"Buttermilk."

The sheriff felt woozy as she climbed the porch steps. Beside the kitchen sink was a drinking glass from the same set as the one on the yard, but full. Beside it stood the quart jar of buttermilk, now half-full.

"Jeez," Schwem said, "who poisons somebody?"

"I think it must have been meant for Patience," the sheriff said.

Sie nett, Mrs. Lapp had told the girl at the hospital that morning. *Always be nice to people in the uniform.*

"I don't think she meant to poison Deputy Luck. I think she didn't know there was poison and meant offering a drink to be a thoughtful gesture. Then she saw what happened and she took the opportunity to run. Take the jar and the glass into evidence. I'm guessing it's something like Killex. Search the house and property for a pesticide container, but my guess is whoever did this didn't leave one behind."

She turned at the sound of boots on the porch. Interim Chief Deputy Bender entered the Goodgolly home. He went straight to the glass of buttermilk and sniffed it. Then he looked at her through his smudged glasses, seeming to measure her for a bolt of upholstery. She awaited her Benderism.

"Came to help you chase your tail," he said.

"Thank you, Dick. Please head back out to where you have reception. Tell Denise to put a BOLO out for a young woman in a long dress and a black bonnet, riding a swaybacked brown horse, carrying a sawed-off shotgun."

"Pretty hard to lose something like that in the first place, some might say. Twice."

"Good point. Then come back here and direct a search with Schwem, please. We have all the probable cause we need. Take this place apart."

She felt a new kind of sick as she reached the porch steps. The yard looked a long way down. She felt overheated again. She grabbed the rail and sat heavily.

Abruptly her mouth burned with a strange taste, and her windpipe narrowed while her esophagus bubbled and fizzed.

She spat toward the grass.

She took her hat off and fanned her face.

As she unbuttoned her wet uniform shirt, she wondered if she had ruined her phone. She had not. While she had been fighting for Deputy Luck's life, Oppo had reached out again.

103°−96°

Fri, Aug 9, 1:33 PM
To: Dairy Queen (dairyqueen@blackbox.com)
From: Oppo (oppo@blackbox.com)
Subject: Two Things

---

1. New Rickreiner Tidbits: failed high-school English Lit twice for plagiarizing; failed EMT urine test for using someone else's urine; failed field-sobriety test by vomiting on Chief Deputy Elvin Lund (deceased) who drove him home to Babette and came away with $500 in Liquor City discount coupons.

2. Silver Alert: Leroy Fanta not responding to multiple contact efforts since asking for information yesterday PM about Golly Bros. property in Town of Leavings.

CHAPTER 27

Fanta made his move. "Why not bring the world to you?"

Faith Golly had put the boy to work watering sod roofs. Jim Golly, with his dog's help, towed by the harness handle, had herded Leroy Fanta back to the creek for cooling. The madman had shucked his saffron robe. He sat nude on the bottom, immersed to his eyes like a hippo. Fanta sat on the bank, soaking his hobbled feet. His headache had somewhat receded. His brain had slowly clarified. *Lamb of God*. He shuddered.

"Newspapers and magazines are dead," he made himself declare. He would never believe this.

"That's not how it works anymore," he continued anyway. "We don't need *Life* magazine. The world is digital. Everyone is a journalist. People tell their own stories."

Since the arrival of Golly's "Lamb of God," he had listened long enough—hours, it seemed, dappled shadows traveling across the water—to recall and confirm the specific delusion that drove the man. On August 26, in Biarritz, France, at exactly high noon—"new midnight"—outside the hotel where the G7 leaders would be meeting, Golly would immolate himself—*like the great martyr Thich Quang Duc*—in defense of Mother Earth. In Golly's retrograde planning, magazine photographers would be there. After that, leaders would lead, and mankind would be saved.

But Golly feared he wouldn't live that long.

My vegetarian therapy has been too indirect and too slow . . .

And you, Mr. Fanta, don't look much better than me . . .

This did not mean that he would be spared, Fanta understood. He was going to die anyway. He had blundered right into Hell Hollow, had interrupted a glorious martyrdom, and Golly couldn't let him go. Not that he cared much about his own death, Fanta had reminded himself, which had been a work in progress for years. With his remaining powers, he was ad-libbing a half strategy to save the boy, and now he blundered on.

"Boris Johnson, Emmanuel Macron, those guys can see you right here in the Bad Axe. Justin Trudeau, Shinzo Abe. You don't have to go to France. You can bring France to you."

He could tell that Golly—paddling cool water against his neck goiter—wasn't hearing. The man existed entirely within the spongiform angel food cake of his brain. Briefly Fanta considered trying to shock him to attention by asking a few of the many painfully obvious questions.

So Faith will drive you to France in my Tercel?

Are you going to charm all thirteen thousand security gendarmes?

Do you think you should wear pants?

Dear Mr. Secretary: Look out the window.

Look out the window? Do you think they'll all be partying together in Angela Merkel's hotel suite?

Never mind. In Golly's obsolescence, Fanta had glimpsed a special opening.

"Thich Quang Duc," he proceeded, returning to the Buddhist martyr on fire in the middle of a Saigon street, "would livestream himself on YouTube. The entire world would look into their smartphones and see him burn in real time."

This got the man's attention. Golly rose shedding water and glared through dappled shade. Through his uncorrected blur, Fanta felt the murderous indignance of this decaying hustler, this tumor-clad berserker. Fanta had affronted him.

YouTube. Smartphone. Real time.

These words had reached Golly. Fanta thought of the newspapers he had seen on the floor of Derp Hubbard's truck. If Golly read other people's old newspapers, then he recognized these nouns, but he had never witnessed the action of the verbs around them. His notion of how truth was constructed revolved entirely around canonical poetry, news articles, letters to the editor, and photojournalistic essays. The man was stuck in print. And in his gathering blindness it was unlikely that he could read print anymore. He had lost whatever grip he once had. Fanta felt his desperation.

He also felt his own traction. *Thich Quang Duc. YouTube.* Now he had to cycle carefully back toward *bring the world to you.* He had to show he understood, admired, and approved of Golly's crimes. His lungs felt weak, but he squeezed out the words.

"You are a very smart man, Jim. And very well informed."

Golly, re-sinking below his shoulders, nodded and coaxed fresh currents across the goiter on his neck.

"You read my *Broadcaster* series on chronic wasting disease."

Golly grunted and nodded again. Across three articles that ran during deer hunting season, Fanta had used the expertise of

Dr. Blaine Kleekamp to describe for readers how whitetail deer shed the chronic wasting prions in their urine, feces, and decomposing flesh. Plant roots absorbed these prions, incorporated them into stem and leaf—deer food—which was how the herd reinfected itself. Deer ate themselves, basically.

"Your scientific knowledge, Jim, is impressive. You're right that prions can be consumed intact, in food. Based on that, all kinds of things are possible. Creutzfeldt-Jakob's could be caused by mad cow prions in infected ground beef, and chronic wasting prions in infected venison could have made you sick. It absolutely could be that the Lyme disease spirochetes in you have opened the door to horizontal transfer. Your scientific acumen . . . Jim, these are marvelous deductions. Breakthroughs, really."

Golly grunted and passed gas. The dog moved away and the editor held his breath as a mighty bubble broke the creek surface and dissipated into tree limbs and moth-worm shrouds. Fanta now approached the crux, the insanity, the make-believe science behind Golly's idea that he could replace his infected animal prions, his bad betas, by consuming clean new alpha prions, from humans.

"As I said, Jim, I know that white truck. I offered Derp Hubbard twice what it was worth. He didn't bite. He wanted to be buried in that truck. That just tells you what a no-good bum he was, a nobody. A lower human."

Golly raised his naked eyebrows.

Fanta asked, "So you ate Derp Hubbard?"

"He was trespassing."

"And others?"

Fanta waited, feeling the dog's breath on his ear. He tried to guess the time. From where he sat, the sun had just slipped behind the limestone bluff carved from ancient ocean bottom by the tiny creek. Time? Eons.

"Faith finds people," Golly said.

From lower human to higher human.

"You used plant roots to bind their alpha prions," Fanta continued, "which you then ate as vegetables? And those alphas are pushing back against your infected betas? I have to say, Jim, that is brilliant. But now you're out of time and desperate to speed things up. You need to accelerate your therapy. You need an alpha-prion bomb. Here I wander in, but I'm too old, too sick. Do I have that right?"

Jim Golly swirled creek water with his swollen hands, making it cycle in front of him. He showed his purpled teeth. Then he lifted his hands and made two peace signs, followed by a heart.

"He'll do nicely," Fanta agreed.

He had to stop this.

"But don't you want to hear about an even faster way? How you can bring the world to you?"

CHAPTER 28

With aching arms from hours of labor, Sammy Lamb of God tosses two wet canvas buckets off the sod roof. He remembers that when he works hard, the voice mostly leaves him alone. He remembers hoeing an endless row of beans in the field beyond the window that he broke.

After the buckets have slapped to the ground ten feet below, they look like two of the many tawny-colored rocks that bulge through the unruly grasses and wildflowers of the meadow surrounding. This place, this farm, seems like some sort of promised land, before things got ruined, before money and greed, before pollution, before floods and fire and disease and war, but he feels too hot and hungry to wonder more about it. He has never been anywhere so hot. He has never been anyplace where the color green burned his eyes. His arms have never hurt this badly. But the woman with I BRAKE

FOR PEACE and MAKE LOVE, NOT WAR on her old green car has
promised him fifty dollars on Monday and a ride back to the
city. Though he doesn't know what city, or when Monday is,
he knows what he will do with fifty dollars. He will send it for
the window that he broke.

Once more an airplane drones just beyond the narrow
wedge of sky above. As the woman has instructed him to do,
he ladders down and conceals himself where his backpack
rests beneath the shaggy eave, under drooping grass and
wildflowers. Anyway, he needs to escape to shade and let the
numbness recede from his arms. The buckets are heavy. The
work he was hired to do has turned out to be hauling water
from a stone cistern along a path that corners several mud-
block buildings, one structure to the next, each half-buried
into the bluff that climbs through thick buzzing forest to
the sky. He hauls full buckets up a homemade ladder onto
the roof over the main house, where he gives water to the
parched sod. From up on the roof, the collection of grown-
over buildings and weedy gardens almost disappears into the
meadow.

The woman, Faith, toils inside the structure next door, a low
lean-to that stoops her almost double as she guts out plum tomatoes and drops them into glass jars. She pauses at the snarl in
the sky and swings her head to find him. She is making sure that
he has come down off the roof, he thinks. She stares exhaustedly
through him while a small yellow plane gaps the valley, flings its
oversized shadow down the near bluff, across the meadow, then
up and out.

But she still stares as the buzzing engine recedes, her face sagging, her hands hanging heavy, wetly red. He gives her a peace
sign, then a plus sign, then makes a heart with his two hands

paired. She drops her head and snicks her blade across a whet-
stone and resumes knifing tomatoes.

Sammy Lamb of God. He likes it. Best yet. It sounds
like the spiritual answer to exploding sheep. Cassie said that
fighting for the future, for all living creatures, was a spiritual
duty.

He travels to the cistern, fills the buckets, and climbs back
into the almighty sun. He sloshes out water as instructed, starting at the point where the roof merges with the hillside, one
bucket per one square foot of thirsty sod, working left to right,
then starting over. When his buckets are empty, he gazes over the
other sod rooftops, then across the irregular grid of small rectangular gardens half-obscured by tall grass and flowers leaning
over them.

He can't help it anymore. He descends the ladder with the
buckets, rounds the house beneath its eaves and starts along
the arbored trail as if bound for the cistern, but then he drops
the buckets and forks off at a crouch through the high flowers
and grasses, disturbing them as lightly as he can until he in-
tersects a garden he has spotted from above: bright green with
the lacy tops of carrots.

His heart skittering, he yanks up four thick ones and de-
vours them soil and all, unbreakably grinning through the
dirt on his teeth. Then he hears rustling in the grass and up
rises half-chewed carrot in his throat. He had promised not
to steal again but then he did. He had fought the police and
awakened in a hospital, unknown to himself. Within an
hour of being awake, the voice had arrived to tell him who
he was.

Do-nothing.

Sleeping while she burned.

You know how people are.
You know what they'll do.
You know what she wanted. Stop them.

His darting eyes come to rest in the next garden on familiar round-lobed leaves. He sees they shelter yellow-striped green melons. He pivots slowly on his haunches to confirm that he is hidden. He listens for the rustling again, listens. He shouldn't steal. *Chickenshit.* He crab-runs across the carrot rows into the melon patch.

The wilting leaves prickle and cling to his skin. He searches for a ripe melon, but they all seem too small and hard. As he sifts through the sticky leaves and hollow prickly vines, the soft earth depresses unevenly under his crouch, tipping him off balance as his heels sink. A low woof turns him. Tipping back while flailing forward, he takes up two fists of melon vines, flails, gets half-upright, and then as the dog woofs again he topples onto his back, the full leverage of his fall ripping up an entire plant by its wide web of roots.

The tangle drags over him, reeking putridly and shedding dirt. He recoils as across his face drag five ligamented fingers, entwined in root hairs, then the gooey puzzle of a wrist, the wrist gripped by heavier roots and dangling from a radius bone stuck with mealy tissue to its ulna. This rotten mess lands upon him. He hurls it off and thrashes to his knees. Before him boils a cavity of dirt, nubby white worms wriggling everywhere.

Then the tall grass shivers and parts. The dog has found him, so close he can smell its black breath. Faith follows with her red knife.

"Didn't!" His words burst. "Monday!"

He points. *Bones!*

She kicks dirt over the decomposing arm. With her knife, she steers Sammy Lamb of God back to his buckets. When he has climbed the ladder and stands numbly trembling on the roof, she takes the ladder away.

CHAPTER 29

Sheriff Kick had driven past Leroy Fanta's house in Town of Hefty—his car was not there—and then called him once more, unsuccessfully. Coming into town from that direction, she had made an appearance at the cooling center in the high school gym to thank the volunteers. From there, being just two blocks away, she had taken a domestic disturbance call—a newly separated young couple, fighting over custody of an in-window air conditioner. Next, she called the hospital: Deputy Luck was stable. Finally at the Bad Axe County Public Service Building, she had changed into a clean uniform, brushed her teeth, challenged her unhappy stomach with a few swallows of Mountain Dew, and checked with Denise on the BOLO for Patience Goodgolly.

"A clean whiff," Denise said. "Nothing. She's staying off the roads, I guess. Or hiding in the woods somewhere. So you're headed back to the hospital? Talk to her dad? Or uncle? Which-ever?"

For a moment the sheriff's throat burned too much to speak. Outside the dispatch window, the flags hung limply. The shrubbery drooped. Heat waves wriggled on the highway. The slant of shadows made the sheriff squint at the time on Denise's computer screen: it was already nearing four o'clock.

"Yes."

"OK, then, so you asked me to run the records on Jon and Jim Golly. Jon is clean as a whistle. Jim was discharged from the Army for unsuitability—that's usually behavior—and went on to be a five-time repeat drunk driver. He beat up some guy on a beach, and some other guy outside a nightclub, got three months in Palm Beach County Jail for the second one. He did five years' probation for possession of a Schedule II drug. I did some digging. You wanna guess what drug?"

|||||||||||

Once again, leaning over his hospital bed, the sheriff turned Jon Golly's head by his Gabriel Goodgolly beard.

"We have a deal," she told him.

His blue eyes came open and looked zoomy. Probably his pain meds were taking him on a trip. She gave the beard a sharp upward yank to let him feel the violence brewing in her heart. *I don't know exactly why yet, but I would love to rip your head off.*

"But if one syllable of what you tell me turns out to be a lie, your immunity goes poof and I'll use every scrap of truth to put you away. My dispatcher just told me about your brother's military discharge and his criminal record in Florida. No lies and no half-truths, Mr. Golly, do you understand?"

He nodded that he did. For a moment her adrenaline flagged and she felt ill again: fluttering sensations below her ribs, the not-quite urge to gag, the sense that she was about to fall from a great height. She backed away, used her palm to rinse her mouth at the sink. Had she ingested poison clearing Lyndsey Luck's airway? Was she feeling it?

"First of all, what's gone on between you and the Rickreiners? You and Jim, and Ronald, Babette, and Barry?"

His mouth came open and his tongue moved, but nothing came out.

Catch your breath and ask a proper question, Heidi. One at a time.

"Did you know Ronald Rickreiner?"

He moved his head vaguely.

"Yes or no."

"Yes."

"Starting when? And how?"

"Me and . . . me and Jim . . . we hadda buy on credit . . ."

He puffed weakly from the lung not punctured by the gimlet.

"Hadda bad year, winter just about killed us, we hadda buy seed and diesel . . . and machine parts, chemicals, feed, firewood . . ."

She waited. His eyes seemed to sink inside his face.

"We fought about it. I thought God would save us. Jim said nature didn't give a damn for God or no one. Jim won. Jim always wins. We took Rickreiner's terms."

"Which were?"

"Forty percent interest, lien on the property."

"You couldn't borrow from a bank?"

"We . . . we couldn't deal with any banks. We left some things behind in Florida, put it that way. We took Rickreiner's terms and two years on we still couldn't pay and he came back and threatened us with the lien to take the only thing we had, which was the land. So, Jim . . ."

He stopped. Oppo's message from 4:33 this morning echoed in the gap.

Throat slit, May 2003 (body in vehicle pulled from manure pond).

As for guessing Jim Golly's Schedule II drug, the sheriff had figured it was cocaine. Denise too, at first. But no, he had been arrested with over two hundred doses of thirty-milligram Adderall, prescribed to other people, stolen and black-marketed. And the charge was just possession. No intent to deliver. He was eating it.

"So Jim did what?" the sheriff demanded of his twin. "What did he do about your debt to Ronald Rickreiner? One false word, Mr. Golly, and our deal goes away."

"All Jim's idea."

"Sure."

"I worship God the Father. Jim . . . the law of nature, Mother Earth, survival of the fittest. We argued. But, as usual, Jim was right. He followed Rickreiner out of a tavern and ran him off the road. Sliced him like a hog. Rolled him and his truck off into Gullickson's manure pond. Gibbs talked to us as suspects. Jim acted offended by that. After we were cleared, we left."

"What do you mean, you left?"

"We didn't really leave. We didn't have one red penny to leave on. We had nothing but the land and those few buildings. But Jim told people we were moving back to Florida, said we'd take hurricanes over being suspected for crimes we didn't commit. Faith was with us by then. We moved way back inside that land and started as pioneers all over again."

Patience had to have a mother. Was this her? Faith? The sheriff changed angles.

"Faith who? Does she have a last name? Where is she from?"

"I couldn't say except Jim met her in a bar over in Iowa."

She paused to swallow back a wave of disgust that left her throat stinging.

"'With us,' you said. Faith was with who?"

"Us," he said again.

"Mr. Golly, whose partner was Faith?"

He closed his eyes. "We never really did decide that."

She gritted her teeth—resisted cracking his face with the back of her hand—calmed herself enough to stay with the purpose of her question. "Whose child is Patience? Yours or Jim's?"

She watched his answer, a shrug beneath the sheet. Her stomach rolled and her right hand closed into a fist. *Let it go, Heidi. Unless and until it matters.*

"But Patience lived with you."

"Patience went with me when I came back out to the farm after a year and a half. Jim had another break, in his mind. He wouldn't tolerate the crying and he made Faith give her up. But he was still my brother. I came back out looking Amish like this and told any English who were curious that I had bought that farm. I kept folks untangled from Jim as best I could, the way I always have, and nobody ever asked twice about it."

"You tried to join the Amish?"

"For show. I knew they wouldn't have us."

"You spoke German?"

"Our mother was German. I studied from an Amish Bible. I only spoke German to Patience. Pidgin German. It's all she's got."

"Why the name, Mr. Golly? You were trying to hide in plain sight. Why not Gabriel Smith?"

"Gotteskinder."

"What?"

"I only ever said that I was Gabriel Gotteskinder. It was the

Amish who started calling me Goodgolly, with a wink. Those
people never say directly what they know. I played dumb and
went along. No one cared anymore. It just stuck."

"How old is Patience?"

"Seventeen."

"Where is her baby? Or babies?"

"Born dead."

"One untrue syllable, Mr. Golly . . ."

"One was born dead. The other didn't last a week."

He turned his face away. She turned it back.

"To whom do I owe the rape charge, Mr. Golly?"

"It's because of the lien."

"I'm sorry?"

"They still have the lien on our land. They're the only non-
Amish who knew we never left."

"Who do you mean, they? The Rickreiners?"

"She still holds the lien. The son waited until Patience turned
thirteen before he told us he would repossess the property
unless . . . unless he could 'take her to the bowling alley for a
hamburger,' the son said. He said that because his mother had
just bought the bowling alley. He took her out again and again,
every time saying he would take the property away if she didn't
go with him to the bowling alley for a hamburger."

She took his beard in her fist, then felt repulsed and let it go,
let him turn away and shake with shame.

"Now we know why she stuck that filthy tool in your
chest."

*And now we can guess where Patience is headed with a shotgun.
And why the Rickreiners are so desperate to* BARRY *me.*

"His mother, Babette, she knows about all this?"

"The lien is hers, legally. What the son was doing, she maybe
didn't know."

"Why didn't she collect on the lien years ago, before Barry started taking Patience for hamburgers?"

He shrugged faintly again. He was losing strength. She took her phone out and re-studied Oppo's most recent message, by now nearly four hours ago.

Silver Alert: Leroy Fanta not responding to multiple contact efforts since asking for information yesterday PM about Golly Bros. property in Town of Leavings.

"Is your brother still 'way back inside the land'?"

Jon Golly nodded and she let him rest. The sky in his window—pink-orange scorch marks on high cirrus clouds—reminded her that time was slipping away. She still had to check on Deputy Luck down the hallway. She still had to brief her night-shift deputies. And—oh, by the way—she had a family, one she hadn't eaten supper with for over a week.

She stared out at the escaping day. It would be a terrible idea to arrest Barry Rickreiner—on just Jon Golly's word—and then not make the charge stick. She needed Patience for that. As hideous as she found the idea, she had to give BARRY HER a heads-up. There was a plausible threat to his safety. She had to be a sheriff here.

Her stomach clenched. Her tongue stuck. Her head spun.

"Mr. Golly, is your brother still somewhere on that land?"

"Yes," Jon Golly whispered finally. "Jim is still back in there."

"Where?"

"Hollow of that middle feeder creek."

That told her nothing. Hollows. Feeder creeks. There were

hundreds. The Gollys owned hundreds of acres. The forests would darken in an hour.

"What kind of man is Jim these days, Mr. Golly?"

"What kind of man?"

He was fading fast. Again she hadn't asked the right kind of question. A nurse's shoes squeaked behind her. Yet somehow it was *the* question.

"What kind of man, Mr. Golly?"

It felt familiar, what Jon Golly whispered fiercely as he closed his eyes.

"You said it yourself. Jim is my *brother*."

CHAPTER 30

"He'll do nicely, yes," Fanta said.

He sandbagged Jim Golly one more time, after the man's monologue on martyrdom, global population shift, and coral reef bleaching had rounded back to the homeless young man hired to water Golly's sod roofs.

Fanta's pig valve fluttered dangerously. Night approached. Between gypsy moth shrouds, he could see a lopsided moon rising in a darkening blue sky.

"But Jim," he resumed cautiously, easing into the twist he hoped would tilt Golly off course, reviewing in his mind's eye the famous *Life* magazine photographs of Thich Quang Duc's suicide in the middle of a Saigon thoroughfare.

Every person Fanta knew had seen the photos. He had been with friends in junior high school, appalled and enthralled at a table in the school library. First the elderly monk's religious

brothers had doused him in gasoline. Then Quang Duc had set
himself ablaze, slowly turned black, and tipped over.

"You realize," he said to Golly now, "that Thich Quang Duc
lit himself on fire in 1963. I'm guessing that you think his sacri-
fice ended the war, but it was only 1963."

Golly frowned and stiffened. Fanta glanced behind. The dog
had departed. He clung to his purpose. Golly's timeline was off.
His understanding of the burning monk's motive was apocry-
phal, twisted to serve his self-interest. Fanta knew the history
well. Quang Duc had protested the Diem regime's mistreatment
of Buddhists, not the war. His death had sparked change, but not
the kind that Golly falsely remembered.

"From the standpoint of U.S. involvement, Jim," Fanta
continued, "Quang Duc's suicide represented actually more of a
beginning. More of an accelerant. That was the moment when
John F. Kennedy stepped into quicksand and sent in 'military ad-
visers.' That happened just months before Kennedy was gunned
down in Dallas. Quang Duc on fire ended nothing. His death
was a beginning."

He watched Golly seethe at the correction. But Fanta's ac-
curacy was personal. Seven long years *after* Thich Quang Duc's
martyrdom, as Fanta lay broken in a mud puddle iridescent with
swirls of Agent Orange, the insanity of the war in Vietnam had
just been peaking.

"It was Kim Phuc," Fanta continued his correction of the record. "It was the picture of Kim Phuc that ended the war. Much
later, 1972. Remember her? She was the naked little girl burned
by napalm, wailing in pain and terror as she ran down the road."

Golly trembled, glaring at Fanta.

"It was a *live child*, Jim, not a *dead martyr*. The spirit of the
war died with the suffering of Kim Phuc. She lived. Her life
changed history."

He pressed on.

"Jim, there is no *Life* magazine anymore, no set of black-and-white photographs that the whole world accepts as truth. No one reads newspapers or magazines anymore, and no one looks out the window. That's not how it works."

At this, Golly lurched up. Finding his balance, he wallowed aggressively across the creek, his entire body flushed with fever, his skin tags abruptly crimson and vividly trembling. He slapped the water and howled from William Butler Yeats into Fanta's face.

"'Turning and turning in the widening gyre, the falcon cannot hear the falconer! Things fall apart! The center cannot hold! Mere anarchy is loosed upon the world!'"

"Jim, listen. I can bring the world to you. Tomorrow."

"'The blood-dimmed tide is loosed!'"

Fanta turned his face away from Golly's rancid breath. "Yes," he said, staring up through a mass of caterpillars backlit by the merciless sky. "The blood-dimmed tide is loosed . . . on YouTube and Twitter."

"'And *everywhere*,'" Golly railed against the aching bones of Fanta's head, "'the ceremony of innocence is drowned!'"

"Yes, Jim," he tried to agree, fighting with a sticky throat, "but this isn't World War One or Vietnam. Go ahead and burn yourself if you believe you have to. Tomorrow, if you want to. Just don't eat anyone else. All we need is a video clip."

"'The best lack all conviction, while the worst are full of passionate intensity!'"

"Yes. Yes, believe me, I know. I'm looking at it."

"I will live!" Golly roared.

Between them, another great gout of gas broke the surface. Fanta stopped his in-breath, waited, waited, refusing to inhale the digested out-breath of a cannibal.

"Somebody knows that I came here," he wheezed at last,

remembering yesterday's call to Vigdis Torkelson at the library. "I'm a friend of Sheriff Heidi Kick," he added. "I promise you she's looking for me, and she'll be here soon."

Golly floundered back, pushing waves, and whistled sharply through his teeth. In moments Tippy appeared out of the deep forest shadows, Faith trailing with her rifle.

|||||||||||

"Kneel," Jim Golly told Fanta minutes later, after Fanta had hobbled at gunpoint across Hell Hollow to the shallow grave that must have been dug and escaped from yesterday by the dead man in the ditch.

"Face away."

Fanta looked at Golly one last time. Still nude except for his water shoes, he had pinched thick glasses onto his swollen head so that he could see to shoot. *Kaleidoscopic.* Fanta understood now why the man in the ditch had been shot so erratically from point-blank range. Faith rounded up the victims. Golly did the honors.

Now she handed him the rifle. Fanta knelt, faced away, toward the looming early moon.

"Whatcha think, Faithy? He just seems like potatoes to me."

She scowled at the ground, her heavy shoulders slumping. She had brought a shovel.

"The sheriff knows I'm here," Fanta tried again. "I'm a friend of hers."

"But I'll be in the history books by then," Golly told Faith. "So it's gonna be your medicine, your call. You'll be on your own."

Fanta watched her lips move silently.

"You don't need time, or France," he told Golly once more. "You don't need to go anywhere. Just bring the world to you. All you need is—"

Golly cocked the weapon behind him.

It's OK, Fanta told himself. *You were killed a long time ago in Vietnam . . .*

With all his dwindling voice he bellowed his final words—"Jump! Run!"—and the last two things he saw were the fuzz of a live child vaulting off a sod roof, and the fast-departing swish of Tippy's tail.

. . . You just didn't die until today.

CHAPTER 31

By the time Sheriff Kick called from the ridge road, heading home in final daylight, the sky was deep indigo, with stars pushing through and hung with what seemed like an over-sized and faintly pink gibbous moon. The Charger's dash said ninety-five degrees.

"Denise, before you punch out, contact that outfit that's spraying for the gypsy moths. I want to go up with them first thing in the morning. I need to get up high and look for somebody living deep off the grid. Pay them whatever."

"Ten-four, my queen."

The obvious struck her. "How did you know that Fanta was asking about the Golly property in Town of Leavings?"

"What?"

"The emails you've been sending me. Aren't you Oppo?"

"Emails? What are you talking about?"

"You won't lose your job, Denise. Trust me, by tomorrow Rickreiner won't be running for sheriff anymore. And thank you for the tips. I'm putting it all together."

The sheriff turned on her headlights and the air exploded with insects, a billion motes of alien energy hopping and swirling and flowing over the Charger, ticking its surfaces like hail.

"Heidi," Denise said, "check behind your ear for a tampon."

||||||||||

At home, Harley met her cheerfully in the front yard and towed her into the porch light to show her the first good news she had seen all day: two sealed white business envelopes that read in scrawly blue crayon *from taylor kick.*

"He did it, hon! These are his apologies for pushing people at the pool yesterday. This one is for Dylan and Grammy Belle."

To this envelope, Taylor had attached a red T. rex sticker— favorite color, favorite creature.

"And, of course, this one."

To the envelope for Becky Rilke-Rickreiner and her boy he had affixed a sticker of a green germ.

"That's hardball right there," her husband joked. "He might have a future in politics."

She put her forehead against his thick chest and listened to his heartbeat.

"Oh, God, Harley."

"What?"

"Rumors."

"Of course. What now?"

"You're snipped."

"I'm what? Oh, snipped. The hell I am. But so?"

"And I'm pregnant."

He froze for a moment. Then he pushed her out to arm's length and looked into her face.

"Are you?"

She had no idea what she would say until her voice came out and she heard herself spackling over the truth. "Harley, it's a perfect rumor. Don't you see how it works? You don't want more kids because the ones we have already are so bad. Meanwhile, Sheriff Mommy is a fraud and a whore, having an affair with her handsome Latino deputy. Launch that from a barstool and it travels at the speed of light around the gossip universe. You and I are the last to know, of course. But guess where I heard it."

His chin dropped.

"Mom, right? I'm sorry."

"Yeah," she said. "And as always, she has only the best sources."

"Heidi, I'm sorry. She's protective. That's why she believes crap like that."

"Yeah," she said, letting go of what had steamed inside her since yesterday, "but let's not pretend this is not emotional violence by the people spreading the rumors. Let's not imagine that it doesn't trickle down to the kids. Play it through the mind of an anxious little boy. Your daddy is sorry that he had you. And your mommy wants a different one of you, and a different Daddy, both. Meanwhile, your beloved sister is off becoming a bigger boy than you will ever be—imagine *those* rumors, Harley—and all this time everybody keeps saying blah-blah-blah how much they love you."

She had pushed herself to tears. She had nothing else to say.

Harley wrapped her in his arms. Then he turned her body surely and gently, her perfectly practiced lover, until they were shoulder to shoulder, and in that embrace her husband walked her around the corner of the house, where by the light from the family room window Dylan and Taylor played in their plastic kiddie pool. Father and mother stopped beyond the boys' sphere of awareness and watched. She wondered if every parent of identical twins saw what she did: completely different people.

"We're going to be OK," Harley said.

"I think I need a bite to eat," she answered him.

"Mom made macaroni salad. You can pick out the green onions, I guess."

"Then I'm going to drive Taylor to Rickreiner's place and drop off his apology."

Harley pulled away and looked at her.

She answered the look. "I know it's late. I know it's bedtime. But then he's clear to go on the field trip tomorrow."

"Heidi—"

"I have business with Rickreiner anyway."

"Why don't you just deliver it?"

"Because it's from Taylor. It's his all the way. No short-cuts."

She saw his eyes agree. He tried to re-gather her in his arms. "But, hon, it's nine o'clock. Prickreiner's probably got a load on. He never really quit drinking, I heard. Can't you do it tomorrow?"

"I can't. He might be in danger," she said. "Not tomorrow, tonight. And he also needs to give me an alibi."

"You have deputies. Do you need to confront him right now?"

Now she pulled away.

"He's all mine. I'm not taking any shortcuts either. Taylor will be fine. And if I can eat your mother's macaroni salad, I can look the devil in the eye."

| | | | | | | | | | |

In minutes she was loading Taylor and his envelope into the Charger, reassuring him as the locks clicked down. She had buckled his booster onto the backseat, and she talked through the window space.

"I'm proud of you for being a big boy and doing the right thing. And I'm so glad you got to play in the pool with your brother. Dylan and Daddy are proud of you too. And guess what? Now you can go on your field trip to Elmo Pond and help at the farm breakfast tomorrow."

Her little boy gazed back wordlessly into her mirror as she turned out the end of the driveway onto Pederson Road. In a half mile they were rolling past the spot where in late July from a potato field Opie's friend Rosie Glick had seen him hitchhiking and had run to tell her father. Amos Glick had barreled down the road in his fastest horse and buggy to snatch up Taylor and bring him home.

"We're all very proud of you," she said. "We would have a hundred more boys just like you if we could. But then we'd be too busy, so we'd rather keep things just the way they are. With Opie home, of course."

He just stared at her. He was every bit just a common seven-year-old boy, she thought . . . yet such a mystery, and so . . . *formidable*. It was impossible to explain to non-parents how even the littlest children were *people*. You did not define or control them—not without committing abuse, anyway—and it was equally impossible to explain, she thought, the unrelenting aloneness of parenthood. You created this life. This was yours to care for.

Am I doing it right?

About halfway to Rickreiner's, she frowned and stuck her arm out the window, trying to scoop in moving air toward her sweaty face. Taylor had begun to hum behind her.

"What are you humming, bud?"

The answer to that would remain private, apparently. He only vaguely smiled at her.

|||||||||||

In another quarter mile, she parked the Charger alongside Rickreiner's mailbox, in the outer glow of the motion-sensing floodlight that cast its beam across his yard.

"Hop out, Taylor. Drop it in the box. Shut the box. Hop back in."

He did.

"See? You did it. Now you're done."

She put on her duty hat.

"Now I have to do one little sheriff thing and I'll be right back. Just sit tight, bud."

She locked him in, then looked back from the floodlit phalanx of red-and-white campaign signs staked in the yard and smiled reassuringly at her son's face, bunched in the window. She felt weary and tight as she raised her hand to knock. Any sheriff does a thousand difficult things—telling a mother that her son has died. *Just another tough moment, Heidi.*

Becky Rilke-Rickreiner answered the door in zebra tights and stood wide and mute behind her screen door.

"Hi. Sorry to bother you. I need to speak with—"

"Barry!" she screeched and disappeared. "You won't believe this! Nine-thirty, you won't believe who's at the door!"

"Two things," she began when BARRY HER slapped into view holding a beer and wearing wet red swimming trunks, blinding her with his pale, soft, nearly nude body, a grub who would be sheriff. "One, I need to make you aware of a possible threat to your safety and recommend that, until you hear otherwise, you open this door only to friends and family and use caution when going out."

The grub rolled his eyes.

"Two, I need to know where you were between ten A.M. and two P.M. today."

"What kinda shit is this?"

"This? This is what a sheriff does. Take notes if you want."

"Threat from who?"

"I'm sorry, Mr. Rickreiner, but that information is part of an ongoing investigation. Use caution is all I can tell you. You went to law enforcement school, I'm told, so you know how it is. Stay home if possible. You're at risk if you don't. I need an answer: where you were between the hours of ten and two?"

"What kind of question is that?"

"Am I wrong? You didn't go to school?"

"You're making something up against me, is that it?"

"All you have to do is tell me where you were."

"Get a lawyer!" screeched Becky from somewhere. "Tell the bitch you got a lawyer and get her ass off the property!"

He winced. The sheriff said, "It'd be way cheaper just to tell me where you were. You weren't doing anything you shouldn't be doing, I'm sure. Anyway, a sheriff's life is pretty much an open

book. Everybody knows your business, all the time. Accountabil-
ity, right? You'd be practicing for later."

The glint had drained from his eyes. "I was here," he said to
the doorframe.

"Someone to verify that?"

"Her," he said.

"Thank you. Mrs. Rickreiner?"

"He was here!"

"Thank you."

Back in the van, she told Taylor, "And now Mommy's all done
too. Let's go home."

But the energy had turned strange at home. Harley sat alone
on the porch steps. Taylor vaulted from the Charger and hustled
away toward the barn to feed his rabbit, a bedtime chore.

Harley said, "Dylan's upstairs. He won't open his letter."

Her phone buzzed and she ignored it.

"What do you mean?"

"His apology from Taylor. He won't open it. He got into bed
and we were talking about the field trip tomorrow, about the bus
ride, how the bus was going to stop so they could feed the goldfish at Elmo Pond. He got real quiet, and I thought maybe he's
thinking Elmo Pond is kind of near where you found the body
yesterday. But I doubt he even knows that, or cares. I said, 'Isn't it
great that Taylor can go along with you tomorrow?' I said, 'Let's
see. Show me your brother's letter. Let's see what he wrote to you.'
But Dylan won't open the letter. I might have pushed him too
hard. He started to cry."

She slumped down beside her husband on the front porch
steps. Her phone buzzed again—a text this time, from Denise—
and she looked at it with some small sense of relief. Finding Jim
Golly from the air would be quicker and safer. It would allow her
to plan without alerting him.

Yes from Crockett Crop Dusting. Meet at the airfield in Lansing, Iowa, 4:30 AM tomorrow.

She leaned her head against Harley's shoulder.

"Dylan is protecting his brother." He sighed. "I guess. But I just don't understand why he needs protecting. Gosh. I mean, what's out there?"

CHAPTER 32

Jump! the voice had commanded Sammy Lamb of God.

This was hours ago now, and miles ago, he thinks—unless he's gone in circles. After she had taken the ladder away, he had watched the valley sink in shadow and the sky catch fire. The melon plants where bones were buried had disappeared behind fog rising from the creek. He had watched Faith and Papa and the dog walk the old man at the point of a rifle. Across the black grasses and closing meadow flowers he had seen three heads, then two as the old man went down.

Jump!

He had jumped from the roof. He had landed on the beaten earth. His leg bones had jarred up into his hips, his hips into his spine, and his neck had snapped back. He had been stunned, pain shooting through his ankles up his shin bones, his head filling with a sick, dull ache.

Run! the voice had commanded.

He had gathered his backpack and begun to limp aimlessly along the dirt path that led to the cistern.

Run which way? From what?

Something had crashed through the tall meadow grass, coming toward him. The dog. Two gunshots had cracked and echoed overhead.

He had limped a dozen more steps without direction. He could not outrun the dog. He had stared at the cistern—cemented stones, head high and round, fed by a joined-wood gutter funneling water down the hillside—then heaved his backpack up and over the rim. He had found toeholds up its mossy stone wall. He had cleared the rim and rolled in, cold water closing over him. The barking dog had sounded squeaky, trailing away. He had held his breath, heard Faith holler past, come up for air.

The dog was heading up the bluff behind the house, gathering its deep black haunches and exploding upward like a bear through brush and tumbling rocks, reaching the height where the sun still struck with setting light. Faith had carried the rifle past the cistern and ducked underneath the dripping wooden gutter that sluiced in the water. She couldn't climb with the dog. She had whistled at it. Behind Sammy Lamb of God, Papa bawled a jumble of words and curses as he flailed without help through the meadow.

He had ducked back underwater and held his breath until he couldn't. When he came up, Papa leaned against the cistern, wheezing, not three feet away. The dog descended in a cascade of loose rock. Papa had gasped at Faith, "Bring him back or it'll be you."

"Who'll cook me?" she had growled in response. "Who'll cook for you?"

"I'll tear you like a vulture."

He had ducked under again. When he came up, Faith and the dog were gone. Papa gasped horribly beneath the eaves of the house, spitting after every breath.

Underwater, he had put his backpack on and crab-walked to the opposite side of the cistern, where the water poured in. He had risen under the spout, chinned himself, thrown a leg over, heaved out, then scrambled up the gutter like a monkey as it zigzagged up through thick forest along the steep hillside. From where the gutter ended at the spring that fed the cistern, he caught a glimpse of Faith and the dog hunting him through the gray grasses at the high end of the meadow, like he was a pheasant.

He was hidden, but he had nowhere left to go. So he had waited there for night. *Chickenshit*, the voice had caught up to remind him. *Cassie never ran from anything. Cassie ran into the fire for her horses.*

But you told me to jump.

Yes.

You told me to run.

Yes. And it is also me who chases you. I am them and I am hunting you. I am inside you and outside you now. I am everyone and everywhere. You can't escape.

He had opened his backpack and taken the shattered highway reflector, had scraped and torn the skin of his forearms like Cassie taught him until they bled into the spring and gently trickling water was the only sound he heard.

|||||||||||

A long, blank time later, still hot, when at last a flesh-colored moon in partial decay had risen overhead, he had scooted back down the gutter to the cistern. Listening from there, he had heard through the dirt walls of the house a terrifying commotion, Faith shrieking and Papa bellowing, the dog woofing excitedly, things falling and breaking.

With a memory of this morning, he had eased off the cistern's rim to the ground. The rough road he had arrived on had exited the forest between two huge stumps. From there, to his first glimpse, the cluster of low, grassy-topped structures had looked like a hobbit shire in Middle-earth, a paradise. Now he was groping through moon shadows along the forest's edge, looking to escape through those stumps again. A door squealed open.

"Tippy! Get!"

The beam of a flashlight had struck him in the back, casting a black ghost of himself forward as he fled.

|||||||||||

Finally, slick with sweat and dry with thirst, no more breath to run, he lies heaving and bruised where he fell among the scoured rocks and tumbled timbers of a deep dry wash.

You can't escape.

After his first fifteen seconds of flight, he has never outrun the dog. The dog has been with him this whole time. But it has always waited, panting, growling, and snapping, for the woman to catch up. So Sammy Lamb of God has limped and rested, limped and rested, night heat somehow heavier than day heat, an hour, two hours, a redundant terrain addled by moon shadows, uphill scrambles and downhill plunges, holes that look like shadows, shadows like holes, always fetid water on low ground, tilting hummocks, sucking mud, swarming mosquitoes, then another brushy climb with thorns tearing at him, going in circles, he fears, with the dog trotting menacingly behind him, now and then baying to guide Faith as she lumbers and crashes along. The dog can go forever, so it is her against him, who can last longer, and it seems that she will never quit.

Finally she is near. He can hear her staggering strides, her laboring lungs. Then he sees her zombie shape lurching down-hill toward him. The dog shows her. She aims. Then something rolls beneath her and she falls, firing the rifle into the treetops.

He starts to crawl down the gulch. She fires again, hits rock. He finds the breath to scramble out and rise to a crouch behind a tree trunk. He turns his back to her, sees a lane to the bottom, and lets gravity pitch him headlong downward. The dog gallops easily at his heels. But the bottom is a bog. He staggers ten strides into muck and sinks to his hips. He is stuck.

I am everyone and everywhere.

The dog paces the margin of the bog, then hurls itself at him—and is stuck too, all four legs, teeth snapping just out of reach. Now here she comes, sidestepping down the hillside, hugging tree trunks, with the rifle slung on a strap over her shoulder.

He has one minute, maybe. If he wants, he can reach the dog's heavy leather collar, the woven-leather handle that Papa grabs to be towed. Or he can reach several of the heavy broken branches that litter the rim of the bog. He catches the narrow tip of one and pulls the branch to himself and threads three feet of the narrow end through the harness handle. He jams the ragged point down into the muck. The dog squirms and yelps. With his weight on the thick end of the branch, he levers himself, belly flops, strains, and reaches another branch farther out, hauls and claws and worms his way to solid ground. She fires again but doesn't hit him.

He limps on and on into screeching, howling night, long after the sounds of the chase have faded. Once, he staggers out of the forest to the edge of a cornfield, a vast, black-silver abnormality straining at the moon. He follows its outer row to a road, walks along heat-exuding asphalt, but a car approaches—*everyone and everywhere*—and he bolts back into the alien corn. Later, scratched raw by leaf blades, he follows a cold creek, rinsing arms and legs and face in it, drinking from it, hobbling on its sharp stones. But then an engine roars above his gulping breaths, headlights fracture black forest, tree limbs shatter, and a white truck crashes through, Papa's swollen head moonlit in the driver's window. He hurries back the way he came.

Later still, utterly empty, he surrenders to a soft patch of hot earth, curls upon his bedspread, and crashes into sleep.

He awakens to a bestial snort and a barrel in his face.

He is caught again, he first believes.

But it is an old horse, lathered and blowing. Standing beside it is a barefoot girl in a long dress and a bonnet, her raw thumb on the hammer of a short-nosed shotgun aimed squarely at his face. He can't erase his rigid grin, even when she reaches into her dress pocket and shines a small flashlight on his raw arms.

She lowers the gun. She peels her sleeves back to show him. Neither says a word.

She turns in the moonlight and vaults aboard the horse. She scoots forward. He rises, shoulders his backpack, mounts behind her, and rides with his arms around her hard, narrow waist.

94°−101°

Sat, Aug 10, 2:13 AM
To: Dairy Queen (diaryqueen@blackbox.com)
From: Oppo (oppo@blackbox.com)
Subject: Opposition Research

Found Hubbards truck and Fantas car way back in

CHAPTER 33

Way back in . . . where? Why didn't Oppo finish the message?

The plane went up predawn, its navigation lights strobing green and red through clouds of rising river fog. As the tiny vessel thumped through air pockets, Sheriff Kick vomited into a Piggly Wiggly sack while a pilot from Iowa named Jack Bristol hollered tour-guide information.

"That's the Guttenberg Dike down there!

"There's the Bishops Ferry Pronto station! Great cheese curds!

"As the crow flies, a guy can hardly sing 'Happy Birthday' between Iowa and Wisconsin! Gotta pull up or hit these bluffs! That's Battle Rock! You ever been on Battle Rock?"

As soon as the plane had climbed high enough to clear the Mississippi bluffs, Jack Bristol abruptly swooped low and with a deafening hiss unleashed plumes of *Bacillus thuringiensis kurstaki* across treetops in Town of Irish Ridge.

"It's completely harmless to humans!" he yelled over his engine and propeller.

"Very low toxicity!

"If you eat fresh fruit or vegetables, then you've eaten plenty of this stuff!

"And look at you! You're fine!"

He pulled up and looped back through his plume. She thought she tasted rubber, and overripe bananas.

"We only spray at dawn and dusk!

"Or if there's no wind!

"Lately there's no wind! We can spray all day!"

He hauled back on a lever and released another gusher.

"Die, you sonsabitches! Die!"

She twisted shut her barf bag and tried to focus on the horizon. She had never seen the Bad Axe from above. Her place on earth was both a mote and a motherland, draping itself in every direction over the planet's disappearing point. As she stared, the fragment gnawed at her. *Found Hubbards truck and Fantas car way back in . . .* What was Oppo doing out at 2:13 A.M.? Who was Oppo?

The plane nose lifted. In the same gaze she could see both ridges and coulees, the rising sun gilding fields and pastures while shadowing watersheds as they fingered down into streams reflecting blue-pink sky.

"Liberty Hill!" hollered Jack Bristol.

Looking east, she saw the landmark flattened by perspective but still outstanding among lesser hilltops, as it must have been, with a tall flag flying, to Grover Cleveland campaigning from his railroad car. The Golly land extended ruggedly behind it, north. The plane tilted south toward a blue-green glint a mile or so away.

"Elmo Quarry Pond!" the pilot hollered. "A couple more

passes, we'll be heading over what you want to see! What exactly are we looking for?"

"Lay of the land," she yelled back. "A road in. A homestead."

"Never seen anything like that!"

"Somebody lives in there."

"News to me!"

"Maybe a white truck or a green car."

"OK! My eyes are peeled!"

She had to close hers and try to feel better. The morning had begun well enough. The entire Kick family had risen at farmer o'clock so the twins could get ready for the 4-H bus that would take them on their field trip to help set up the Bad Axe County Farm Breakfast, with the traditional sunrise stop to feed the mythical giant goldfish. There had been a minor conflict over how much stuff Taylor had in his backpack, which seemed ridiculously heavy, but she and Harley had exchanged eye signals and agreed to let it go. Then Taylor had been upset when the bus, because it arrived early, came all the way down the driveway to the house. For some reason he had wanted to wait by the mailbox at the road. But he had recovered and waved to his mom and dad from the window.

Her stomach was leveling, and she was feeling glad for Taylor when her phone buzzed.

Rhino said, "I can't reach Bender."

"Bender? He's off. He should be home."

"A lady friend—I didn't know he had one, did you?—called around three A.M. to ask when his shift would end. I said, 'Eight o'clock last night.' I thought maybe you assigned him somewhere."

"No."

The plane banked over Liberty Hill and the Jon Golly farm—"Ten-four," Rhino said, "will deal, sorry to bother"—and then cleared the nearest ridge to the north. For no more than three seconds they were passing over a narrow coulee bisected by a tiny rill of a stream. Upon the meadow landscape, still in shadow, she made out vague geometric sketches in the late summer foliage. Accidental shapes? She had hardly had time to wonder before the plane had flown beyond, looping back toward Elmo Quarry Pond.

She pondered over Deputy Bender for several seconds—that he had a "lady friend," for one thing, and if he was missing, where was he, and was he OK?—then looked down to see the short green 4-H bus parked at the quarry pond with specks of kids at the water's edge. Maybe from up here she would see a spot of gold finning in the bright aqua water.

No, of course not. But—

"Stop!" she cried, twisting in her seat belt.

"This is an airplane, Sheriff!"

On the road a half mile from the pond she watched a single speck—a child?—walking along the road—and an old white pickup drifting up behind him.

"I mean, go back, go back, circle back!"

CHAPTER 34

By dawn she had reined the horse aside twice to dodge him, the atrocious Papa, who was careening erratically down empty roads—*I'll tear you like a vulture*—half-blind, steering that old white pickup. She had stiffened and hissed as he passed. Another time she had skirted them wide around the echoes of the dog baying for Faith.

Now, at the brim of a paved road with a yellow double line, as twin beams prick a gray fog wall, she utters her first syllables.

"Hup-hup-schnell," she tells the horse, and they clatter at a new pace across asphalt, feeling its fervent yesterday breath.

Past the ditch they disappear into high corn and turn toward a dome of thinner sky that suggests an awakening town.

The dome dissolves as they approach. She hups the horse across a soybean field, through a tangle of shoved-up earth and shoved-downed trees, through a broken fence, across a small empty parking lot behind a cinder-block building, and around to the front of a store called Liquor City.

She dismounts. The horse wheezes beneath him. She aims the shotgun butt and with a blow to the window's geometric center she obliterates the Liquor City emblem. An alarm starts to bray as she clips jutting shards from the window frame. She gathers her dress and steps in. She walks up an aisle sweeping the gun barrel along a shelf of bottles, scattering the floor with broken glass and a spreading pool of alcohol. She grabs a bottle as she rounds the aisle and comes back the other way drinking from it, leaving wreckage in her wake.

She hands the bottle up to him.

It tastes like fire.

Then she climbs back inside his arms.

"Hup-hup," she tells the sagging horse. "Schnell."

CHAPTER 35

"Circle back over the pond! Hurry!"

"This old bug-smasher can't go over seventy-five knots! With this spray tank under me, she gets wonky if I tilt her more than thirty degrees! Hang on!"

She yelled at Rhino: "I need someone heading toward Liberty Hill and the quarry pond!"

"The log on Bender's GPS indicates he been near there for several hours. But I can't raise him."

"Just get someone moving!"

The plane wallowed so wide north, then so far east, that they passed over the borders of Vernon and Richland counties.

"Deputy rolling, Sheriff. What is he looking for?"

"The 4-H kids are at the pond! I might have seen Hubbard's white truck! We're circling back! I'll update!"

So slow. She aimed her finger to call Harley and saw that he had texted her.

Dylan left his letter. I opened it. Pic attached.

"Here we come! Better look!"

They approached the pond again. The bus remained there, the kids. But now the road was empty. The solo child and the white truck were gone. Desperately, as the plane slid away into irrelevant space, she twisted one way, twisted the other, lunged against her seat belt to see beneath the wing, but the truck had vanished from the landscape.

She looked at the photo of Taylor's apology letter that Harley had attached.

I am not sorry. I will never be sorry. No one will make me sorry when I am not sorry. HE will see who is sorry.

Then Harley was calling.

"Heidi, the bus driver did a head count. Taylor was there. Now he's gone."

"No."

It was all she could say.

"He ran away, Heidi. When they stopped at the pond."

"No."

"They just did a roll call. Taylor wasn't there. Dylan said he and the other kids saw him sticking his thumb out on the road. The driver made him come back. But he must have snuck off again."

"No. I'm sure he's there."

"Heidi . . . he had a hammer in his backpack."

"No."

"Dylan saw him put it in there. That's why he insisted on taking the backpack. Dylan didn't want to tattle."

She wrenched around to look behind at nothing.

"Put me down," she said.

As the plane came around to the south and outer Farmstead appeared beneath, Jack Bristol reached across and squeezed her hand.

"Soon as I can."

CHAPTER 36

As the little yellow plane zooms over rooftops, she slides off the horse to the pavement and drives her shotgun butt through the window of Dollar Heaven. The glass shatters. Her free hand swirls with the alarm, seems to be conducting it, invoking someone or something.

He watches her roam the aisles. In quick succession, she plays with dolls, stuffs her rough feet into hot-pink flip-flops, tries gum and spits it out in surprise. She puts on a Disney princess mask before she shoves a shelf over, then another, until they all go down like dominoes.

She wears the flip-flops and the mask outside.

The horse spooks but she settles it.

She cracks the shotgun, loads two shells from her dress pocket, climbs aboard, and they ride on.

CHAPTER 37

It was all the sheriff could do not to shove the door open and jump. When she saw Bristol was heading toward the Mississippi, she hollered, "No! Not in Iowa!" She pointed at the road scrolling under them. "Put me down right there!"

"No can do, ma'am."

"Land it."

"I got a big belly full of juice."

"I don't care. That's Hefty Road. Put me down."

"Not safe or legal."

Rhino filled her other ear. "Sheriff, I've got alarms going off at two Rickreiner properties. Babette is on my other line. Your permission to ignore?"

"Ignore."

"OK, I've got everybody moving, and I've just put out a three-state Amber Alert. Denise is on her way in to help. Take your time and be safe. We're all on it."

"Stay on the line, Rhino."

She ordered Bristol, "Land it on the road."

"I'd lose my license. I can only do that in an emergency."

"This is an emergency."

"An *airplane* emergency, ma'am. Problem with the plane."

She pointed at a cabled lever on her side of the cockpit. "What's that?"

"That stiffens up my rudder flap in high winds."

She kicked it clean of the dashboard.

"It looks broken. Land the plane."

||||||||||

She did not expect to be picked up by Interim Chief Deputy Dick Bender, driving Lyndsey Luck's Tahoe. Bender was rumpled and perspiration-stained and appeared exhausted, a mad gleam in his eye as he told her, "Rhino sent me."

She didn't want to get in.

"Where have you been all night, Deputy?"

"Off-duty."

"Not my question."

"You're wasting time."

"Where is your vehicle?"

"You'll see."

"Goddamn it, Bender. I don't trust you. Get out. Leave the keys."

He didn't budge. He gripped the wheel with his small hairy hands and stared ahead. Sweat rolled down his temple and along his unshaven jaw. Over the radio, Rhino announced another break-in, this time at Dollar Heaven.

"Bender, get out."

His right hand released the wheel and trembled as he reached to lower the radio volume.

"No, Sheriff. I'm Oppo. I know where the white truck is going. Get in."

||||||||||

As Bender rocketed the Tahoe toward Town of Leavings, she felt so agitated that her tongue stiffened and her body went numb. Beneath her crashing heartbeat, she heard her interim chief deputy begin to explain himself. Yesterday afternoon, Denise had sent him to the Bad Axe County Library to window-dress the Vigdis Torkelson improper-campaign-activity complaint, just to shut up Becky Rilke-Rickreiner. From Mrs. Torkelson, he had heard about Leroy Fanta's interest in a Town of Leavings property still owned by the Golly brothers.

"I thought them two jokers were long gone. I had to take them food from my church one winter. As far as I knew, they sold out and left after Gibbs cleared them for the Ronald Rickreiner murder."

She did her best to listen. While he was at the library, Mrs. Torkelson had fed Bender the tidbit about Barry Rickreiner cheating in her high school English class. Later, Deputy Schwem had reminded him that the candidate had also cheated on a urine test as an EMT, not long after Babette had bribed him out of a DUI charge.

"We've all been watching out for you," Bender said, "one way or the other, once we saw who our next boss could be. I'm Oppo," he said, "but I've got a team."

He had pushed the Tahoe up to ninety. She hardly felt movement, though the vast feedlot of Vista Farms had come and gone in a flash.

"By this point," Bender was telling her, "Prickreiner's campaign and this Greevey-Goodgolly mess began to seem, to my mind, like different parts of the same shitstorm."

He braked and separated from the highway with a reeling right turn. Ahead were the steep hills and sharp curves of Muchlander Road. Bender sped in the style of a local, using both sides of the center line.

"So last night after my shift I tried to track down Fanta. He wasn't home. He wasn't at his office. I spent until midnight searching the taverns. By then I was worried for him. I had a hunch—that name Goodgolly just rings all kind of bells—and I drove out here, where we're headed now. I thought I might find him at Goodgolly's farm."

He pumped his brakes for a doe crossing the road, timing her, then came to his senses. He slowed hard and stopped Luck's Tahoe to wait for two fawns to skitter out, halt in panic, and gallop after.

"That time of day," he muttered. As he accelerated, her tongue came unstuck.

"Dick, I thought you hated me."

"Personal feelings got nothing to do with it."

No sooner had he rammed the Tahoe back up to speed and crested a sunlit rise than he had to hit his brakes again for an Amish wagon rolling down the backside. A plow horse shuddered against the weight of the wagon and its precarious heap of cut hay. Two wide-eyed tykes in straw hats rode at the very top of the heap.

"How the hell they don't fall off of there . . ." Bender grumbled. With blind curves ahead, he had to be patient. She had to be patient with him.

"Well, I appreciate—"

"I will just be goddamned," he blurted, pumping the brake, "if Prickreiner is going to wear that badge."

"I appreciate that. You don't have to like me."

"I'll quit if he gets elected. But I'm afraid of that. I don't know what else I'd do."

"Dick, I appreciate that."

"It's good to be appreciated."

"I appreciate you, Dick."

"Good."

At last he got enough straightaway to ease around the hay wagon. Clear, he flattened the accelerator, throwing her head back. Four roller-coaster miles later, he took the final turn and launched the Tahoe east on Liberty Hill Road, spewing dust and gravel behind.

Halfway into Jon Golly's driveway, she jumped out, pushed open the heavy swing gate, and jumped back in. As Bender hit the gas, she felt disembodied, as if someone else had just done that. *Oh, Taylor. Oh, God, please.*

She felt blind with terror as they bounced through Jon Golly's sun-scorched yard past the house and clothesline, the sawmill and barn and wellhead pump, then out the tractor road on the north end of the farm where a steep green coulee wall rose and filled the windshield. There was Bender's Avenger, parked beside the stream that cut the coulee. The sight startled her back to the task. The Avenger's tires were knifed. Its windows were smashed. The radio and onboard computer were damaged. A failed attempt to penetrate its trunk had ended with an old-fashioned farm tool, a scythe, embedded in the lid.

Bender shut off Luck's overheating engine.

"I had a hell of a night, Sheriff. There wasn't anybody around when I got here. I came this far to look. I meant to turn around and head back, but then from that direction . . ."

He pointed across the stream, toward the coulee wall beyond which he had found Jim Golly's hidden homestead. The tractor road emerged on the opposite bank. From there it arced through tall thistles across unused pasture, then bent sharply and headed parallel to the stream across a scree of sandstone below a bluff and disappeared into heavy forest.

". . . I heard gunshots. I heard someone whistling and a dog barking. I shouldn't have left the car here, I guess, but I didn't want to get stuck driving across, and there was nobody around. I decided to wade across and quick-see. I know I shouldn't have left the car . . ."

"I don't care about the car, Dick. We'll get you a new one."

She felt short of breath and sick to her stomach again. The small relief of night had already dissolved in the new day's thick heat.

"Release the tail door and give me Deputy Luck's keys. Then what happened?"

As she opened Luck's gun vault, Bender said behind her, "Well, when I got into the woods over there, I found some bloody clothing hanging in a tree. So I kept going."

Luck's tactical rifle had been the sheriff's own, back when she was the rookie. Still, she fumbled with it.

"I figured Daniel Greevey ran out of somewhere over there, gunshot, throwing off clothes to slow down a dog. He stole those rubber boots here. He took off on the Goodgolly buggy and got tossed out where we found him. So I figured what I was hearing might be someone else over there getting chased like Greevey was."

Bender opened the trunk of his ruined car and lifted out his own rifle. She still fumbled with her old weapon. How did the magazine load again? And the scope had been rotated for storage. How did she align it?

"It's sod buildings in there, Sheriff. It's goddamn pioneer times. Dark as hell. Somebody moaning inside one. I found Hubbard's truck and Fanta's car. But sure as hell Grape's little Toyota didn't get across this crick. Too much water here. That truck could handle this, but Fanta must have gone in another way, maybe a backup route since the trouble here yesterday, maybe followed whoever lives back there."

"Jim and Faith Golly," she said. Her chin dripped sweat. Her slick hands felt like someone else's. But finally the magazine clicked into place.

"When I came back, I found my car like this, and there were lights on inside Goodgolly's house. A vehicle took off, a hot new engine."

"Rickreiner," she said, "looking for Patience."

"I didn't have much juice left in my phone. I had planned to charge it from the car. I hiked out to Liberty Hill Road and got part of a message off to you before it died. It was a long goddamn walk until somebody picked me up on the highway. I was just getting back when you called from the airplane."

He watched her struggle with the rifle scope, then gripped the jittering barrel and held it level.

"Right. There you go." He pointed across the stream again. "We hike across that hillside and up a canyon—you can just see it, the break in texture—where a little feeder joins this creek. A few hundred yards up that feeder is where the ground levels out into a meadow not much bigger than a baseball field. That's where the place is. We'll cross the feeder and bushwhack our approach high on the opposite side, away from the buildings, so we can stay out of sight. The whole trip is just about a quarter mile. Except it seems like two hundred years into the past."

She tightened down the scope.

"Let's move."

CHAPTER 38

At Supercuts, the window glass surrenders with a bright chime. She snaps across the wreckage in her new pink flip-flops, shucks the Disney princess mask, towels off her hot face, and spends a minute inches from a mirror, plucking black hairs from her chin and upper lip.

Then she flings her bonnet away and hops into a chair. She tells him something in her strange language. Then she tries to make it English.

"Hurt me, many, not hamburger. He koam, I kill. Boam!"

She taps her sweat-damp dress between her breasts, concentrates on her words.

"Jailhouse. Safety."

At her command, he uncoils her braid and with a pair of long sharp scissors he hacks it off. It falls like an old rope to the floor.

CHAPTER 39

A long time ago—long to Taylor Kick—in the days just after his and Dylan's seventh birthday, but before the end of the school year had separated him from his special teacher, Miss Garland, Taylor had seen the first mean sign about his mother from the window of the school bus.

The sign was where the bus stopped on Ten Hollows Road to pick up Chad Mooney, in Taylor's first-grade class. It was stuck into Chad Mooney's yard, his mother waving nearby it with a baby on her hip. Miss Garland had been telling him, *Read everything you can, all the time. Practice. The world is full of words.*

The sign was red with white capital-letter words that were stacked on top of one another, a pattern he had later described to Miss Garland as easier for him to read, and she had told him that is not how you write words, unless you are in China writing Chinese words. If you want to be an American, she said, always put words left to right and always read them left to right, even if your brain and eyes are trying to tell you something different.

KICK
HER
OUT

It had taken him a few moments. Then as the bus pulled away fierce tears had filled his eyes. Chad Mooney had goofed his way down the aisle like always, but when he had tried to sit in his usual spot, next to his classmate Taylor Kick, Taylor had nearly put a boot up his wormy little butt.

Soon after that, school ended, the heat wave began, Opie left for camp, the caterpillars came to strangle the trees, and a different mean sign began to appear everywhere.

BARRY HER

Taylor had been in a secret bad mood about many things for a long time. When he saw that sign, suggesting his mommy would be dead—because dead is when people got barried—his bad mood became so bad that eventually he had put a hoe-point into Dylan's arm when Dylan said, *Just ignore the signs.* After he hurt Dylan, he was alone.

Then what happened at the pool. Turd-mouth Riley Rilke-Rickreiner had said to him, "Don't you know your mom likes Mexican weiner? She's going to have a Mexican baby. My dad told me, and my dad is going to be the sheriff. He's going to barry her."

He had shoved Riley into the pool. When Riley's mother had started screaming, he had taken a good run and shoved her in too. But it didn't change the problem. *My dad is going to barry her.* He had already been thinking of a ski mask and a hammer. He didn't know where the Rickreiners lived—it was on a different bus route—but last night his mom had taken him there.

| | | | | | | | | | |

The man who pulled up beside him wore weird glasses that pinched his bald head and sucked his buried eyes forward and made them look like giant frog eggs. He had no hair. Gray lumps hung on his dripping face.

"Where you headed, hot dog?"

He had practiced his answer.

"Home. I live at four-thirty-eight Sunset Ridge Road. The white house with the triple garage past the Town of Blooming Hill water tower. If you don't know where that is, I can show you where to go."

The man began to hum, not saying if he knew or not. Then he smiled, showing chalky purplish teeth.

"All aboard for Sunset Ridge Road."

CHAPTER 40

"I saw lights in one of the buildings last night," Bender whispered. He pointed from the brushy hillside. After leaving Jim Golly's forest road, they had crossed a rivulet of springwater in one long stride, then bushwhacked painstakingly through underbrush, mindful of a dog, until they could look down upon the same vague geometric shapes that Sheriff Kick had seen from the airplane: arcs and partial rectangles, limned by just-visible gaps in the natural meadow plants. She strained to see clearly through ground fog that drifted up and became lustrous as it intersected with sunlight. As she focused, she began to understand what Bender meant by "buildings." She began to see depth, a perpendicular plane. She was looking at walls.

"Otherwise I would have bumped right into one of them," Bender said. "Those are sod buildings, like pioneers, natural bricks, dirt and root and grass, blend right in. But there were lights and moaning coming from the bigger one on the far right."

The coulee looked about a hundred yards across and three hundred yards long. Birds called cheerily as they flitted through its layered fog and light. The tiny creek, rocky and fast, barreled down the center, bobbing jewelweed and oxeyes. She counted four structures, two rounded, two squared.

"Some are sheds," Bender whispered, "storage probably. There are two more of those round ones that we can't see because they're right under us. That other square-cornered one is a garage where I saw the vehicles. Both the square ones are dug back into the bluff behind them. We're just looking at the front. The one on the far right, I guess that's the house."

"You saw lights? You mean lanterns?"

"No, incandescent lights. No power lines. No generator running. So, solar. Batteries from his brother. He had to have support to live this way."

Bender pointed toward the opposite ridge, where the sun ignited a stagger of tall red pines.

"Off that way is where I heard the dog barking again, kind of trailing away, and more gunshots—"

He stopped.

"Sheriff, speak of the devil."

A great black dog galloped out of the pines and down a tarn of tumbled limestone toward the coulee bottom. From the last rock the creature leapt and disappeared, its progress toward them marked by stirring goldenrod and asters. Then it reappeared, trotted out between the two rounded sod buildings, and leapt over the creek. Now they could see the dog wore a harness with a handle. Once across the creek it advanced more slowly, head raised, sniffing in their direction.

"Or maybe that's the devil's guide dog," Bender muttered as he raised his rifle.

She stopped him, pointing down the near bluff. Below them,

three lean and ragged coyotes pawed through a mound of earth, haunching up and squirming backward, yanking on something buried. The dog had picked up the coyotes' scent.

It released a low woof. Alerted, the coyotes squared to the challenge, bristling and hunching their backs. The dog stopped at thirty yards and woofed louder. It knew better than to fight. At the same time, the coyotes seemed to know they had been vanquished. Sure enough, a gunshot fractured the stalemate and the coyotes skulked away looking over their shoulders. The black dog followed woofing and snarling at a distance until all four disappeared.

Now a heavy old woman limped down the opposite hillside. She gripped a rifle. With each lumbering footfall, a long gray braid swung behind her. She dragged herself stiffly between the several smaller sod structures. Then, as she entered what Bender had identified as the house, she seemed to vanish directly into the hillside.

"Stay here and cover me."

When Bender was ready, the sheriff descended two hundred feet through buckthorn and berry brambles and reached level ground through a reef of red-tinged sumac. The first low sod building had a rounded roof that merged with the terrain on either side and framed a hobbit door of hewn wood. She bandoliered her rifle and opened the door. From inside came a sweetly nauseating stench, mysterious until her eyes adjusted to make out shelved walls stacked with canning jars, some ruptured and billowing mold. A root cellar. She swallowed back her revulsion as she closed the door.

The next structure, another low, freestanding dome, contained tools and hardware, cans of diesel fuel and gasoline, coils of cable and wire, lumber, nails, the requirements of self-sufficiency. She hunched beneath the roof and probed the corners with her Maglite. Nothing else to see. She closed the door.

She crossed the creek on stepping-stones. The contents of the next structure astonished her: bundles and bales of decomposing, mouse-chewed newspapers. With hesitant fingers she separated the layers of one bale, mid-heap, and found a masthead: *New York Times, Saturday, December 5, 2015.* Above this was a *Broadcaster* of the same vintage. Below it, a *Minneapolis Star-Tribune.* The bales were bound with twine.

As she ducked and followed her flashlight into what Bender had called the garage, she held her breath, sick with fear at the sight of Leroy Fanta's old Tercel. Beside it was a rusted, mud-spattered Bronco, its last renewal tag 2009. Next was an empty slot.

She reeled out into blinding sunshine. As she tried to signal Bender—*No white truck!*—she heard the door of the house creak open behind her.

CHAPTER 41

Taylor could not read the road signs. He worried that the man couldn't see with his frog eyes and would drive them right off into a ditch. This had almost happened twice, and by the time Taylor saw any signs the words were flashing by too fast.

But then they were on gravel and he knew.

"Sir, this isn't the right way."

The man kept humming, kept going even faster, kept leaning up until his glasses were inches from his windshield, and even then he could barely keep the truck on the road.

Taylor's backpack sat on the floor between his knees. He crept his hand to the zipper, slowly opened it two inches, and saw the handle of his hammer. He looked up. The truck's shadow lunged long in front of them, spreading all over the road.

"Sir, I would like to get out, please."

"What's your name?"

He had practiced this. "My name is Riley Rilke-Rickreiner.

I'm going home. But this is not the way to my house. I would like to get out. Please."

"Your name is Riley?"

"Yes, sir."

"Rickreiner?"

"Yes, sir."

The man's bloated hand dropped off the steering wheel and snatched up the backpack. As he held it close to his face, the truck's outer wheels caught the shoulder. Gravel flew. The truck jolted left and right, then plunged into a deep and rocky ditch, shearing off small trees until the road surged back up beneath them.

The backpack still dangled from the man's fist. He dropped it into Taylor's lap to show exactly where Grammy Belle had stitched *Taylor* down one shoulder strap and *Kick* down the other.

"You," he said, "are the sheriff's little boy."

"She will find you," he blurted, tears rising.

He waited for a reply, but the man kept humming and driving.

"Wherever you take me," Taylor said, "my mom will come there, with a gun, and a whole bunch of other people will come there too. Fast."

The man stepped on his brake. The truck fishtailed into the opposite ditch. He bulled it out in reverse and began to turn it around.

"Exactly," he said. "Bring the world to you, a friend of mine told me. I was blind but now I see."

"I have a hammer," Taylor warned him. But it came out as barely a squeak.

"Good boy. We're going to need a hammer."

CHAPTER 42

The woman staggered toward Sheriff Kick, her large raw hands gripping what looked like the same rifle the sheriff had seen her carry down the hillside.

Bender bellowed from above, "Stop! Drop the weapon! Get on the ground!"

She didn't seem to hear, or maybe from the look on her face she didn't care.

The sheriff reached a hand to her rifle strap. She needed two seconds to swing it around and bring it to a useful angle. She could get shot in that amount of time.

"Ma'am, Mrs. Golly, stop."

"Jim's not here," she said, still coming.

"Ma'am, stop. An officer on the hill has his weapon on you. You will be killed. Drop the rifle. Sit down on the ground. Keep your hands where I can see them."

"He's gone," she said, her voice a croak, escaping her down-turned mouth as she worked her way across a mound of earth. "He must have found a way."

Bender came crashing down the hillside and stopped at the creek. He went to one knee and aimed. "Drop the weapon and get on the ground!" he bellowed again.

"Mrs. Golly, please. Stop exactly where you are. Talk to me. He found a way to do what? Tell me. *Do what?*"

As if she seemed to hear this finally, the ragged woman paused, her head and shoulders swaying side to side, the rifle moving with her. Her words came out as cries of pain.

"Jim thinks it's his call to save us all."

"From what?"

"He was calling people, warning them. No one believed. He must have found a way," she repeated.

"To do what, Mrs. Golly?"

"The newspaperman said bring the world to him."

"Meaning what?"

"Meaning I'm free," she wrenched out.

"Mrs. Golly, put the rifle down."

"Free," she repeated.

She took another step and Bender shot her.

The impact spun the woman and dropped her onto her face. The birdsong stopped. As the woman convulsed and tried to crawl, Sheriff Kick lunged and picked up her rifle. It was unloaded, she saw, its chamber struck hollow by the first rays of light to touch the bottom of Jim Golly's abruptly silent abyss.

CHAPTER 43

More glass shatters. To the wail of a fourth alarm, she drags him inside a bowling alley, where they swill soda and roll bowling balls. It seems like she has never used a straw before, doesn't understand until he plunges one into her icy Coke and fits the other end between her lips.

"Never hamburger," she tells him for some reason. "Many hurt. Bad men. Never hamburger."

She doesn't know which fingers to put inside the bowling ball until he shows her. She rolls with startling strength, claps her rough hands when she hits anything.

But she moves from one thing to another in a hurry. After half a dozen rolls, she ignores her returning ball and takes his ball away and drops it and walks him to the red vinyl seating. There she kisses him. She moves her shotgun off the cushion, sits him down, and places his hands upon the pins that close her dress.

"Love."

He turns toward police sirens.

"Love me," she commands.

He pulls six straight pins and the dress falls.

"Love me beautiful."

As she fumbles with his filthy shorts he has an uneasy memory of how this went with Cassie, back when, awkwardly in the dark, high on the same bunchgrass hillside that later caught fire and swept down.

Wanting to resist, he fails the moment that she touches him. Instantly trembling, he carefully kisses her everywhere, then lifts her and lays her gently on the vinyl. He kisses her everywhere again, begins to worry again. But she gasps, shuddering and hitting and keening strange words. He seems to be in shock after that, gliding from the chaos of pleasure into a deep wild dream.

He dreams he flies upon a horse that lands upon a sailboat. A great bird flaps over. Then he and Cassie are riding on the bird, which answers to the name of her horse, and the earth spins brightly green and blue below.

Later, he only dimly senses the absence of her smell and weight. He believes she is still there and tries to hold Cassie from inside the dream.

But he stands and finds she has vanished.

He wanders in a vacant fuzz, hearing many sirens now. Beyond the broken window, the frightened horse tosses its head, rattling the dumpster where she tied it. Her dress and slip are where he dropped them.

But the shotgun is gone. So are his shorts, his shirt, and his backpack. She has dumped out his rock, spike, fork, and reflector, his blanket, phone, and chalk upon the floor.

A stuck-tongue, do-nothing chickenshit like you, the voice awakens to tell him, *funny you could ever think she loved you.*

But he stares at what she's drawn.

And kneels to draw the truth around it.

CHAPTER 44

Bucking out Jon Golly's driveway in Luck's Tahoe, the sheriff set her phone to dial dispatch, tossed it on the seat, and concentrated on a prayer she was trying to remember.

Oh, Lord, protect . . .

But she was too frantic to put abstract language together. She blasted through the swing gate, felt it clip the Tahoe's rear end. She was throwing gravel behind on Liberty Hill Road when Denise's voice rose through the commotion.

"There you are, Heidi! We've been trying to—"

"Get EMS help for Bender on the Golly property. He's in there with a shooting victim, critical when I left. Tell them to drive through the stream where Bender's car is and follow that old road. Put everybody else in a contain pattern on the roads looking for Derp Hubbard's white truck. It's Jim Golly. He's the telephone ranter, From Hell Hollow. He has Taylor."

"Heidi—"

"Assume Golly is outbound with a big head start. He's had way too much time since I saw him from the plane."

"Heidi, no, he's inbound. The truck was just sighted south-bound on Sime Road. He's heading into town."

Her mind froze. Where was she even going? She was only going.

"Talk to me, Denise."

"OK, I'm talking. Meanwhile, Heidi, we're having a weird string of break-ins that I don't think we can keep ignoring. Alarm calls first at Liquor City, five minutes later at the Dollar Heaven, eight minutes after that the Supercuts went off. Someone saw two kids on a horse. By the time I sent Schwem over to Supercuts, the alarm at Bad Axe Bowl was going off, so Schwem is headed over—"

"Denise!"

"Right here."

"The pattern. All Rickreiner properties, inbound from the northeast."

"You're right."

Neither spoke for a moment.

"Never mind the bowling alley, Denise. Redirect Schwem to the newspaper office."

"Ten-four."

She tried to reach Harley, who didn't answer, and then she was trying to text him without entering a soybean field at lethal speed when Denise called right back.

"He's there."

"Who's where?"

"I'm getting calls. At the *Happy Valley Shopper*. The white truck is there. Somebody saw a man in a robe smash the door. Now he's inside the building with Taylor."

||||||||||

When after a sickening blur of time she at last cornered onto Second Street, the white truck was parked crookedly over the curb with Deputy Schwem's Tahoe behind it, red-and-blue lights sparking. Both the building's door and front window had been smashed. The alarm shrieked over Schwem's strained voice as he wrangled with Barry and Babette Rickreiner on the opposite curb.

The instant she saw Taylor's brown cap with gold letters move across the shadows inside, she felt herself enter sow-bear mode. She blocked the street with Luck's Tahoe and leapt out with her duty weapon drawn. She ripped open the door of Derp Hubbard's truck and saw her little boy's unzipped backpack. No hammer. Extra underwear. An apple. A Ziploc bag of crackers. His favorite Matchbox car, the Torino. *Oh, Taylor . . .*

"Golly!" she bawled from her guts, looking for something to shoot at. "Let him go!"

Taylor's cap had disappeared. Nothing else happened. Thank God. She had yelled and waved a gun. Stupid. Starting now, she had to act like the sheriff.

Trying to hide her shakes, she turned to assess the periphery. A few old-timers had shuffled over from Norse Nook with coffee cups in hand. The custodian and manager of Farmers Bank watched beneath their sign: 6:21A.M. and 94 degrees. A few cars had pulled over on Main Street, drivers stepping out to watch. Jaywalking across the Main Street–Second Street intersection came a slender barefoot kid in a filthy shirt and filthier cargo shorts, carrying a worn black backpack against his or her chest. The kid's face looked vaguely familiar. But now Schwem was barking back and forth with the Rickreiners.

"Put that away," he ordered BARRY HER. The deputy dripped sweat, in octopus mode trying to restrain the on-charging mother and son. The candidate had liberated his sidearm from its thigh holster, a heavy semiautomatic.

"No, you will not 'organize a posse to go around back.' I said put that away. Ma'am, do *not* touch me. And, sir . . . Hey, dipshit, I'm talking to you." Schwem was losing it. "Return that firearm to its holster immediately." Her deputy caught his breath and found some more suitable language. "For your own safety. And everybody's."

"He has an open-carry permit!" Babette kept screeching. She pointed at the sheriff. "And she's doing nothing!"

Schwem spoke like he had grit in his teeth. "Ma'am, if you touch me again . . ."

"Kick her out!"

Abruptly done with Schwem, Babette tried to get the small crowd to chant.

"Kick her out!"

This jolted the sheriff back to action. She holstered her weapon and popped Luck's back end—rifle again, plus loudspeaker—but what was she supposed to do now? Hostage training was long ago, and it was just that, training. *Your little boy is the hostage* was not covered in the manual. But the number one concept boiled down to this: Don't force anything. Take your time. Put the safety of non-hostages first.

"Get back!" she hollered. The strange teen, barefoot in dirty cargo shorts, still coming toward the scene, changed course silently, keeping the backpack close in an odd grip. "All the way back across the street."

Then time seemed to melt and slip—ten minutes? sixty seconds?—until into her ears and straight into her soul arrived a yowl of pain.

Where the window glass once read BAD AXE BROADCASTER, EST. 1938, L. FANTA, ED-IN-CHIEF, her child had emerged, yanked to his tiptoes by the fist of a bloated beast in a filthy yellow robe spotted with sweat. Jim Golly held Taylor close against him as a shield. In his other fist he gripped Harley's framing hammer, cocked above Taylor's skull.

She used her loudspeaker. "This is Sheriff Heidi Kick. You don't need to hurt anyone. Tell me what you want."

He seemed at peace. He restrained her squirming little boy from behind and kept the hammer poised as he squinted into the blazing street.

"As Mother Earth's demands are urgent," he called out, "so are they simple." He held fast as Taylor squirmed. "Noon is our new midnight, people, and it's time to wake up."

So this was Fanta's letter writer, *FROM HELL HOLLOW*. Denise's voice crackled from the radio at her shoulder: "Heidi, you gotta look out for Patience Goodgolly. She's in town. The report of two kids on a horse, that must be her and someone else. I just heard there's a bonnet and a long, brown braid on the floor of the Supercuts."

"Ten-four."

She kept her eyes on Golly. "And right now," he called out, "Mother needs some of her carbon back." He paused, looking pleased with himself. "I need some gasoline!"

He strained to see if anyone moved. The sheriff said to Schwem, "Get it for him."

Her deputy seemed rooted, doubting. But she had just felt the arrival of a hunch about Golly, springing from a memory of his rant. *Those who face the darkness are meant to shine the light. You will be saved by fire.*

She had to get this right. *Don't force anything. Take your time.* As much as her mother's instinct said otherwise, the cop in her had begun to sense that Golly didn't want to hurt Taylor. Where was the gain in that for him? Taylor would get hurt only if she rushed Golly, forced him off his plan. He was the hero here, the show. Taylor was the man's bait, not his purpose.

She forced her fear into the background and said to Schwem more quietly, "We're going to humor him. He wants gasoline, get him gasoline. He also wants attention. We're going to give it to him."

She pointed toward the old-timers outside the café.

"One of those guys has chain saw gas in his truck. Get going."

Now her deputy moved. She watched Golly smile.

"A couple gallons would be good," he called after Schwem.

"And now," he appealed cheerfully to the swelling crowd on the far sidewalk, "who's going to do the YouTube?"

CHAPTER 45

To a boy who runs slower and reads slower than his twin brother, who writes crookeder and spells worse that his twin brother, whose smaller 4-H rabbit has one squinty eye and only half a tail . . .

To a boy whose sister will soon be a far better brother than he could ever hope to be . . .

To a boy like this comes a special sense about the thin margins of survival. And so he sits on the floor exactly in the spot where the man told him to sit, and he stays there even on broken glass, not moving—though the man has let go of his collar and set the hammer down on Mr. Fanta's desk—though the man has become busy calling someone on the telephone and drinking liquor from a bottle out of Mr. Fanta's drawer.

"Oh, no, don't bother calling the cops. The cops are already here. Show starts in thirty minutes."

Taylor has been in this office before, on a school trip where

Mr. Fanta gave a tour and spoke about old newspapers and then spoke in unclear words for a long time about many other things and then cried. But Taylor had paid attention to what he could understand, and he remembers that this building exists because a rich man built a saloon and a pool hall beneath six hotel rooms. So where Taylor sits is the old saloon floor, which he remembers is from hickory trees, cut down in Town of Zion and made into floorboards by Quaker people. Behind the old saloon in the old pool hall is where Mr. Fanta used to make the newspaper before there were computers. In there, behind a curtain with pictures of ducks, is a urinal the size of a bathtub, and beside that tilts a rust-stained toilet that has a black seat and no lid. The stairs go over the toilet to the balcony above Taylor, where Mrs. Fanta used to work on the very first kind of computer, and that balcony used to be the hallway to the hotel rooms that Mr. Fanta told the class were crammed with old historical papers that nobody cared about but him. Taylor thinks of all this because several minutes ago the man had asked his mother for gasoline, which means he doesn't know that underneath the hickory floor there would be a simple drain valve on the big tank that Mr. Fanta explained was in the basement, fuel oil to run the boiler that pushes steam to the radiators in the winter.

Or maybe the man does know. A boy like Taylor develops a sense of when to be quiet, which is almost always, rather than be behind, or wrong, or both.

Shut up, a voice often tells him. *Just shut up.*

He senses acutely a bull's-eye on his back, and he often wants to cry like a baby in front of people, the way Mr. Fanta had cried in front of his whole first-grade class. Yet he is neither a baby nor an old man. He is a big and lucky boy, people tell him, loved by everyone, they tell him, but he doesn't feel big or lucky or loved, and hearing this over and over without believing it feels like the wheel of a great valve screwing down on him and turning him off.

He has messed up his plan to appear in a hunting mask and hammer-smash the mouth of Riley Rilke-Rickreiner's step-dad. He never should have said he had the hammer, for one thing. Before that, he should have kept his thumb back, taken a chance, and waited for a better-looking ride. And before that, anyway, the stupid early 4-H bus had come all the way to the house so he couldn't get his dad's orange mask from where he had re-stashed it in the newspaper tube at the end of the driveway. So turd-mouth Riley's turd-mouth stepdad is still out there yelling nasty words at Taylor's mother, who is angry, Taylor worries, because she isn't coming in to get him, and she would have come in to get Opie or Dylan or his dad, by now, for sure. In fact—he searches—his mom has vanished.

So he sits there stiff as a stump in front of the man while not his mother but Deputy Schwem walks up with a red plastic gas can and sets it on the top step. Then Taylor and the gas can just sit there, waiting for something.

"What time is it in France?" the man asks into the phone. "Perfect. Thirty minutes. New-midnight, French time."

CHAPTER 46

"Heidi," Denise said, "I just found out he's called all three La Crosse TV stations."

Sheriff Kick had gone around the building to inspect the alley. Too narrow for fire trucks. With her phone at her ear, she started back toward Second Street, feeling seasick with adrenaline as the alley seemed to pitch and roll beneath her. She had to be right. Had to. She could not image life without . . . could not imagine life going forward if she was wrong. Golly didn't need to hurt Taylor. That did not seem to be his kind of insanity. She just could not bear . . .

"He told them he has your little boy hostage. He told them to come and see the show. Seven A.M., which he seems to think is noon in France, they said."

Denise tapped keys and hit switchboard buttons. "Actually it's two P.M. there. He thinks they care? Or he's in France?" She said to someone else, "We're not looking for a girl on a horse anymore. Get here now." Something clattered. "Heidi, Golly invited the TV people to 'the summit,' he said, to 'witness history.' And they're coming."

"Send the fire trucks," she said.

"The guy from Channel 8 said he was rambling about some burning monk who died in Vietnam fifty years ago and some naked little girl running from a firebombing who survived. What does all that mean?"

"It means send the fire trucks," she repeated.

"Harley's on his way. I said leave Dylan with the neighbors if he could. Your mother-in-law was yelling. I tried not to tell him very much."

"Thank you."

As she reached Second Street, a voice behind her said, "Where do you want me, Sheriff?"

She turned to see Deputy Lyndsey Luck in uniform stepping from the battered gold minivan that served as Farmstead's only cab. Deputy Luck looked wan and weak, a shell of her sturdy self. Somehow her duty boots must have gotten misplaced in the hospital, because the cuffs of her uniform trousers sat atop light blue terry-cloth slippers. But here she was. The sheriff exhaled and steadied herself. It was a small thing, maybe, but the rookie's toughness calmed her.

"You can move people back and set a perimeter at two hundred feet. Nobody but police and fire inside that."

She scanned the swelling crowd for the Rickreiners. The jackass who wanted her job had his firearm unholstered again and was asking for volunteers to rush the newspaper office, citing posse comitatus.

She called her rookie back and pointed.

"We can't let him escalate. Give him ten seconds to lock that thing inside his vehicle. Over there, that red El Camino. He takes you to eleven, Taser him, cuff him, and take him away."

"My pleasure," Deputy Luck said.

Now here came Grammy Belle and Harley.

"Just the way I heard it," her mother-in-law was saying, "she's doing nothing."

"Ma, stop."

"Don't tell me to stop."

Belle was red-faced, sweat-lathered, in full voice around a half-smoked cigarette.

"That's my grandbaby in there. Do not tell me to stop. I'm going in to get him."

"Stop, Mom." Harley yanked her back. "Heidi, why is everybody just standing around?"

She could hardly croak her terrible answer. Her decision was not up for examination or discussion, not even by Taylor's daddy or his grandma. "Please don't bother me. I'm working."

"Working? That's our boy. You're his mother."

"Harley, let me do my job."

"Ma!" Again Harley had to catch Belle by the arm, stop her from charging the newspaper office in her bikini top. The jolt sent her cigarette flying. Harley stepped on it. "*Mother*," he said.

"I'm not just going to stand here."

"Yes, you are. Heidi, what's going on? What's the plan?"

She managed to get a breath to the bottom of her lungs. She had to be right. "You're looking at the plan. Wait. Watch."

"She's letting him just sit in there with a monster!"

Just then she heard the fire trucks shrieking away from the public safety building a half mile north of town. They would arrive in sixty seconds and she needed to direct them.

"Go away, Harley. Now. Take Mom with you."

Two minutes later, she had positioned the fire trucks so that TV vans could get around them onto Second Street. Golly hauled Taylor forward and squinted out until he found her.

"Sheriff, be a doll," he called, "and leave the hoses on the trucks."

She hesitated. Taylor's cheeks gleamed. Golly raised the hammer. "I mean that."

She gave the order and Golly retreated, towing Taylor into the shadows of the office. Then she heard him exclaim happily, "Aha!" She didn't know what he had found until Grape Fanta's antique rock music began to swirl out and set an eerily festive mood.

The sun burned down for the ten longest minutes of her life. The TV vans arrived and set up. A dozen or so Bad Axers held up smartphones, recording. She prayed that she was right. There was no need to hurt her child. A chilling reverence had set in. Then it began.

First, Golly emerged from the shadows of the office behind Taylor dangling from his fist, the hammer re-cocked as a weapon over her little boy's precious skull. Next step, at the end of Golly's grip, it was Taylor who picked up the waiting gas can. Now Taylor and the can dangled as Golly awkwardly backed up and then went sideways into the frame of the broken window. From there, he reached back and spun Fanta's old wheeled wooden desk chair until he had positioned it behind himself. He toppled back into it, keeping Taylor in front. He said something to Taylor. Taylor screwed the nozzle off the gas can.

His intent appeared: he wanted Taylor to douse him. But it was difficult. Hefting the heavy can, Taylor missed broadly twice, splashing himself and the floor. Then Golly found the answer was to push Taylor to arm's length, bend forward in the chair as far as his bloated body would allow, and have Taylor empty the can over his neck and head like man getting a bath in a bucket. Taylor splashed more gas on himself in the process.

Then Golly pulled Taylor onto his lap and showed the cameras that he had a lighter.

Sheriff Kick expected him to give a speech now. France. Monk. Vietnam. Look at me. Look at us. Noon is our new midnight. The urgency of our war against ourselves, to save the planet.

Instead he seemed to lose himself in emotion. His head dropped, his gasoline-soaked robe slipped, and for one long minute his warty shoulders shook with what appeared to be grief. He recovered, and as he began to speak, her heart felt as if it would be crushed between her sudden fear that she had been wrong, and her desperate hope that she had guessed right.

"You may pretend to be astonished, to wonder why," Jim Golly began. "But you have the facts. I've shared them many times with all of you. Not that you didn't already have them. Not that you don't live them. You *are* the facts. You know why."

She expected him to cite his facts anyway, to deliver an apocalyptic climate screed like she had heard him raining down on Leroy Fanta. Instead, after a long pause, he said again, "And still you will pretend to wonder why. Oh, how you stroke your precious innocence. But anyway, I'll show you why."

He whispered into Taylor's ear.

Taylor looked up beneath his hat brim.

Golly nodded and let go of Taylor's jacket collar.

Slowly and uncertainly, Taylor descended the concrete steps and drifted squinting into the blazing sun. Then he tried to sprint so abruptly that he tumbled, rose with his face in a mask of naked terror, and sprinted again until he crashed into his mother's duty belt and gripped her waist.

"The future," Golly said. "That's why."

He flicked the lighter and exploded into flames.

CHAPTER 47

As Golly had planned, water from the hoses arrived far too late to save him. He flared, sizzled, and toppled below the window frame as flames jumped up.

The price of delay was the building. Fire tore across the spilled gas on the floor and hit Fanta's desk, which acted like a heap of dry tinder. Those flames reached the paper-crammed balcony before the hoses were even unrolled. By the time the water arrived, the windows of the upstairs rooms were blowing out and raining glass shards down upon the firemen in the street.

Quickly, the only goals left were to keep the fire away from the fuel tank in the basement and to stop it from spreading down the block. After five minutes, both seemed attainable. The firemen soaked the insurance office on one side and the vacant former pizza parlor on the other. They pumped the basement full of water so that if the floor collapsed it would fall into a pond. Meanwhile, the fire moved up and back, sweeping through the

old hotel rooms. One brave volunteer scampered up a long ladder just in time to hack through the roof so that water could rain
down. Steam hissed high into the sky. Flames shot back out the
windows. Charred scraps of newspaper floated everywhere. An
already hot day in downtown Farmstead had become a steaming
inferno, and Leroy Fanta's old *Broadcaster*, all of it, was lost.

Sheriff Kick had drifted out of body. The adrenaline, the heat,
the loss, the salvation—maybe she was in shock. At some point
Taylor had released her waist and Harley had retrieved him.
While another old woman warbled "Amazing Grace," she could
hear her mother-in-law squawking at her to come and give her
brave boy a hug, and of course, drifting that way, she wanted
nothing more.

But it didn't feel over.

Still, warily, she let herself be drawn toward family. Her little
boy had been saved. There could be celebration. But her guts still
churned, her fists still closed and opened, her eyes still searched.
It just did not feel over.

"C'mere," Belle commanded her heartily, "hug your little
hero."

She and Taylor were just reaching for each other when Barry
Rickreiner squawked, "Get away from me!"

She looked over her shoulder. He had been marching toward
his El Camino, running his mouth, but now he found his way
blocked, first one direction, then the other, defiantly, by the
barefoot kid in the filthy cargo shorts. Just as Taylor grasped her
hands, she stiffened. Paired with the action of harassing Rickreiner, the kid's face made sense.

Patience Goodgolly!

The sheriff pulled away and sprinted.

"What is this shit?" BARRY HER squawked. "Get away from me!"

Now the backpack dropped to show the sawed-off shotgun.

Then the girl showed its purpose. He recoiled, stumbling on a fire hose as she trained her weapon on him at point-blank range.

"Who the fuck are you?"

She held the shotgun steady. He backpedaled toward empty space, starting his El Camino remotely with a key. She stalked, culling him from the innocent.

"Patience."

"The fuck?"

"Patience," she was telling him a second time when he turned and ran for his vehicle. Her gun barrel followed, aimed from the hip. Coming at a cross angle, Sheriff Kick launched herself and dove, twisting through the shotgun's path, ducking her head as she tackled BARRY HER out from under the blast, feeling shot rip through her hip and lower ribs in the same instant when the El Camino exploded.

Except for steam hissing high into the air from the *Broadcaster* building, there followed a ringing, sweltering silence. Sheriff Kick half rolled and tried to rise. But Deputy Luck had corralled Patience, who was not resisting.

She fell back. As BARRY HER struggled beneath her, this was what she stared at: black ash and white vapor climbing in a harsh blue sky.

EPILOGUE

The miscarriage occurred in her surgical recovery room at 4:47 the next morning while she was alone watching cable news on mute, specifically during a commercial for a device that allowed you to pedal your feet in tiny circles from a sitting position while you watched TV.

The surprise event began as a swoon that she thought was exasperation with human weakness, but then it took her deeper than that, into a full minute of synesthetic heartburn that tasted like coyotes howling.

She thought, *Uh-oh.*

Heidi, your wires are crossing big-time.

She turned off the TV while experiencing a cramp that bit just like a menstrual cramp except it hung on.

Then she felt a deep inner spasm, followed by a slow, trailing wetness that when she looked—incompletely able to bend over her shattered rib and repaired skin—had carried out of her a blurrily shaped magenta clot the size of a soybean.

She wept until just after sunrise, when a nurse came to bring her crackers and apple juice for breakfast, then cleaned her thighs, changed her underpants, gown, and sheet, fixed her with a pad, and took her baby away.

|||||||||||

Her shotgun wounds, the pesticide she may have ingested, the heat, the stress—one of those, or some combination, or all of them together could explain it, Dr. Patel told her. Or possibly some other cause entirely. There was no way to be certain.

Later in the day, she had visitors, each one bringing something she could focus on. Denise came by before her dispatch shift and smacked a kiss onto her forehead and delivered to her, first, Leroy Fanta's file folder of Jim Golly's letters to the editor, and then a joke.

"How do the Golly brothers tell when a girl is old enough to breed?"

"I don't think I want to hear this."

"You do. They make her stand in a barrel. If her chin is over the top, she's old enough. If she isn't, they cut the barrel down a bit."

"Oh, God, that hurts. You are so bad, Denise."

"Builds scar tissue, hon," Denise told her. "How we women survive."

It was the subtext of the ugly joke that made them both quiet for a while. They had no place to put Patience Goodgolly, no relatives to take her, no confession or expression of remorse, nothing beyond the eerie calm yet angry stare of an abused young woman that the sheriff had first seen when Patience explained in German that she was walking on Liberty Hill Road *because she couldn't fly.*

At least she hadn't killed anyone.

At least she wasn't dead like Kim Maybee.

At least, according to security footage, she had gotten drunk, played with dolls, plucked out her mustache hairs, drank soda, rolled bowling balls, and had sex that she wanted with a boy her age—kind of a scrambled, high-speed childhood, it seemed, before she planned to pay back Barry Rickreiner for the pain he had caused. She would have to testify against him. Based on motive and opportunity, she would likely face charges for stabbing her father-uncle, Jon Golly. It wasn't clear yet whether Faith could have done it, and there were no other suspects. Perhaps the boy in the security footage would know something, but so far Patience either didn't know or wouldn't say who he was or how he was involved. He had been seen last night wearing her dress and traveling on her horse through a pasture in Richland County. Deputies there hadn't found him yet.

"So I read your mind," Denise said finally.

"You are way too good at that."

"I took a detour coming in to work and stopped by your neighbors the Glicks. I kind of had to beg them, but Dawdy Glick made the call, and he said that for now, yes, until we figure things out, Patience can stay with them . . ."

||||||||||

Bender showed up later that afternoon, saying he happened to be in the neighborhood after arresting Jon Golly in his hospital bed, his first official business as acting sheriff.

But he gave himself away by bringing her a cold Mountain Dew, which she pretended to drink while he filled her in on the aftermath yesterday at Golly's *compound*, as he had been calling it. The dog had been a problem, he told her remotely. She got his drift and didn't pursue. He kept talking.

"EMS tore the muffler off the ambulance getting Faith Golly out of there."

"I'm not surprised."

"She didn't make it."

"I know."

"I had to."

"Yes."

"But there will be questions."

"There will."

They were quiet awhile. She pretended another sip of Dew.

"People are real hurt about Grape Fanta," Bender went on finally, his difficulty with the statement showing that he was one of them.

"I am too," she said. "The Bad Axe will never be the same."

"Heck . . ." Bender was struggling, his thin, badly shaven throat pulsing. "Heck, my birth was announced in the *Broadcaster*. My marriage. My wife's passing. Janice always loved to read Grape's . . ."

He had to stop.

The sheriff said, "He touched a lot of lives. In the end, I think he saved some."

"There's a goddamn bunch of bones in there," Bender said in almost a moan. "Bodies same as poor Fanta's under them vegetable gardens. He was a stone-cold killer and a goddamn cannibal until he found a better way."

It was her turn to struggle. She would never stop seeing gas-splashed Taylor in Jim Golly's grip, her child's terror-stiffened face, then his pell-mell sprint toward her with madness and flames tight on his heels. She imagined the moment had been burned into the memories of the millions who by now had seen it worldwide.

Then Bender said, "You won't be surprised that suddenly a certain kind of folks are coming forward to tell us they've seen Faith Golly driving Hubbard's truck all over for the last couple months and felt something might be wrong. Or to tell us that they've known for years that those sod buildings were back in there and something bad might be going on. They had trespassed through there, hunting or mushrooming or joyriding on snowcats, and they had got shot at, or chased by that dog, and now they're proud to be part of the story. Just this morning some old guy called us from Chaseburg and said Faith Golly fits the description of the woman who has been picking up his recycled newspapers for years. On the subject of tips, I went and spoke to the Amish bishop, Stoltzfus. I said you people need to talk to us. See something, say something. How he answered was, 'Ja, that might be a good idea.' Which in Amish I think means, *We'll keep minding our own business.*"

Bender stared at his hands and seemed to be gritting his teeth. Enough silence passed that she went back to skimming Jim Golly's letters. The man wanted to be heard but not caught. His more recent letters, probably once he started killing people and using them for fertilizer, were salted with misdirection in case someone came looking. *They ship my grain to China . . .* He grew no grain. *The great river I see from my bluff used to be wild and clear, not dammed up and muddy . . .* His sod home was on low ground thirty miles from the Mississippi.

After a few quiet minutes, Bender recovered to complete his report. A volunteer group was heading out to retrieve Fanta's body. Vigdis Torkelson had begun making memorial arrangements and she figured the event would fill Farmstead's baseball stadium if they could get a permit. Until the sheriff was stronger, Bender would be directing the interrogations of Patience and Jon

Golly, and organizing a forensic search of Golly's compound. At last he dropped a sour little Benderism: "I guess we'll find out just how hard the top job really is."

She smiled at him.

"Well, when you find out, Dick, let me know, OK?"

|||||||||||

Yesterday's remarkable display of team spirit aside, Lyndsey Luck wasn't feeling well enough yet to work a duty shift, but after Bender was gone she stopped by in jeans and her DEATH ROE SURVIVOR T-shirt. She brought a flower arrangement that she must have driven sixty miles round trip to acquire. The sheriff and her young deputy had their first real conversation.

"What I wonder," Deputy Luck said as they concluded, with the sheriff's family waiting in the corridor, "is, like, I'm starting out, and things just seem *so* complicated, and every week stuff seems to get even more complicated, and I'm starting to wonder when I'll ever stop feeling like a rookie. You know?"

The sheriff thought for a moment.

"I do know. Yes. So, when you become sure that things are truly far *more* complicated than they ever seemed when you started . . . *that's* when you'll know you're not a rookie anymore."

Just then Dylan burst into the room ahead of Taylor, shouting, "Mommy! All the stupid signs are gone!"

"All the stupid signs are gone," Taylor added.

Harley confirmed.

"Every last one. You are now officially unopposed. It's a couple months early, but congratulations on your reelection."

|||||||||||

Through the nine more long days that she had to wait before going home, the heat wave persisted while her department's investigation proceeded and the gears of justice turned slowly and squeakily. She mixed work-related visits with family time, and between naps she spent hours on the phone. The remains of three bodies were recovered, then five, then six. Father Paul McCartney was helping with the effort to identify those he could. Denise and Bender gave her updates. District Attorney Baird Sipple had called her. Pending results of the ongoing investigation into Barry Rickreiner's alleged crimes, he was working on charges of murder (Kim Maybee), statutory rape (Patience), destruction of police property (Bender's Avenger), and he was considering a charge of attempted murder (Lyndsey Luck, via poison meant for Patience). But he had mostly called to bark at the sheriff, to say that he was countermanding her promise of immunity for Jon Golly, that every scrap of information Golly had provided would be disallowed in court, and to scold her for thinking on her feet in the heat of battle.

She didn't care. Lives were saved. Anyway, Jon Golly had heard his Miranda rights, and in an effort to secure himself a deal for what he knew about Rickreiner and his brother, he was telling his story all over again. The sheriff read transcripts and listened to recordings that Bender played for her.

"What I don't understand," she told him, "is why the Golly brothers still owned that land at all. This whole time, Randall Rickreiner's heirs, Babette and Barry, still had a legal lien on it? Right? But they never collected on the lien?"

"Legal is debatable," Bender said. "I talked to Kevin Smallwood, Babette's attorney. The debt was all in one brother's name, Jon's, and the lien was on joint property. Smallwood told Babette years ago that it probably wouldn't hold up in court."

"But the Golly brothers never knew that."

"Of course not," Bender said. "But eventually that girl got old enough and Barry figured out how to use the threat of it."

"Do we know whose daughter she is?"

"Faith's," he said. "By one brother or the other." He seemed embarrassed. "I asked a bunch of times. Jon Golly truly doesn't know." He moved on. "He said Faith hated both of them and wanted her girl back. From that I gather that she was out looking for Daniel Greevey, who got away from her and Jim, when she came upon the buggy crash, where you were, and then the scene at the farm. It must have been obvious to her that Patience had beered her courage up and stabbed Jon. So Faith staged that crime scene and took the girl to Derp Hubbard's empty house for safekeeping. She hoped to blame the gimlet to Jon Golly on Greevey, and blame Greevey's gunshot wounds on Jon Golly, like they got into something together. I guess that's why she dumped a shovel and that rifle down the outhouse. When we get the ballistics, we'll find out if that's the rifle they used on Greevey. Then all she had to do was let Jim die of whatever the hell his problem was, and she'd have her little girl back at the end of it."

Let Jim die . . .

Faith had not survived to tell her story, and Jim Golly was ashes. There would be no postmortem. But was it possible that his sickness wasn't from bacterial tick bites and infected deer prions, which was what he complained of in his letters? Was it possible, part of the pattern, that Faith had been poisoning a man who abused her?

"Dick," she said, on a hunch, "has Jon Golly said why he booby-trapped his house and his barn? Maybe Faith was trying to get at him?"

Bender appeared exhausted as he sorted through his pages

of notes. "No," he concluded, still scanning. "I thought of that, but no."

After a minute, he summarized, his voice wooden with disgust.

"Patience had started resisting Rickreiner, refusing to go with him 'for a hamburger,' sassing off and acting like she might tell someone. So Rickreiner started coming around and threatening her and Jon Golly." He flipped pages. "That was what the booby traps were about. But once Rickreiner started running for sheriff, Jon Golly was afraid the guy would kill them both to keep his fairy tale alive. Golly finally told us yesterday that he hid some motion-activated cameras. We'll look through the footage."

"When you do, you'll see Barry Rickreiner putting pesticide in the buttermilk," she predicted. "To shut up Patience, same as he did Kim Maybee. That's the piece the DA needs."

"We'll look," Bender promised.

The sheriff closed her eyes in anger.

"Sex crimes, exploitation of underage girls. We've been down this road in the Bad Axe before."

"That's what makes it a road," Bender said.

There was a fine Benderism, indeed.

But he wasn't done. She waited.

"And jumping in front of that sonofabitch is what makes a sheriff a sheriff," he said, looking almost vehemently away. "A fella might even say he felt proud to work for a sheriff like that, being as himself, if he had to, he couldn't have done it."

||||||||||

The heat wave continued through the whole nine days. On the morning of the day that she finally went home, a thunderstorm broke the spell for a short while. Alone in her room, she watched it rain for thirty minutes in drops that seemed as big as marbles, steam rising from pavements and fields back up into the downpour. It felt cooler outside, even through the window. Her eyes were relieved.

While this happened, fifty miles south in Fennimore, where it wasn't raining, the Grant County Sheriff's Department got a report of a horse tied off in a Piggly Wiggly parking lot and arrived to find a teenage boy in an Amish dress drawing on the sidewalk. He seemed disoriented and became combative. Officers eventually delivered him to the local hospital, where he was fed, medicated, and observed. Within mere minutes they had charged the kid's phone and spoken to his mother and knew his name was Aaron Robert Zimmerman, seventeen, from Silver Falls, Oregon, a high school straight-B student until a year ago, now suffering from schizophrenia, alogia, and grandiose delusion. He had told Grant County deputies that he had been homeless and on the road for a week or two, but in fact he had been missing from a juvenile mental health facility since March. As she heard this—*since March!*—a storm broke inside Sheriff Kick and tears as heavy as the raindrops ran down her face.

|||||||||||

An hour later, it was a hundred degrees again and humid. Harley helped her get comfortable in the relative cool of the shade on the front porch.

"Hopefully he can relax a little now."

Her husband meant Taylor, whom they could see over by the barn trying to attach a spear, an old tool handle that he had sharpened, to the handlebars of his bike, given that Dylan had just figured out that if he filled his water bottle, put it in the holder, and left the top off, it would keep him cool by splashing up and hitting him in the crotch every time he went over a bump, an invention he planned to showcase when Opie came home.

"Look at us," Harley said. "All of us just out here waiting when she's only just left the camp. It's a long van ride. Two hours is going to take forever."

She, they were calling Opie these last couple days, falling back into the word like a familiar old chair.

"Well, since we have time, there are a couple things we can talk about," she said. "If you're up for it."

"Beer," came Harley's answer, and he returned from the kitchen with a cold can of PBR for himself and a cold brown bottle of Bundaberg ginger beer for her.

She began, "We need to stop hoping that we don't have to take our little boy to a therapist because we're worried that it's a small town and everyone will talk, and because we know he's not emotionally bulletproof like Opie, and so we're afraid he'll carry it the rest of his life. We have to stop the wishful thinking and do our jobs as parents."

"I know, hon."

"Who makes the call to the therapist, me or you?"

"I will."

"As for the Bad Axe," she went on, "and our continued residence here, we have to face the fact that as smart and perceptive as Opie is, she made it all the way to nine years old without understanding what a lesbian is."

Harley sighed. "Yeah."

They had spoken to a camp counselor before telling Opie that her mother had been shot, feeling it was a relatively minor but real family situation that first the camp and then Opie should know about. The counselor had suggested stalling for a couple of days and then talking to Opie themselves, because she—the first telltale *she* in reference to Opie—was working on something to explain to them.

They had waited nervously. Then Opie's news had turned out to be that she was not actually a boy, as she had once thought *when I was so immature*, she said. No, she was a girl who loved girls, loved her best friend, Rosie Glick, to be precise, whom she wanted to marry and have babies with, and this had confused her into thinking she was really a boy in the wrong body, because only boys were supposed to love and marry girls, or at least she had never heard anything different *back when I was so immature*, she said. At camp a woman with a penis named April—*Jeez! The woman is named April, you guys, not her penis! Stop!*—had helped her figure this out, and helped her understand that Rosie Glick, or any other girl she loved, might or might not love her back in the same way, and all of this was normal and therefore *easy-peasy*. As soon as she got home, Opie had promised, she would explain to them *the huge difference, you guys, between gender and sexual identity* . . .

"She sounded so happy on the phone," Harley said. "I mean, she's a happy kid anyway. But she sounded like her feet were off the ground. It's great to know who you are, right?"

"My point being," the sheriff said, "that we have choices. We can leave the Bad Axe."

"Yes."

"Which we never talk about, because you and I love it here. We can't imagine being anyplace else. And we just hope the kids are OK."

"Yes."

"So."

"Yup."

Dylan hammered over a pothole and squealed as the water hit his crotch. Taylor seemed to get his spear affixed.

"Meanwhile," she said, "we have another child we hardly ever talk about because the other two are using up all the air, who just goes about the business of being a perfect little boy."

"Hmmm. That worries you?"

"So you heard me say 'perfect'?"

"Yeah."

"I think he feels a lot of pressure not to disappoint." She paused. Though they were healing well, her wounds hurt and she shifted away from the pain. "His siblings are a load. His daddy is a baseball all-star. His mommy is high-profile."

Harley squeezed her hand.

"Maybe you should take a job at the bank, hon."

"Sure." She squeezed back. "And maybe you should start striking out more, maybe hit about .230."

"I don't know how," he said. "I can't."

"And I can't work at the bank."

She sighed then.

"Oh, Harley, I just love children. I love our children. I worry about them. Our children, all children, everywhere. That's not crazy, is it?"

"Of course not."

"It's not crazy to worry about bringing children into this world? To not totally want a baby?"

"No, of course not."

She turned her hand over and knit her fingers into his.

"So, then," she began, "I have something that I need to tell you."

"Sure."

But she was fighting tears and then she waited because she looked away and saw Taylor pedaling his speared bike as hard as he could out their long, long driveway, three hundred yards to the mailbox.

Pedaling, pedaling, farther and farther.

She squeezed her husband's hand hard, and then harder, her breath stopping as their little boy reached Pederson Road, looked inside the newspaper tube . . .

Then turned back home.